A ZEBRA REGENCY ROMANCE

Seeking Celeste

Hayley Ann Solomon

Can a lady-turned-governess teach a lord about love?

ZEBRA
U.S.$4.99
CAN $6.99

EAN
ISBN 0-8217-6629-5
9780821766293
50499

"SHALL I GOVERNESS YOU, TOO?"

Anne's well-modulated tone was caustic, for she could only ascribe her tumultuous passions to fury.

A strange curve crossed Edgemere's wide, masculine, hopelessly sensuous lips. Anne was too drawn to them to look up and see what might be reflected in the golden eyes that regarded her, she knew, with steady avidity.

Amusement? She thought not, for her traitorous pulses were raging in her temples and a wave of heat threatened to envelop her entire, untutored body.

"That could be arranged, my dear, though I fear the lessons I seek are not strictly as dry as the curriculum you have outlined."

Anne looked up sharply. "Then, you shall have to look elsewhere for your lessons, my lord."

"You have a hard heart, Miss Derringer, but I accept your terms."

"Beg pardon?"

"You shall invest my siblings with some modicum of common sense, some degree of formal education, and a good dose of happiness. I am not so shortsighted that I cannot see what is at the end of my nose. As for myself . . . much as I may desire to be schooled by you, I shall forgo the pleasure in the interest of your ongoing virtue."

"Oh!"

"However . . ." Edgemere drew closer, and Anne thought she was likely to faint. "If you continue to blush so rosily at every utterance I make, I cannot answer for the consequences."

SEEKING CELESTE

Hayley Ann Solomon

Zebra Books
Kensington Publishing Corp.
http://www.zebrabooks.com

ZEBRA BOOKS are published by

Kensington Publishing Corp.
850 Third Avenue
New York, NY 10022

First Printing: June, 2000
10 9 8 7 6 5 4 3 2 1

Printed in the United States of America

One

"Robert, you are a beast!"

The voice would have been a wail, had it not turned out to be a sad and rather quavery squeak. The eighth Earl Edgemere sighed.

Contrary to the belief of his two rapscallion siblings, he was not, as they would have him believe, a monster. Indeed, even now he was experiencing a curious mixture of remorse, regret and resignation at the pain his pronouncement was causing.

Katherine—or Kitty, as she was more affectionately known—was undoubtedly the apple of his eye. True, he had been blessed with only one sister—and a half one at that—but had he a dozen to choose from, he was certain that none could have been dearer. In spite of her defiant copper curls and stubborn, decidedly roguish chin, she was an Edgemere through and through.

Her eyes were blazing now, and he rather wished she would have done and pour the pitcher of blackberry cordial over him, or at least brandish a prized house plant in his direction. Heavens, there were enough of them around! One of the ornamental cycads or even a potted palm would have served the purpose perfectly. Anything but the sorry sniff and the tiny trickle of tears he detected beneath woebegone lashes.

He hardened his resolve and coughed impatiently. If

Lady Lucinda had been alive, none of this would now be happening. Unfortunately, she was not, and now that the mourning period was over, it was time to take action. Heaven knew, the whole of the ton seemed set to remind him of his responsibilities.

"Robert?"

He placed his hands squarely behind his back and sighed. "I am not a beast, Kitty, and you know it!"

"But you still mean to send us away!"

"Miss Parson's Academy for young ladies is most unexceptionable, I assure you! I have spoken with Miss Parson myself, and though she may appear a formidable creature to begin with, I am perfectly certain she has the best interest of her charges at heart. It is not as if it is forever . . ."

He stopped as reproachful eyes upbraided him unmercifully.

"And what of Tom? Surely you cannot mean to . . . to . . . *abandon* him, too . . ."

"Abandon? What nonsense is this? Kestridge is one of the foremost schools in all of England! It is not as if—"

"Robert, we shall be *lonely!"*

The words impaled the golden-headed, sublimely good-looking gentleman before her. Garbed impeccably in a morning coat of sapphire superfine, he seemed unaware that his profile singularly resembled one of the marble statues it was his passion to collect. Though he sported several fine white ruffles on his shirtsleeves, he preferred to remain otherwise unadorned. Modish but Spartan. My lord Robert never had much use for fripperies.

He wavered, for a moment, for the young girl who entreated him with anxious eyes and a profusion of sadly disordered curls made an excellent point. After the warmth of Carmichael Crescent, his little half brother and sister would be lonely. He closed his eyes and pushed the image away roughly.

"You shall make friends, I assure you! Lady Dawson has been most kind in her offer to present you when you are of age. It is no small thing to have her as sponsor, though she will undoubtedly balk at introducing such a harum-scarum miss as you are to the ton. Let Miss Parson afford you some polish, my dear, and I assure you, you shall never be happier."

Kitty could see by the set of her beloved Robert's mouth that his mind was quite made up. She swallowed hard, but there was a lump in her throat that made it curiously impossible to say anything at all.

Her brother, divining her thoughts, assumed a gentler tone, for despite the troublesome larks his kin were inclined to get up to, he loved them dearly. If their last governess had not been so *unforgivably* prim, the scamps might not have been inclined to ruffle her feathers sufficient to cause such a hasty and indignant resignation. Then he, at least, would not have had to look for other options. He sighed.

"It is better so. Tom cannot be in leading strings forever, and a household of women can do him no good."

"If you came home more regularly . . ."

The eighth Earl Edgemere felt a stab of guilt.

"Speak sense, Kitty! I have to take my seat in the House of Lords. It is not my will, but my duty. Besides, I am too often away on King's business to reliably reside out here in the country. Tom will have to go to Kestridge, and there is an end to it." His words were final as he rang the bell and indicated to the hovering lackey that Ravensbourne, his man of business, was to be admitted.

He was not so hardhearted a brother, however, that he did not first tousle her ringlets and produce an exquisitely crafted wooden marionette from his drawer. He watched in indulgent amusement as unmitigated delight danced with mutiny on Miss Carmichael's expressive, childlike face.

"Not such a beast, after all?"

"Oh Robert, you know I speak without thought! I just wish . . ."

"So do I. I wish your mama had not been taken from us. I wish, too, that Papa had not contracted inflammation of the lungs all those years ago. You hardly even knew him. You would have liked him. Stubborn as a cart horse. Just like you."

He grinned all of a sudden, and Miss Kitty Carmichael could not help allowing the corners of her lips to quiver with an answering quirk. Robert could be so engaging when he chose. His smile, God bless him, was quite impossible to resist.

She shook her head, unaware how her bouncing curls bobbed impetuously down her shoulders and across her face, quite heedless of the grown-up pins Lauder had painstakingly placed that morning.

"Stubborn like *me?* I think, Robert, you must really mean like yourself!"

"Baggage!" The harmony between them restored, they allowed the conversation to run to other things before coming back to the point that hovered silently between them.

"By the by, Kitty, I have secured for you a place with a most unexceptionable travelling companion—a Miss Danvers or Danforth or some such thing, I must check—to convey you to the seminary. Tom shall go by chaise, as is fitting his title." His lordship's eyes softened, though he hushed Kitty firmly with a finger to his lips. "Now, Miss Curly Tops, I want no more tears. Miss Ellen shall see to your packing, and you and Tom may have the whole day off."

With that, Miss Kitty Carmichael was forced to be satisfied. He resolutely refused to notice the hazel eyes, so like his own and brimful of tears, that scorched his person long after the door had closed.

* * *

"Good gracious, Samson! You cannot mean to leave me stranded!" Miss Anne Derringer assumed her most baleful look and glared at the coachman who had been paid a most handsome consideration to set her down at the village of Kingsbury. Though she was not three miles from her final destination, the weather was inclement, and she found herself disinclined to set her finest pair of kidskin boots to the dubious rigours of the country road.

"Beggin' yer pardon, ma'am! This 'ere be Kingsbury and Kingsbury be yer final stop!"

"But I had thought . . ."

"Never do that, ma'am! Don't never do no one no good to be thinkifying! That be for the gentry folks, and beggin' pardon, ma'am, that is somethin' you are *not*. Leastaways," he corrected himself, "not no more."

Anne nodded quietly. Samson had always born a grudge. Now, she supposed, he was enjoying her situation twofold. She resolved not to show him her discomfiture, but rather to hold her back as rigidly straight as she always had and to step out of the conveyance with as much dignity as she could muster. This, fortunately, was no real hardship, for she was a lady possessed of quite singular poise and a self-restraint that belied her tender age.

Samson scowled as he handed down the corded bandbox and set it flatly upon the cobbles. A few tears or pleas would have suited him better than the imperious nod of the head and a back half turned in his direction.

He considered, for a moment, divesting Miss Derringer of more than the last guinea he had already extracted for the ride. Perhaps she felt the vile direction of his thoughts, for she turned and the flint in her eyes was unmistakable. No wonder they called her the ice maiden.

He shook his head and cursed. The wench would probably put up the devil of a struggle, and there was no saying who was likely to shortcut the pike to ride on, past Kingsbury, toward Hampton. Since he had no desire to be taken before the magistrate and sentenced to rot in Newgate or worse, he merely permitted himself a snigger and a few earthy profanities. Unfortunately, the redoubtable Miss Derringer appeared not to hear them, so he shrugged, turned the horses round and began the long journey home.

Anne released her breath. She refused to allow the cold misery that coursed through her veins to take hold. If she did that, she knew, she would become an embittered little spinster, no better than Lady Apperton or the equally spiteful Miss Chatterley. She shuddered at the thought, for despite her well-bred bearing, she was an imp at heart.

Not at *all* suitable to become the companion of the ageing Countess Eversleigh, but there! She had no choice. She had gambled her last farthing recklessly—daringly—on the merchant ship *Polaris*. Not because it was better than any of the other prospects she might have chosen, but because of its name. Polaris of the night sky, the polar star, the guiding light. She had hoped for some small return on the competence she had invested. Instead, *Polaris* had sunk. And with it, her cushion between gentility and outright poverty. Only the offer of twenty pounds a year and ample board now stood between her and total ruination. No one in her right mind, she had been firmly assured, would employ a young, impossibly attractive woman with curling lashes and tourmaline eyes to be governess in any household worth its salt. The temptation to its male occupants would be too great a hazard.

The three miles to Kingsbury were not as irksome as Anne might have imagined, for the air was crisp, light streamed through the thin, spring-time clouds and her long, lithe legs seemed to take on a life of their own now that they were released from the confines of Lady Somerford's cramped and rather poorly sprung chaise.

True, the bandbox felt, after a while, as though it were filled with rocks. Anne had to remind herself sternly that sensible gowns and neat linen shifts could not simply be abandoned at the side of the road. Only the thought of her few precious books, tucked snugly at the bottom—at the expense, one might add, of a rather elegant muff and several fine brocade spencers—saved the whole wretched lot from being ditched. Despite the burden and the rather novel sensation that her arms might drop off at any given point, Miss Derringer found her spirits to be unaccountably lightening.

She wondered what the stars would be like in this little country village. London, with its odour and gaslamps and trails of dirty smoke, was no longer a good vantage point for her to carry out her nightly studies of the sky and its heavenly secrets. Talking about secrets . . . she must take good care not to let her treatise on comets be found upon her person. She had been labeled a bluestocking once before with disastrous effects upon her first season. Better that her employer find in her an unexceptionable companion rather than a learned and—yes, to herself she would admit the grim truth—scholarly one.

She sighed, then scolded herself for being such a flibbertigibbet. No use having a sudden fit of the dismals. Doubtless the stars would be spectacular and she would, after all, have an excess of time to regard them at her leisure. Why did the thought not console her? She put the question from her mind and breathed deeply.

Anything—anything was better than sinking into a decline. With her usual firmness of nature, she set her delightfully dainty foot forward, then emitted a yelp of pain as her ankle twisted hopelessly upon a clump of vines that had enmeshed themselves upon the path.

"Double damnation!" The oath was out before she had time to reflect upon the entirely unladylike nature of the tone. She set down the carefully corded bandbox and examined her foot. The delicate, turquoise kid boots—her one concession to vanity—were still tangled in the muddy vines. She brushed them off quickly, then set one ungloved finger to the aching spot.

The pain told her instantly that the sprain was more serious than she had first feared. In despair she looked at her trunk, merrily corded in canary yellow and weighing, to her mind, a ton at least. She shifted herself off the footpath and considered her narrowing options.

If she did not make Kingsbury by nightfall, she would undoubtedly miss her connection to Staines, thereby angering the dowager countess, who would have sent a trap down to wait upon her arrival. On the other hand . . . she could not very well walk in her present condition, so she had no option but to cheerfully wait upon the foot path and hope that some friendly passerby would notice her plight and help her into the village. The stream and little trickling waterfall to the left of the path looked inviting, so she abandoned her worldly goods and eased herself slowly onto a pile of the velvety green grass. The effort was worth the accompanying pain, for she reasoned that if she had to wait, she might just as well do so in a modicum of comfort.

Fortunately, her serviceable blue merino, whilst not the very height of fashion, was nonetheless the very thing for a crisp spring morning: warm and remarkably resistant to damp. It was in this position, then, that she shifted her plain, untrimmed chip straw hat, resigned herself to her fate and settled for what might turn out to be a long and tiresome vigil.

After what seemed like an age but was really closer to the far side of an hour, Miss Derringer began to feel the faintest prickle of misgiving. Surely, by now, a cart should have passed her way, or a horse and trap. Even a lone rider would have been comforting. She shifted position and winced. Her boot, once modishly loose, now seemed jammed to her swelling foot. She fiddled furiously with the laces, but the damage was done. The kidskin, she realized, would have to be cut, but since she had nothing so practical at hand as a knife, she desisted from her efforts.

"Allow me!"

Anne startled and swung round, as best she could under the circumstances. Too late she realized the indecorous manner in which her long, slender legs revealed themselves to appreciative eyes.

Colour danced to her cheeks as she immediately swept the blue merino down over lengths and lengths of excellent white linen petticoats.

The gentleman, clad indecently in buckskins that left little to the imagination and a severe dark riding coat that appeared faultless in its elegance, discarded his gun and advanced a trifle closer.

To Anne, who had fretted that no one would find her that day, the gentleman's amused chuckle came as a mixed blessing. On the one hand, she had undoubtedly been found; on the other . . . well, she did not wish to reflect on the other, for her pain was suddenly forgotten in the confusion of several emotions that seemed to have taken over her foolish, dreadfully immodest person.

The slight flush turned to crimson as the gentleman dropped down lightly beside her and peremptorily took hold of her boot.

"Sir!"

"Is that indignation or gratitude I detect in your tone?"

"Neither!"

"How so? Either your maidenly instincts rail at me for making free with your . . . eh . . . delicious charms, or your common sense applauds me for having the foresight to carry a knife!"

"Let me go!" Anne glared uncivilly, for she was curiously loath to be a source of amusement to this arrogant fellow.

"I shall, with regret, once I have slit the leather." The gentleman, *odiously* unabashed, slipped an ungloved hand into a near invisible pocket of his riding coat and withdrew the promised knife.

"Now, I shall endeavour not to hurt, but I shall not offer you false coin and make untrue promises."

Anne nodded. The gentleman, after all, was merely trying to help. If his eyes lingered over her longer than was strictly pardonable, well, she had only herself to blame with her hat askew and her hair all but tumbling from its pins.

"Wait!" he ordered.

"Beg pardon?"

"Don't squirm! My aim may be unerringly accurate, but I beg you not to handicap this delicate operation by wriggling. A person may replace a boot—they may not as easily do the same for a leg!"

"You are pleased to make fun, sir!"

"And why ever not? It is not every day one comes on a sylph on one's lands."

"Hardly your lands, sir! This, I apprehend, is the common toll road to Kingsbury."

"Then, you have been misinformed. This is a private path that leads, admittedly, in that direction, but nevertheless well within the boundaries of Carmichael land."

"The devil!"

The gentleman appeared not to have heard the unladylike epithet, but his lips twitched nonetheless.

"I take it you have been apprised otherwise?"

"And hoodwinked out of my last guinea piece! The coachman assured me it was for the toll."

"You were robbed, for the toll road lies north of this boundary. There!"

The boot shot off Anne's foot, catching her momentarily by surprise.

"Oh!"

"Yes, it hurts a little, I don't doubt." The amusement vanished from the man's face as he explored the ankle with sudden, unexpected tenderness. "Worse than I first suspected. You make a brave face, miss . . . ?"

"Derringer."

Aristocratic brows arched in her direction.

"Indeed? You appear a trifle too young."

Anne looked at the gentleman in sudden confusion. Young for what? And why was he regarding her now with a sudden tightening of his eminently masculine lips? She tried to ignore the warmth that coursed through her being as he lifted her as if she were nothing more than a troublesome child.

"Put me down, sir!"

"And abandon you to any passing crofter? Not likely!"

There was a faint sternness about him that caused Anne to resign herself to this extraordinary and unlikely fate. She felt, however, honour bound to make one last protest before the fluttering of her pulses overset her entirely.

"My bandbox . . ."

". . . shall be collected in due course. Come, if you wish to impress me with your good sense, you will cease remonstrating and allow me to get you over this paddock and across to Carmichael Crescent without further ado."

"My hat!"

"You should have thought about that before allowing your pins to go hopelessly astray." His voice was firm as he regarded her uncompromisingly, but since he was holding her quite high and facing him, she could not help noticing that his lips were perilously close for comfort. She wondered if he noticed, too, then immediately shut her eyes to the positively indecent image that presented itself to her obviously overset imagination.

When she dared peek at him once more, she found the sternness gone and her bandbox nothing but a tiny hint of yellow in the distance. He grinned.

"That is better! I can't abide gabbling females. And by the by . . . yes."

"Yes, what?"

"Yes to your errant thoughts, young lady."

If Anne could have blushed deeper than the pretty pink that already all but stained her cheeks from the crest of her head to the modest shadows of her well-laced bodice, she would have. Instead, she indignantly turned her head and pretended not to have heard the odious, pointedly ungentlemanly teasing.

Two

The Earl of Edgemere seemed to have a stride that made wide, lush paddocks disappear faster than Anne could ever have expected. She had a faint sensation of hedgerows and oaks passing behind her, but she hardly paid much heed. What caught her interest was the strong, masculine heartbeat that brushed up close to her ear. The man's warmth acted as a soothing drug upon her disordered senses.

All notions of maidenly conduct seemed to vanish deplorably into the crisp morning air as she snuggled up and brazenly resigned herself to her fate. The earl, feeling her relax, smiled more broadly than ever and allowed the faint glimmers of a whistle to emanate from his delicious golden lips.

"Not far, now. You shall have a hot posset and apply a cold pack to your ankle. I daresay after all your adventures you shall require a little light supper before bed."

"Bed?" She glared at him, horrid visions looming before her. He nodded. "My housekeeper has prepared an excellent chamber for your use. I confess, we had not expected you to arrive so soon, but since you have, I suppose it is for the better."

Did Anne imagine the sudden restraint in his tone? Again, he eyed her with renewed disfavour.

"You are certainly younger than I had thought."

"Evidently. You have mentioned that twice already."

Anne kept her tone tart. If she concentrated on annoying him, she might not be quite as prone to throw her arms about him in wild abandon. She thought she must be going mad. Nothing he said made sense, and never—never in all her seasoned four and twenty years—had a man ever produced such a dangerous, rackety and entirely wanton effect upon her person.

She reminded herself sternly that she was Miss Anne Derringer. All the hurts of past seasons welled up inside her. "Prissy Miss Derringer," "Miss Derringer the ice maiden"—titters behind fans—"Miss Derringer the bluestocking." It wasn't working.

She did not *feel* like ice. On the contrary. As for her learning . . . in this man's arms she was perfectly certain she could not now parse a simple sentence if she tried.

"How old *are* you actually? I collect from Lady Markham that you are three and thirty."

"Well past my last prayers, in fact."

Indignation mingled with relief. She was not going mad. The stranger was obviously suffering under some misapprehension. Whoever Lady Markham was, she had not been writing of Miss Anne Derringer. Anne had never encountered the woman in her life.

"Sir . . ."

"I would not have phrased it in those disparaging terms, but yes, I had expected someone a little older. You are hardly out of leading strings yourself!"

Anne almost giggled. From the sublime to the ridiculous. She straightened her back, but that had the effect of causing this odious man to slightly alter his grip. His hands were scorching upon her merino. If only he had possessed the common decency to wear gloves. . . .

"I will have you know, sir, I am four and twenty if I am a day!"

"Really?" His tone rang with disbelief. "You look

hardly an hour above eighteen. Quite unsuitable, in fact, to accompany Miss Kitty the requisite thirty miles."

"Sir, set me down!"

"Whatever for? I may be disposed to turn you off, but it shall not be without a character or before you have at least enjoyed the hospitality of my home! It is the least I can do, Miss Derringer."

"Really? Well, I shall have you know, sir, that it is not enough!"

Mild surprise entered Lord Carmichael's brilliant, deep-set, hazel bright eyes. He stopped in his tracks.

"Devil a bit, woman! Whatever can you mean? I believe I am more than generous under the circumstances."

"The circumstances are exactly what eludes me. Now set me down, sir. I fear you are a victim of some unfortunate misapprehension."

Robert stared at Miss Derringer in bemusement. He wondered whether her delicate pink lips ever curved into the delicious smile he suspected them capable of. Actually, smiles were not the only thing her lips caused him to ponder about. . . .

"Sir!"

"Be patient, Miss Derringer, we are nearly at the manse. See?"

Anne did see. The house was unmistakable with its huge, wide arches, pilaster columns and marble steps. My lord ignored her feeble protests and increased his pace. Anne decided it would be useless to argue with anyone headstrong enough to blithely ignore her express injunctions. No doubt he would soon enough realize his mistake, and when he did, she hoped he would be sufficiently humbled to offer her a profuse apology. Three and thirty indeed!

The stairs to the front entrance were taken at a leisurely but thoroughly efficient pace so that it seemed, to Miss Derringer's bemused estimation, that it was no time at all before they were being heralded into an imposing morning chamber of royal blue relieved by elegant hints of silver and a tall, impossibly beautiful epergne filled with a profusion of cut flowers.

"How wonderful!" The words escaped her just as the stranger set her down on an elegant, Egyptian style chaise longue of deep velvet.

"My sentiments exactly." Robert's eyes danced, for he could not resist teasing the straight-backed, slightly prickly Miss Derringer. She might challenge him with an ascetic tongue, but he could have sworn she was less resistant to his tender ministrations than she would have him believe. His own instincts on this matter, he righteously chose not to explore.

"No need to gape, Augustus! The young lady has met with an unfortunate accident. See to it, if you will, that her portmanteau be restored to her forthwith. It is to be found by Tom's stream at the south boundary."

"Very good, my lord! And will that be all?"

"Apprise the Viscount Tukebury and Miss Kitty that Miss Derringer has arrived. No doubt they will wish to make their bow and curtsy."

"Very good, your lordship."

The door all but closed behind him.

"May I look at your ankle?"

"Indeed, you may not! Quite improper, my lord! I collect you *are* a lord?"

"Yes, but you are aware of that, Miss Derringer. No doubt Lady Markham filled you in on *all* my particulars. She has a remarkably sharp tongue for one so advanced in years!"

Anne was momentarily diverted, wondering what *else* the unknown Lady Markham could tell her of this handsome man, so stern and cool, yet with such a mirthful dimple bubbling beneath the surface. She would like to explore it. . . .

"Miss Derringer!"

"Oh! Beg pardon, my lord! You were saying?" She looked at him inquiringly.

"I was saying that either you present me with your ankle or I shall advance upon you and unceremoniously retrieve it from under your skirts myself."

"Oh! How very unhandsome of you, my lord!"

"Very! I am not known, my dear, for my handsome nature."

Did the voice hold a slight warning? Anne very prudently decided not to press the matter but rather, with great delicacy and a quite inordinate degree of feminine modesty, presented the offending foot meekly.

The earl stared at her hard, and a strange but fascinating smile threatened to break the severity of his quite captivating lips. He said nothing, however, but regarded the swelling with a small tightening of his brow.

"Miss Derringer, I should like a doctor to have a look at this."

"No! My lord, it is perfectly fine. A good night's rest and I shall be right as a trivet. I need to travel tomorrow—"

"I have already explained, Miss Derringer, that you are travelling nowhere without suitable escort! I don't care whether you are thirty, forty or a mere green girl no older than my Kitty! You have been summarily discharged from your duties—I confess I was deceived a little by Lady Markham's letter of reference—but I am willing to make good my error. You shall be paid your fee, so be quiet, I beg you, and bother me no more about trifles."

"Trifles? Trifles? My lord, my life is not a trifle, and I intend, tomorrow, to continue on with my journey!"

The earl glared at her, unused to being ridden over roughshod in his own home.

"Miss Derringer, have I not made myself plain enough? You are going nowhere until I have delivered

Tom to Kestridge and returned to fetch Kitty myself. Then, once she is safe in the hands of Miss Parsons, I shall return you personally to London."

"In your chaise?"

"Yes, Miss Derringer, in my chaise! Do you require to know whether I drive a curricle or phaeton or merely an outmodish barouche?"

"No, my lord, for these matters cannot possibly interest me, beyond the fact that riding twenty miles in a closed chaise with you would be enough to quite ruin my reputation forever. However, since I cannot expect you to care a ha'penny farthing for such inconvenient trifles, I merely require you to know that you seem to be labouring under some *absurd* misapprehension . . ."

"Absurd? Miss Derringer, I am many things, but I assure you, I am not absurd!"

The eighth earl glared at the impossibly composed young woman before him. How *dared* she look so neatly imposing when her delectable raven's hair was falling about her face in a most improper manner and it was she—*she*—who was at fault for believing she was a suitable travelling companion for someone like his hubble-bubble sister. Why, as she had almost implied herself, it was *she* who needed the chaperoning. Little vixen!

"My lord, I believe we shall get on a great deal better if—"

"If what?"

"If you give me a moment to explain."

"I believe I have another plan for getting along better, Miss Derringer!"

"And what is that, my lord?" Anne tried desperately to still the inconvenient hammering of her heart. Drat the man! He had no right to play havoc with her senses, no right to kneel next to her and smell of apple blossom and soap. . . .

His mouth was upon her. Light, but as devastating as

if he had forced her lips open and commenced a concerted assault. Anne determined to push him away, but found, instead, that her arms were tangling themselves against his chest, and her traitorous mouth, far from being outraged, seemed curiously satisfied with the caress. For a moment, she experienced a warmth flood her being that convinced her, once and for all, that she was no ice maiden.

"Angel, my dearest angel." He was murmuring endearments into the base of her neck. Anne could not believe how tender a man's tone could be, nor yet how beguiling the touch of a finger on flesh.

Then, very unfairly, but quite properly, she disentangled herself, straightened her elegant back and delivered a stinging blow across one deplorably handsome cheek.

My lord gasped at the gesture, his eyes narrowing quite dangerously. Anne drew in her breath and awaited the inevitable reprisal. It never came, though she could sense his jaw tightening.

There was an uncomfortable silence in the room as both parties glared at each other, yet felt wholly miserable within. Anne, always fair, drew in a breath to apologize.

"Spare your platitudes, Miss Derringer! I apologize for so far forgetting myself as to take advantage of an employee—nay, a *guest* in my home. Unforgivable and I assure you the event shall not recur."

The stiffness of his tone was unmistakable. Anne felt quite dreadful as she noticed how streaked his profile was. She had never intended actually *hurting* the man; she had merely wished to discourage unwelcome advances. Unwelcome? Ever distressingly truthful, it was *her* face that burned when she remembered her curious response.

She opened her mouth to speak, but she could not formulate the words that would remove the hauteur from his eyes or the grim set to his lips as he regarded her.

"Think no more on the matter, sir. I must have said

something improper to encourage you to believe . . ." Her voice faltered.

Robert, had he been alone, would have cursed out loud. How could he have been so maladroit as to allow a situation like this to arise? Worse, how was it that despite the most humbling of set downs, his pulses still raced quite excruciatingly, and the impulse to take her in his arms and repeat his offense again and yet again remained disconcertingly strong.

Instead, he tightened his lips, hardened his tone—more against himself than the offending young lady—and decreed that no more was to be said on the matter. When the silence between them grew uncomfortable and there was *still* no sign of his truant siblings, he decided that the interview ought to be brought to a speedy close, for his self-control seemed strangely unreliable.

"Miss Derringer, I shall have a trap sent round for Dr. Harley. I suggest you heed his advice, for he is quite notable in his field. In the meanwhile, I shall convey you to your chamber whilst I consider what is to be done with my sister."

Before Anne knew what he was about, she was in his arms again, and he was heading for the archway that led through to the private chambers of the west wing. It was all she could do not to curl her arms about his glorious, sun-streaked hair and bury her head in the warmth of his superb cravat . . . warm from his neck. She shivered and held herself correctly apart, though she could swear she could hear his heart beating through the lawn silk. Perhaps she was mistaken. It must, of course, have been her own heart that fluttered so wildly under the cover of deep merino.

All too soon, she was deposited in a comfortable chair near a large bay window. The chamber she had been assigned was far more spacious than anything she had conceived, though it was Spartan in its trimmings. True, the sheets of the neat oak bed were crisply turned down, and a little fire crackled merrily in the grate; but apart from a Sevres pitcher filled with water for her ablutions and a small rose hastily set near the cheval glass, there were no ornate decorations about the chamber that marked it as out of the ordinary.

Well, she thought. *It is fitting. I must remember that I am no longer a lady, merely an upper servant. That is how he regards me and how he came to that . . . regrettable lapse of judgment. I must take care, for liberties of that nature are notorious. Perhaps I should tell him that I am not the travelling companion he takes me for.*

"My lord . . ."

"Hush, Miss Derringer. There is nothing more to say. If you need anything, feel free to use this bell. In your condition, I should imagine that even drawing the curtains will be painful. Don't hesitate, if you please, to ask for help. No doubt Augustus and the house staff will be able to assist you."

Anne wanted to scream that she did not *want* the butler's assistance; she wanted the lord and master's. Propriety, however, came to her rescue, so she smiled wanly and offered her thanks for the handsome offer.

"Good day, then, Miss Derringer. I shall not see you until tomorrow."

"Good day, my lord."

Why in heavens did she feel so desolate? Would she not have been furious—outraged, even—had he made the smallest push to linger? Always honest, Anne knew she *would* have been. The knowledge, however, in no way removed the sentiment. She felt bereft. Tomorrow, of course, she would have to renew her journey to Staines and the formidable Dowager Countess Eversleigh. She would have to, in a calm moment, explain the misapprehension his lordship was labouring under. . . .

"By the by, Miss Derringer . . ."

"Yes?"

"My apartments are on the second floor. Your virtue, I assure you, is in no danger at my hands."

Anne thought she ought to be grateful for the information. She was not.

"Excellent, my lord. I shall breathe easier, I assure you." Had he detected the tartness in her tone? And heavens, what else could she have said? No doubt the eighth Earl Edgemere felt himself very chivalrous to desist from dallying with the hired help.

Anne stared after him long after his back was turned and his steps could no longer be heard on the elegant footpath on the lawns beneath her window. For the first time in her life, she succumbed to that most dreadful of maladies, a fit of the dismals, and wept.

Three

The room was dark when she woke up, although she noted some tallows had been lit and the embers in the grate had undoubtedly been supplemented by some sturdy logs and a good smattering of coal. She wondered how she came to be sleeping on the fine brocade armchair, then remembered with sudden, heart-stopping clarity.

She must have cried herself to sleep, a peculiarity that she deplored and consequently denounced most vigorously. "Anne, you widgeon! Not two days into service and you are in a most singularly awe-inspiring pickle! Will tears help? I think not. Now go and brush your hair until it gleams. *That* should take your mind off unmaidenly matters!"

She was just gingerly testing her ankle to see whether it would stand up to such an exertion, when she heard the tiniest sound from behind the dark, cherry curtains at the far side of the room. Her nerves tensed at once. Not, surely . . . but no. Whatever his shortcomings, Anne knew instinctively that the eighth earl was a man of his word. There would be no nocturnal adventures, however depressing she found that excellent fact to be.

What, then? A whispering and a giggle. Anne allowed herself to breathe. The rapscallions, then, whoever they were. She remembered his lordship referring to his relations as such. At the time, her mind had been fixed on other matters. Her lips twitched. If she were being eagerly watched, no doubt they were up to some dire prank or other.

Since none could be so dire as those she, herself, had performed not so very long ago, she was not unduly alarmed. Common sense made her check the door frames for suspended pails of water. Nothing.

She relaxed slightly, yawned and gingerly—for indeed, her ankle was still shockingly tender—made her way to the very inviting bed.

Yes, there it was. A suspicious little lump wriggling its way under the blankets. She wondered if it was a mouse. Too large for a frog, though the toads had been prodigiously large that year.

"Good gracious! Someone has been so thoughtful as to provide me with a pet! I wonder, though, whether he or she had the goodness to rip holes in my blanket? I would hate for the poor creature to suffocate."

Was it her imagination, or was there an uncomfortable rustle behind the cherry damask? Eyes twinkling, she cast off the bedclothes and flung herself across the bed, for the little animal, whatever it was, would be sure to flee at the first sign of freedom.

"Got you!"

Her hand over the lump, she carefully slid the other into the blankets and allowed her fingers to glide to the offending area.

"Oops! *Prickly* little devil! Not a toad, I collect, but a very fine hedgehog! Come out, little sweetheart, and let me examine you."

Carefully, Anne uncovered the brownish creature and regarded it with fond amusement.

"What an excellent specimen you are, to be sure! Now, just hold still whilst I extricate the worst of your spikes from my arm. There! That is better; now we can become acquainted. I, of course, am Miss Anne Derringer. I wonder if my friends behind those curtains gave you a name?"

Was it her imagination, or was the rustling becoming more distinct? Back turned she could only surmise by the briefest of scuffles and the most decided of kicks that some youthful debate was wordlessly ensuing behind her.

Presently, the damask moved with decision, and she could sense, rather than see, two—no, was it four?—eyes upon her person.

"Pardon me if I am not quite presentable. You see, I was not expecting company."

"Miss Derringer?"

She turned around to see two vivid eyes confront her. How familiar was the stubborn tilt of the chin, though the curls were feminine and the youthful expression harboured none of the sensuous lines of the older, more intoxicating male version.

"The same."

"I am Kitty. Tom, come out from there at once. She won't eat you!"

"Indeed, I won't. Though I am inclined to wonder whether our little friend, here, has eaten."

"Not since noon, when we discovered it. Dreadfully sorry about him, ma'am! Robert usually finds us such . . . such *deathly* governesses."

"I infer, then, that you do not immediately consign me to that appalling category?" Ann's tone was dry, but irrepressible humour lurked at the corner of her rather handsome lips.

"Gracious, no! You look to be a *great* good gun!" Tom stepped confidently out of hiding and dusted himself off with the air of a gentleman grown. A quick calculation had Miss Derringer judge him to be around nine, with his older, more worldly wise sister eleven at the least.

"I am relieved! Kitty, may I have your slipper? It looks delightfully soft."

"My slipper?"

Anne nodded. "I am not sure how much longer our little creature, here, is going to stand for being held. Since I am not, myself, over partial to prickles, I should like to set it down somewhere comfortably. Your shoe will make an excellent nest until we can return it to . . . where did it come from?"

"The herbarium."

"Very good. The herbarium, then. Ah, excellent."

Anne took the offered footwear and gently released her charge into the base. Tom and Kitty exchanged guilty glances.

"It did not hurt you overmuch, did it?"

"No, but I am a hopelessly dull sort of person that way. Dreadfully cautious, you understand."

Miss Derringer could have laughed out loud at the baffled faces that digested this piece of very disappointing news.

Kitty snorted, but Tom proved an unexpected ally, announcing that Miss Derringer must be overstating the case, for she did not *look* cautious. A quick glance at the cheval mirror confirmed Anne in her worst fears. The child was right.

Her hair was spilling from her pins in coils, her dress was smeared with mud, her elegant kidskin boot was slit and there was a high and unmaidenly colour upon her cheeks. Worlds away from the proper, calm, self-controlled young woman who had set out that morning.

That young lady had been resigned to the fact that she had come down in the world and was now relegated to a rank only slightly above that of maid servant. True, companions were expected to be genteel, but that was where their similarity with the high ton ended. Companions were not expected to be excited, unnerved, curious or in any way out of the ordinary. They were like pieces of furniture. Elegant, but curiously inanimate. Most of all, they were wholly ineligible for anything but a lifetime of solicitous fetching and carrying, curtsying and withdrawing, needlework and other appropriate but rather unfortunate activities.

Miss Derringer, redoubtable, stubborn, intelligent beyond her four and twenty years and, regrettably, still single, had little option but to view this destiny with equanimity. True, she had wrestled, at times with tears, with wild defiance, even once, with a priceless Sevres vase that had come to a sudden and rather sorry end upon Lady Somerford's hearth. But after the storm had come peace and a quiet resignation.

That was, until the moment of her meeting with Lord Edgemere. Anne pushed the thought of his handsome, woefully beguiling form from her mind. He had overset both her sense and senses quite sufficiently already! It was time for the dull lady of caution to reemerge.

"I *am* dull, Tom, but thanks for your confidence in me! Now, children, I intend retiring to bed before the candles have quite burned in their sockets."

"No!"

"No?" Anne allowed surprise to register somewhat disapprovingly in her tone. Truth was, she was enjoying the scamps. They offered a welcome respite from the gloom of her prospects.

"No! Not before you promise Robert you shall not take me to Miss Parson's Seminary tomorrow."

If the situation hadn't been so absurd, Anne would have chuckled.

"I assure you, Kitty, even if I begged to escort you there, his lordship will not countenance such a thing."

"But . . ."

"No buts! He assured me so himself, only this afternoon!" Anne squirmed to think of the earl's sweeping denunciation of her fitness to escort the young Miss Carmichael. Pay her her fee indeed! Over her dead body would she accept a single brass farthing from his top-lofty lordship. She was good enough, it seemed, to dally with. *Not* so to escort his flesh and blood. The truth smarted more than she cared to admit.

"But that is famous, Miss Derringer!"

"Beg pardon?" Anne was out of kilter with the children's exuberance.

"You shall stay and be our governess instead." Kitty's tone was decidedly firm for a young lady of her tender years. Anne was as much touched by this as she was by the fact that the duo were obviously yearning for something more than the lot Lord Edgemere had so obviously designated them.

"Kitty, Tom . . . I fear that is out of the question. In truth, I must tell you that I am an impostor in this household, for whoever his lordship was expecting, it was not me!"

Four sparkling eyes turned happily upon her.

"An impostor! I *knew* she couldn't be Robert's choice! Miss Derringer, you will not *credit* how stuffy he can be at times."

"Never mind that, Tom! Tell us . . . oh, tell us, dear Miss Derringer, how you came to pretend to be my travelling companion!"

"Pretend . . . good grief, children, I am not so depraved as all that! I never pretended a thing. Your brother, however, persists in labouring under a misapprehension, and every time I try to set the record straight . . ."

". . . he refuses to listen. How very like Robert! Tom! We shall tease him mercilessly over this!"

Anne was horrified. "You shall do no such thing. I forbid it!"

The children looked at her with renewed interest. Miss Derringer was not to be trifled with, then. Somehow, they liked her the more for it.

"Very well, but you will not be such a . . . a . . . *maw-*

worm as to refuse to tell us your story. *Nothing* exciting ever happens to us."

Anne might have pointed out that it was useless, then, to apply to her, for *her* life could be described as disappointingly uneventful. Truth, however, compelled her to hold her tongue. Lord Edgemere may be described as handsome, annoying, charming, distressingly overbearing, but never, never, never dull. Again, her colour rose as she remembered certain interesting elements of their discourse . . .

"Kitty! I hope you do not mean to tell me that 'mawworm' forms part of your every day vocabulary?" Attack, of course, was the best means of defense.

Kitty grinned. "Oh, my language can be delightfully varied! But bother that . . . tell us your story before we *die* from curiosity!"

Anne sighed. She supposed it would do no harm to give Miss Kitty Carmichael and her brother, the little Viscount Tukebury, a carefully expurgated account of the day's occurrences.

They seemed unusually silent when they realized that Anne was forced, by reason of imminent poverty and self-imposed spinsterhood, to reduce herself to service. It seemed that despite their merry, scapegrace ways, they were not entirely insensitive to other people's distress.

Tom broke in on the stillness to ask whether it would not have been better, after all, to have accepted the offers of either Mr. Stokes or Sir Archibald Dalrymple.

Kitty crushed him with scorn, stating that if the gentlemen in question were truly as Miss Derringer had described, she would have had to be "dicked in the nob" to get shackled to either one. Anne had to smile. The analysis, whilst careless and quite deplorably cant, was nonetheless highly accurate. Miss Kitty Carmichael had perceived almost instantly that which she herself had battled with restlessly. Marriage without love was not a release; it was a prison. At least, as a paid companion her savings and her soul would remain entirely her own.

She smiled cheerfully and said as much. Kitty's eyes shone at the thought of such great independence, and Tom promised grandly that as soon as he was of age, Miss Derringer would come and live at the dower house.

Miss Derringer did not laugh at this supreme and lordly gesture. Instead, she thanked him gravely and swept herself into a curtsy that, had her ankle not wobbled precariously, would have been most elegant indeed.

Dawn broke more swiftly than Anne could ever have imagined. She had been dreaming luxurious dreams that lingered, slightly, in the crisp chamber as she woke. Almost she could smell the scent of apple blossom and soap that had driven her sleeping senses wild and caused such tousled havoc with the bed sheets. She allowed her lips to soften into a lazy, secretive smile before awakening, at last, with a shocked start.

"Good lord! I shall miss the stage!" She searched for a clock in the unfamiliar room, but found nothing so prosaic at hand. Instead, her glance alighted on a bowlful of cherry red peonies and her second best morning dress laid out neatly at the bedstead.

"It must be later than I think!" Sun streamed through the damask curtains, still drawn, but nevertheless allowing bright beads of light to escape into the small chamber. Anne groaned as kestrels and humming birds chirped prettily outside her window. The day must be far more advanced than she had anticipated. Dawn would have been a few hours ago at the very least.

She swung herself off the bed and felt the floor carefully. The hot posset and cold pack must have worked their magic, for the swelling was down and thankfully the pain had eased tenfold. She felt a slight tenderness, but nothing that her serviceable boots, well laced, could not deal with. She hoped the earl had not, after all, unduly troubled the village doctor. If he arrived, she would undoubtedly feel more foolish than she already did.

Miss Derringer dressed quickly, leaving only her back buttons undone before placing her nightwear and tooth powder back in the sturdy brown bandbox. She pressed this shut and corded it with expert adeptness, resolutely closing her eyes to all stubborn pictures of dreamy-eyed gentlemen with soft golden curls and lips that curved deliciously. They were like . . . but no! It was pointless and dangerous to follow that idle path.

The peonies smelled heavenly. She wondered who had set them there and why. Probably a kindness of the bustling kitchen staff. She could do with all the kindness that came her way. Relentlessly ignoring her rising dismay at the day's prospects, she plucked a blossom and set it cheekily against her creamy skin. It looked delightful.

She set it down, quickly coiled her lashings of dark hair into a single knot, then thread the blossom through before pinning the whole loosely upon her head. She would have been the picture of elegance had her morning dress not been a drab and serviceable maroon, unadorned by anything more than a single chaste ribbon and the tiny, silver buttons peeping shyly down the length of her preposterously straight back.

These she struggled with, cursing the lack of a lady's maid or hand mirror at the very least. No good, no good! It took nimble fingers far too long to get around them. She would have to alter the pattern when she arrived, finally, at Lady Eversleigh's. Companions were not expected to take overlong over their toilette.

Finally, it was done. The staid cheval glass did her justice, for her colour was high and she looked softer, less like a prim ice maiden than usual, for her tight coils were loose upon her delicate, oval-shaped face. Good! Tomorrow, no doubt, it would be an unbecoming little mobcap over her head. Today, it was the peony.

Anne chuckled at the thought, her irrepressible spirits subtly rising. Today she was going to have an audience, once more, with the Earl of Edgemere. Though it was to take her leave forever, she would make the most of the opportunity to learn his face, his gestures, his scent, his smile. Every person was allowed at least one indulgence. Anne's secret indulgence, she decided, with admirable calm and cool defiance, was to be this.

Four

"Robert, you do not understand what a great good gun she is!"

"I do, Kitty, believe me I do! That does not mean, however, that she is suitable to act as a *governess* to you young rapscallions. You'd have her for breakfast in a minute, and I'd be obliged, as usual, to leave off my pressing business in London to hotfoot it home instead!"

"She is different!"

"So I infer. *Different,* however, does not always equate to suitable. The discussion is closed."

Miss Derringer's ears burned. It was not her habit to listen in on other people's conversations, but if they would indulge in such matters in the public breakfast room to which she had just been politely directed, there was not much she could do about it.

How dare the man! Not suitable indeed! Why, he knew nothing about her. . . . She pressed slender, suitably gloved fingers to hot temples. No, he knew more about her than she did herself . . . more about stirring secret hidden warmths in strange, deliciously wicked places. . . . She had never even *thought* that way before.

Miss Derringer straightened her back and allowed rage to hide the sinful direction of her erring, normally impeccably ordered thoughts.

Not suitable . . . not suitable. . . .! She briskly tapped on the door, then glared at the earl before smiling calmly at his siblings and taking a seat. Anne did not wait for an invitation. She may have been about to lower herself into service, but she had not done that yet! To his high-and-mighty lordship, she would remain, always, a lady born and bred.

"Miss Derringer, tell Robert at *once* that you will stay!"

"Kitty, I do not believe I have been invited. Tom, if you are going to spill your chocolate, do have the goodness to at least aim for the gown, rather than the ice white gloves. Muslin is deplorable to wash."

Tom grinned unrepentantly. "May I practice on you?"

"Vile child, no you may not!"

Was that a faint flicker of amusement she caught flashing across the earl's taciturn features? Anne smiled inwardly. How strange that she could be so angry and breathless at one and the same time.

"Miss Derringer, I trust you slept well? Your ankle, I hope, is better for the rest?"

Polite words, but Anne could feel a current between them that had little to do with commonplaces.

"Excellent, my lord. I have been so cosseted it is small wonder I am feeling better. Do not trouble yourself over a doctor, for with these stout boots I am cured."

Perhaps she should not have drawn attention to her footwear, for the earl would surely, then, not have had the audacity to set his glass at her and peer under the table at her kerseymere skirts and the abhorrent boots that she had praised, only yesterday, for their serviceability.

"Deplorable!"

"Beg pardon?" Anne's cheeks flamed, for she had been thinking the same herself.

"Perfectly shocking how stout boots can make the most delectable of ankles dowdy. Miss Derringer, remind me, I beg, to procure you some new footwear. I fear I have slashed your kidskins beyond all repair and shall therefore nobly suffer the consequences!"

Did he *mean* to insult? Anne regarded him steadily. His mind was unreadable but for the faint twist of a smile upon shockingly inviting lips.

"My lord, the boots serve my purposes admirably. I hope you are not so depraved as to imagine I will accept trifles from you?"

"Miss Derringer, after yesterday, believe me, I will not make that mistake twice."

So! He regarded his kiss as a trifle. Anne would have hit him had he not been leaning negligently out of reach at the far side of the polished beechwood table. Perhaps he read her mind, for in that split second he grinned and caught her furious glare. Two pairs of eyes gazed at their elders curiously.

"What trifle did you give her, Robert?" Tom, sublimely innocent of the charged atmosphere, allowed his interest to be voiced. Kitty, a little more worldly wise, kicked him under the table. Anne would have chuckled had she not felt so suddenly, inexplicably, crestfallen.

"Nothing of any account, Tom. Nothing Miss Derringer could not procure *more* of if she only made the slightest push."

"But I shall not, shall I, my lord? I think we understand each other perfectly. And now, my dears, I think it is time for me to take my leave. It is a long route to Staines, I believe."

"Staines? What has Staines got to do with anything? And I thought I told you—"

"Exactly the problem, my lord! If you had but *listened,* rather than *told* . . ."

Kitty giggled. "I *said* she was a great good gun, Robert!"

"Impertinent widgeon! I have a mind to send you to the nursery for the day. Be quiet! Better yet, take Tom and scarper. There *must* be something for the pair of you to do whilst I decide what is to be done."

Kitty knew that tone. She winked saucily at Miss Derringer, made a great show of gathering her muff and pulling Tom down from his seat, then left before her great bullying half brother could change his mind.

"Miss Derringer . . ."

"Lord Carmichael . . ."

"Miss Derringer, you must realize my position. It is impossible that I offer you the post of governess!"

"I never asked for it, my lord."

"Indeed, I know that, but it seems my siblings have taken the most extraordinary liking to your company."

"Extraordinary seems inaptly put, my lord! True, many have taken me in strong dislike, but I don't think it can justly be termed *extraordinary* that the children have taken a liking to my company."

The earl's lips twitched. "Miss Derringer, you deliberately misunderstand me."

"And you me, my lord! Besides, whilst I have no inclination whatsoever to foist myself on your household, I might say that I have more to recommend myself than a pretty face and pleasing manners!"

"That is a relief, for I would hardly call your face pretty, and your manners, my dear, are abominable."

The words were spoken so silkily that for a split second, Anne hardly grasped the sense. When she did, she gasped, her expressive eyes flashing such outrage that the earl was moved to chuckle. They stood and faced each other.

"Careful, my dear, you might just be tempted to slap me again."

"It is no more than you deserve."

"Is it? I merely point out to you that your manners are . . . unusual. You do not deal in commonplaces."

"I hold that as a compliment, my lord. I abhor hypocrisy."

"Then, we are in agreement. Smile, my pretty."

"You have just pointed out that I am *not* pretty."

"And that rankles? Allow me to be more precise. *Pretty* is for flowers, for trinkets, for watercolour sketches. It is not for your face."

"What *is,* then?" Anne felt her heart beat faster, for Lord Carmichael had somehow breached the distance between them, and she could not, for the life of her, find it in herself to take the necessary steps backward. Again, the scent of apple blossom and soap, the golden tendrils that brushed his shoulder and now her gown. . . .

"Beautiful. Extraordinary. Magnificent. Raven hair and raven heart. Strong words for a strong, strong woman."

Anne felt she could not breathe. When he reached over to pull out her hairpins, she made no demur save a tiny, inarticulate fluttering of the hands. It was enough.

"Miss Derringer . . . Anne. It seems I do you a great disservice. I am never usually so uncontrolled in my passions. I gave you my word and that is what I shall stand by."

The tiny disappointment lasted only a moment. Anne was *glad* that her breathing seemed restored, and the cool calm of reason descended, once more, upon her eminently sensible person.

"How did you know I was Anne?"

"Beg pardon?" The earl, for once, was discomposed.

"Anne. Anne. You called me Anne, my lord."

"How very impertinent of me! I glimpsed it on your bandbox. *Miss Anne Derringer.* Very neatly printed, too."

"You tease me!"

"I only tease my friends."

What did *that* mean? Anne wished he did not look at

her with such unsettling directness. She decided to change the subject.

"By the by, my lord, with respect to my qualifications . . ."

"*Shall* I respect them?"

Why did he twist everything she said? The man was so provoking!

"Indeed you should, for I am familiar with the classics, three languages, mathematics, and the terrestrial globe, of course."

"Of course." Why was there a decided hint of laughter to his voice? Anne felt an answering smile curl at the tips of her lips. She quelled it crushingly.

"I am accounted a master at the celestial globe." How boastful she was! She, who took such care to conceal her learning for fear of being labeled a bluestocking. How very lowering!

"Indeed? I have some interest in celestial beings myself." He was looking at her *that* way again, so she felt she must either melt, throw herself wantonly into his arms or concentrate fiercely on the substance, not meaning, of their conversation. She chose the latter.

"Celestial beings? I would not have thought you would have much time, in London, to foster such an interest."

"Alas, no! I do, however, possess a two-inch telescope of Newtonian design. I must fetch it out some time, for I fear, since Lucinda's death, I have neglected my star-gazing to a reproachable degree."

"You really are interested?"

"My dear Miss Derringer, why would I lie upon such a substantive issue? If you doubt me, you may speak with an acquaintance of mine, one Sir William Herschel . . ."

"The king's astronomer!"

He looked at her sharply. "How do you know that?"

"My particular interest is comets. Sir William is the definitive guide on the topic."

Almost for the first time, the eighth Earl Edgemere looked at Anne of the raven hair with respect as well as admiration and the usual attraction.

"I will show you my observation notebook sometime."

Miss Derringer could hardly bear the pain. She bit her lip and half turned away. "I would have loved that, my lord."

Her voice was so low he only just caught it.

"You mean, I hope, that you *will* love it."

Anne shook her head. "Do not tempt me, I beg! There is no place for me in this household. I came on it by chance and I shall leave it resolutely. I infer you believe me to be a travelling companion for Mistress Kitty. An *unsuitable* one—"

"Bother that! That was my idle, arrogant tongue!"

Anne smiled, finally. How could she not?

The earl drew in his breath sharply. He had never seen a face illuminate quite as Anne's did. The moment, however, was elusive, far too fleeting for his comfort.

"True, my lord, but even idle tongues can speak the truth. I *am* unsuitable, not by virtue of my age, as you think, nor by my behaviour, which I admit is rather more erratic than I am prone to, but by simple virtue of the fact that I am an impostor in your home."

Whatever Lord Robert Carmichael had expected, it was not this.

"Good *God,* woman, what kind of melodrama is this? Imposter, indeed! You are, I understand, Miss Anne Derringer?"

"None other, my lord. I am *not,* however, sent by Lady Markham nor had I so much as *heard* of Miss Kitty Carmichael and her oh so intriguing set of brothers before yesterday morning at the earliest."

Robert's long, wide brows snapped together in surprise.

"No?"

"No!"

"Then, what the devil . . .?"

The inelegant question was never framed. Before he could demand a more satisfactory explanation, his eyes were alighting upon a thin stick of a woman, of indeterminate years but supremely proper appearance. She wore, upon her ageing head, a turban of fur trimmed with two elegant feathers of matching hue. Brown, to an undiscerning viewer, but to high sticklers like Lady Castlereigh, the tone would better have been described as "tawny" or "dusky gold."

My lord, however, was not interested in the minutiae of such definitions. With a sweeping stare he regarded the straight back, the ebony cane and the high-necked gown with a polite but gentlemanly disfavour.

"Augustus?"

The butler coughed. "May I present to you, my lord, Miss Elizabeth Danvers? I understand you have been expecting her."

His lordship was just about to inquire whether Augustus had been indulging in a little too much of his port wine when light dawned. Elizabeth Danvers . . . the name rang a bell. He searched his elusive memory, all the time feeling the burning stare of Miss Anne Derringer upon his elegant person.

Hell and damnation! It was Miss *Danvers* who was to be Kitty's travelling companion! Lady Markham had mentioned her quite specifically by name. Then who, in tarnation, was . . .

Anne smiled. "I believe you now understand my circumstance, your lordship."

"Understand? That is a strange term to describe my confusion! I shall let that pass, however and—"

"Your lordship!"

The tone was ringing. The eighth earl guiltily felt caught in the schoolroom. It was only a mad moment, however, before he retrieved his dignity and turned to the lady in question.

"Miss Danvers, welcome to Carmichael Crescent."

"Thank you, your lordship, and it looks as if it is not a moment too soon, either!"

"Beg pardon?"

"That gown is *far* too low cut for a young lady, miss! It reveals invitingly, and that is one thing I cannot hold with. I am sure his lordship will agree that such an unbecoming expanse of flesh is improper and unsuitable. I shall see, at once, to the alteration of your gowns."

Anne was stunned, startled, then blatantly amused at the impertinence.

"I collect you believe me to be Miss Kitty Carmichael?"

The woman glared at her crushingly. "Naturally, though artifice makes you appear a trifle older. We shall deal with that, too, young lady!"

Robert's brows furrowed. Was this why his siblings went through governesses like he went through glasses of Madeira? If this old crab was a sample. . . .

"I think not."

The woman stared at him in incomprehension. "My lord, I must ask you to be silent on this matter. As a man, you cannot know—"

"As a man, I believe I am best *qualified* to know, Miss Danvers!"

"Oh!" The wicked implication caused Miss Anne Derringer to smother a most unladylike chuckle of amused comprehension. This mirth was not, however, reflected on the leaner Miss Danver's countenance. She poked at the earl with her stick and demanded to know if he had dared sully her ears with gross innuendo.

When he solemnly nodded an affirmative, she gasped in outraged virtue and took a seat upon the instant.

"My lord, I have been sorely deceived!"

"I, too, Miss Danvers!" His eyes danced across the room and caught Anne's in a fleeting embrace of the spirit.

"I have references from no less than Lady Markham, Miss Rochester-Smythe and at least a handful of minor peeresses!"

"I am relieved, for you shall then have no difficulty in procuring employment elsewhere!"

"I have been hired to escort Miss Carmichael, here, to Miss Parson's Academy for young ladies and that I shall do!"

"Miss Danvers, whilst you shall most certainly have your fee for your obvious inconvenience, I have to advise you that Miss Kitty Carmichael is going nowhere, least of all to Miss Parson's Academy!"

"Lady Markham—"

"A *pox* on Lady Markham! Miss Kitty is not travelling anywhere and that is my final word on it!" His lordship crossed over to the mantelpiece and extracted a fine cigar from the silver box marked with his crest and emblazoned, in crimson, with his initials.

"Profanity, my lord!"

"I believe so, Miss Danvers. Now, at the risk of further offense, I must beg you to withdraw to the blue salon, where I assure you your ears shall not be further smirched by my unruly tongue." His lordship smiled so charmingly that the prim Miss Danvers felt slightly mollified at this obvious concession to her gentility. She was moved, however, to question the earl further, something he considered a sad error.

"Miss Danvers, cease worrying at me like a . . . like a . . ."

"Beaver?"

His lordship looked up and grinned. "Thank you, Miss Derringer! How eminently helpful of you. Miss Danvers, desist from worrying at me like a beaver. Miss Carmichael has no need of your services, for she and her brother are to be tutored at home."

"By *you?"* Miss Danver's genteel voice dripped sarcasm.

The earl's voice was gentle, but there was no denying the steel behind the tone.

"Have the goodness, ma'am, to credit me with a modicum of common sense. By the veriest good fortune, I have managed to procure for myself one of the finest governesses in all of London. May I present to you Miss Anne Derringer, of . . ."

"Woodham Place." Anne supplied the information automatically. The earl did not blink or so much as glance in her direction.

"Woodham Place."

"Well!" Miss Danvers eyed her rival in a new light. "Well! And do you teach the finer arts?"

"Naturally, ma'am, I am passing proficient in watercolours, dancing . . ."

"Are you indeed?" The eighth Earl Edgemere turned once more to address her. He smiled lazily, but his sleepy lids did not fool Anne for a second. Her heart began to stammer in that strange, exhilarating manner.

"But, of course, your lordship . . ."

"Familiarity, my lord, not excellence!"

"Very well, then, familiarity. I do, however, require excellence in the *celestial* globe," his lordship stated.

"But naturally." The undercurrent between the pair was now palpable. Miss Danvers, regarding both parties with rising distaste, announced that she had most certainly been sadly deceived, for a household that prized such flimflammery nonsense above basic accomplishments was not at all what she had expected in one distinguished enough to house a peer of the realm.

The said peer came perilously close to a rather wicked comment that upon reflection was best left unsaid. When

Augustus arrived to usher the lady to a less objectionable accommodation, Lord Carmichael merely bowed with studied elegance, carelessly announced that Miss Danvers might make free with both his luncheon and the comfort of his smart, cherry red barouche, placed his hands upon his lips to silence any further admonitions and closed the door decidedly in her querulous face.

Five

"Anne."

"Miss Derringer."

The earl sighed. "Very well. Miss Derringer. I trust, despite the false start, that you will truly stay?"

"It is very bad of me, but I'd do anything to disoblige that old tabby! I had one too many governesses like her, myself."

She neglected to mention that her dislike of Miss Danvers went far deeper than the schoolroom. It was just such prim and prissy cats who had made her two London seasons such unutterable misery.

She chose not to think about it, but the earl noticed the momentary pain beneath the glorious, dark, featherlight lashes.

He controlled the urge to take her in his arms. That would be the very thing to make her cry off the new arrangement, and Lord Robert Carmichael, confirmed bachelor and gentleman of the ton, knew for a certainty that whoever the devil she was, the intriguing Miss Derringer must be made to stay.

"Excellent. Then, it is settled!"

"My lord, lest you forget . . ."

"Yes?"

"I am entirely unsuitable; the children will have me for breakfast . . ."

"—and lunch and tea, *too,* no doubt! Don't hold a fit

of ill humour against me, my dear. I am unused to having my well-ordered plans overset."

"You also have not viewed a single reference. . . I could be a . . . a . . ."

"Imposter? We have already established that!"

Miss Derringer frowned. "Be serious, I beg! I have never acted as a governess before . . ."

"Then, you require practice!"

"On Tom and Kitty?" For the first time, she looked a tremulous combination of doubtful and wistful. The earl moved toward her and placed a finger upon her lips. Anne was silenced, shocked at her trembling, and at the honey sweet intimacy of the simple, silencing touch.

"Lord Edgemere, it is not fitting." His finger remained on her lips, and she could taste him as she spoke. She stepped back, the better to break the invisible bond that was straining, against all odds, to tie them together.

The earl inclined a little toward her, then stepped back briskly.

"If you mean that I am hopelessly attracted to you, Miss Anne Derringer of Woodham Place, then yes, it is unfitting."

Anne had never felt so self-aware before, of the beating of her heart, of the faint tightening in her ribs, of the straining of bodice muslin . . . she could hardly breathe.

"I shall procure my bandbox, my lord. There is nothing more to say."

"The devil there is!" The earl seized her almost roughly.

"Let me go!"

"Not before you promise not to be such a straitlaced goose! You shall governess my siblings and governess them *well!*"

"And you, what of you? Shall I governess you, too?"

Anne's well-modulated tone was caustic, for she could only ascribe her tumultuous passions to fury.

A strange curve crossed the earl's wide, masculine, hopelessly sensuous lips. Anne was too drawn to them to look up and see what might be reflected in the golden eyes that regarded her, she knew, with steady avidity.

Amusement? She thought not, for her traitorous pulses were raging in her temples, and a wave of heat threatened to envelope her entire, untutored body.

"That could be arranged, my dear, though I fear the lessons I seek are not strictly as dry as the curriculum you have outlined."

Anne looked up sharply.

"Then, you shall have to look elsewhere for your lessons, my lord."

"You have a hard heart, Miss Derringer, but I accept your terms."

"Beg pardon?"

"You shall invest my siblings with some modicum of common sense, some degree of formal education and a good dose of happiness. I am not so shortsighted a brother that I cannot see what is at the end of my nose. As for myself . . . much as I may desire to be schooled by you, I shall forgo the pleasure in the interest of your ongoing virtue."

"Oh!"

"However . . . if you continue to blush so rosily at every utterance I make, I cannot answer for the consequences."

"Consequences, my lord?"

"Consequences, Miss Anne Derringer."

The eighth Earl Edgemere drew a little closer. Anne thought she was likely to faint, for she could swear she could taste his mead-sweet tongue even as he drew back and rested lazily against the imposing marble pillar that formed so elegant a feature of the breakfast room.

"My lord, you are pleased to tease!"

"Very pleased, Miss Derringer."

"You shoot yourself in the foot, you know, for you leave me with no option but to decline your quite extraordinary offer."

"Young ladies are not in the habit of declining my offers, Miss Derringer!"

"I warrant you are not in the habit of making them, my lord. Not, at all events, respectable ones!"

"Perspicacious as well as beautiful!" His voice lowered to almost a whisper. Anne could feel his gaze, willing her to step forward. She could push him against the pillar. . . .

"I am leaving right now. With any luck, the countess Eversleigh will overlook my tardiness. My lord, you will excuse me."

Anne turned resolutely to go.

An arm shot out and palpably restrained her. The air of laziness evaporated from the earl's features as he swung her round.

"I will *not* excuse you, Miss Anne Derringer! The children shall never forgive me, and God help me, I should not forgive myself. You will stay, and if my presence is so noxious to you . . ."

"It is *not* noxious!"

"No?" The aquiline features relaxed, slightly, as the twinkle returned.

"You know it is not." Anne abandoned herself and her virtue to truth.

For her pains, she felt her cheeks stroked with infinite gentleness and the pins pulled expertly from her quick coiffure. Not surprisingly, her hair responded by falling around her face and cresting slightly at her waist.

"Silky."

"Mmm . . ."

"You are not to slap me."

"It is a governess's duty to discipline where required."

The twinkle reached his lips and became a quite indisputable grin.

"Bearing that in mind, Miss Derringer, will you warn me before such severe correction is implemented?"

She nodded. "I shall, my lord."

"You are aware that I am liable to kiss you at any moment?"

She nodded. "I disapprove, Lord Edgemere."

"Disapprove but countenance the notion nonetheless?"

A small smile played around delicious pink lips. "In extraordinary circumstances, I countenance the notion."

"Then, come here, Miss Anne Derringer."

She stepped forward with decision. Twenty pounds a year was being thrown recklessly to the winds. She could not, in all conscience, take up Countess Eversleigh's position. Her thoughts were too impure for a highly referenced paid companion.

His lordship's kiss was all that Miss Derringer had anticipated. It was full, satisfying and slightly bittersweet, an apt reflection of her turmoiled emotions. Her wanton surrender to the sensation was a terrifying loss of habitual control. Nevertheless, the passions evoked were so strong, so. . . .

"Lord Edgemere?"

His tongue lingered, for a moment, before he held her from him.

"Miss Derringer?"

"I feel a cautionary slap may be necessary."

"Miss Derringer, if you had the smallest idea of what I would *like* to do right now, I fear that nothing short of a severe beating would correct me."

"Shall you cut the willow cane or shall I?"

He grinned. "Neither, for I shall be virtuous and desist from all temptation. I leave for London tonight."

"So soon?"

"Say things like *that,* Miss Derringer, and you shall overset, completely, my iniquitous sense of honour! So long as you are a governess in my home, your virtue shall be safe."

"Very well, my lord, on those terms I accept. My fee, however, is quite exorbitant! I shall ask twenty-five pounds a year.

"Miss Derringer, you drive a hard bargain. You shall, however, not get a sovereign less than forty a year."

"Forty pounds! My lord, you trifle with your fortune!"

"Miss Derringer, I am no gambler. I believe it a perfectly safe bet that you will earn your forty pounds in the first month. Kitty and Tom are not without spirit!"

"Excellent, for I shall expect them to apply themselves with passion."

"They are fortunate children."

"Help me with my hair, my lord. Your fortunate siblings will be *unmerciful* if they catch sight of me like this."

"As *I* should be."

"Beg pardon?" Anne flushed, not quite taking his meaning, but understanding, at once, his tone.

He sighed. "Never mind. Give me the wretched pins." She did, and turned around obediently as he set the coiffure to rights, allowing only a small kiss to drop down at the nape of her silky neck.

"Lord Edgemere!"

"Your virtue is safe, Miss Derringer! I merely trifle with your affections!"

"Desist, then, my lord! Whatever became of that woman?"

"Which woman?"

"Miss Danvers."

"Gone, I hope."

"Oh, I hope not!"

"Have you lost your wits, you silly woman?"

Anne glared at him, then chuckled. "Possibly, but I have just had the most excellent notion."

The earl eyed her wearily. "That is . . . ?"

"She would be perfect for the countess Eversleigh! If she were just to take your barouche to Kingsbury, then change at Hampton for—"

"Do you always meddle like this?"

Anne's answer was firm. "It is not meddling, my lord, merely *managing* . . ."

"Do you always *manage,* like this?"

"But of course!"

The eighth Earl Edgemere nodded and sighed. "I suspected so, Miss Derringer. I am devastated to have to inform you, however, that I loathe and despise managing females!"

"Excellent, my lord, for I find the attraction between us troublesome. Since you are bound, at some stage, to loathe and despise me, we shall deal together perfectly!"

"Mmm . . ."

"Now, about that awful woman . . ."

"You do not give up, do you?"

"Never!"

"Very well, I shall speak to her about it. If necessary, I shall convey her to . . . where the devil shall I convey her to?"

"Staines."

"Very well. I shall convey her to Staines myself."

Anne smiled sweetly. "Thank you, my lord."

The earl bowed. "It is a pleasure, Miss Derringer."

Anne walked from the room without looking back. Lord Carmichael fingered the last of her pins absently. Anne Derringer of Woodham Place . . . now why did that name sound strangely familiar? Not alarmingly so, or obviously so, but the name nevertheless triggered something . . . some hazy half thought . . . . He would look into it. Something told him that if matters were permitted to take their course, he might have every reason to be interested in *any* affair bearing upon that name. He pocketed the pin, had a last, lingering glance at the ormolu clock, then clicked the door shut quietly.

"Kitty, if you persist in leaning over the rails, at least do it, I beg, with some style! Climb on the flower box so that your back can lean elegantly against the pillar. That way, you will not tumble precariously to a hideous death and I shall not be immediately turned off without a character!"

Miss Carmichael reflected on her governess's instruction. It seemed reasonable even if it erred, slightly, on the cautious. Nevertheless, full of boundless amiability, she altered her position and continued to stare at the proceedings below.

The earl's team had been called up and were now pacing the courtyard a trifle friskily. Lord Carmichael, much to Tom's disgust, had decided upon the landau. This absurdity came in spite of the delightfully clement weather and the fact that his lordship had a spanking-new phaeton at his disposal.

"Tom, can you picture your brother hoisting Miss Danvers up onto the high perch?"

Anne's reasonable query evoked a fit of giggles. She had to smother a laugh herself, for as it was, Miss Danvers's luggage was causing something of a commotion below stairs. She had arrived, it seemed, with seven trunks, a banded portmanteau and several strange-looking objects that the parlour maid pronounced as hatboxes, but which the under butler declared to be "frigging coal scuttles, they be that heavy." Whatever the contents, the luggage was now taking up most of the room in the chaise, and his lordship, of course, had not yet appeared.

That is not to say that Hastings, his valet, was not below stairs and furiously demanding to eject everything but Miss Danvers herself from the chaise. He pointed wildly at the elegant, gold embossed trunks, neatly packed and waiting patiently upon the flagstones for the appropriate attention. His lordship, it seemed, did not travel anywhere without twenty-four starched silk shirts and neckerchiefs, a riding coat with matching Hessians, morning wear. . . .

Anne would have gladly continued to eavesdrop on the catalogue of his lordship's unmentionables, but her attention became riveted on Miss Danvers, who was easing herself toward the carriage window with a decided scowl upon her frigid countenance.

"Have you no manners, young man?"

Hastings's eyes boggled. "Manners? *Manners?* You are nothing but a common—"

"Now, now, Hastings." The earl had appeared. His tone was suitably reproving, but his lips twitched in an unholy amusement that caused Miss Danvers's ire to turn upon him as well as his long-suffering valet.

Anne's heart lurched at the sight of him, resplendent in the most indecently fitting doeskins and a coat that proclaimed itself a Weston, for its styling was severe, curiously devoid of padding and a breathlessly close fit. Lord Carmichael's golden blond curls just caught the sunlight and gleamed entrancingly in the afternoon sunshine. The beaver set at a rakish angle upon his head was black, to match the riding coat and the gleaming top boots. Anne thought she had never beheld so handsome a sight. She drew herself back into the shadows, for her conduct, like the children's, was unseemly. One didn't stare over balconies and indulge oneself in glorious masculine sights. . . .

She sighed. Perhaps one simply peeked. Genteelly, of course. She stepped forward again and resolutely ignored the hammering of her heart. Would he look up? Of course he would; he would want to wave to Kitty and Tom. . . .

"I *knew* he was a great gun!" Tom's voice broke into

her reverie. "See, he is having the phaeton brought round!"

Kitty forgot her elegant posture and curved herself over the rails once more. "It is true, Miss Derringer! I bet he means to *follow* Miss Danvers to Staines."

"Don't be such a gudgeon, Kitty! He means to *lead* Miss Danvers to Staines."

"Whatever! He will be taking the phaeton, at all events."

Anne chuckled. "His lordship seems to have a pleasing sense of self-preservation. He obliges me, but still manages to do precisely as he wishes."

The children ceased dangling over the balcony to stare at their governess in astonishment.

"But of course," they said, almost in unison. "It is the Carmichael way. We *all* do."

Miss Derringer sighed. "I warrant you do."

The business of packing the eighth Earl of Edgemere's London necessities into the landau was not sufficiently interesting to arrest the children's attention for long. Especially not since, after a few brief words with the coachman and Miss Danvers herself, Lord Carmichael disappeared once more.

"Where the blazes did he go?"

"Blessed if I know! Let's find him!"

Anne opened her mouth to call them back, then shut it again. She was not inclined to waste her energies on useless ventures.

Besides, she understood their feelings. If she had not been brought up the soul of discretion, she would be running after him herself. The thought, though wanton, disreputable and faintly intoxicating, was honest. Miss Derringer could have no idea how pretty she looked with a faint flush to her cheeks and her bonnet askew from peering illicitly below.

The crack of a whip and the rolling of wheels on the

flagstones indicated that Miss Danvers, at least, was on her way. Anne breathed a small sigh. With her went the certainty of twenty pounds a year and a lifetime of servitude. Her new life promised more but was less—*far* less—predictable.

"Do you always spy on your employers?"

The colour grew rosier as Anne whirled round. "How in the world . . ."

"There is a secret stair. The children will show you, I have no doubt!"

"I have *every* doubt! Do you mean to say they may suddenly disappear and I shall have to hunt around for secret passageways? I thought that sort of thing went out with the Gothic!"

"It did! This, however, is a Gothic style villa. It could not claim so prestigious an appellation if it did not have its fair share of dungeons and skeletons and—"

"Now you are absurd, sir!"

"And you are beautiful, my lady! And you still do not answer my question. I believe you are being deliberately evasive."

"About spying on my employers? You are the first one I have had, and I will have you know, my lord, that *that* was not spying; *that* was merely assuring myself—"

"That I heeded your managing advice and escorted the old witch to Staines?"

"Which I see you are not doing . . ."

"Fiddlesticks! I most certainly am! My phaeton will pass the landau at the first junction, you shall see. I have at least an hour at my disposal before I need concern myself—"

"Are you aware of Aesop, my lord?"

"Aesop?" For once, the earl looked blank.

Anne smiled smugly. "The hare and the turtle . . ."

"Good God, woman! You don't mean to compare me to a common hare, do you? As for a turtle, the only thing

I noticed in that line was a hedgehog, and why that woman should have a hedgehog hiding in her coat pocket beats me . . ."

Their eyes met in dawning comprehension. Anne's merely twinkled, but the earl so far forgot himself as to allow the corners of his delectable lips to become involved, too. They twitched now uproariously.

"Shall you strangle them or shall I?"

Six

"The hare must fly."

"I disapprove of mixed metaphors, my lord."

"There is apparently much you disapprove of, Anne of the bewitching eyes."

"My lord . . ."

"Yes, yes, I know. You disapprove of that, too. I shall be very proper and say farewell, Miss Derringer. Be diligent in your duties."

"That is better, sir, but would be better yet if you released my hand and did not plant kisses upon my palm."

"How very disappointing and dreadfully dull, Miss Derringer! Nevertheless, since I wish to remain in your good books, I shall release your delightful fingers at once and make haste to catch up with Miss Danforth or Dishwater or whatever."

Anne giggled, though she tried vainly to be reproving. "Danvers, my lord, as I warrant you know!"

"Shall I have to have discourse with the dragon countess?"

"Very likely, for she will wonder at the change of arrangements. I have every faith in you, however."

"That relieves me, though does not promise for any less tedium. Still, I shall endeavour to earn one of your delightful smiles upon my return."

"Which will be . . . ?"

"Heaven knows! A couple of months, I should imagine. There are several bills being passed in the house, and I shall be attending the Tattersall sales . . ."

Anne knew a stab of disappointment, though she skillfully hid it. It was no concern of hers what the earl chose to do with his time. He had not mentioned the galas and balls and ridottos, but she was not so green as to consider he would not be attending. She wondered if there was already some suitable young lady picked out for him and decided, regretfully, that there would be. A man of his rank did not go unnoticed about the ton for long.

"I shall stay away, Miss Anne Derringer, for if I did not, I may break my promise to you, and that I could not, as a gentleman, countenance."

"Your promise?"

She looked up then and read the tender expression on his face. It was fleeting and replaced, almost at once, with one laden with a teasing irony.

"Just so."

Anne blushed.

"Fustian! I am no incomparable to hold you enraptured in my toils! You are perfectly free to return when you choose. Stop talking flummery and admit that some other pressing reasons keep you from home."

"Perhaps." The earl folded his arms jauntily and grinned.

Anne wished he did not look so annoyingly pleased with himself. She bit back a scathing comment, half-ashamed that she should be so piqued at his evident desire to set off.

"You will say farewell to those rapscallions for me. I wish you joy of them, Miss Derringer!"

"You may be sure I shall take good care of them."

"But will they take equally good care of you?"

The laughter was clearly visible in his eyes. Anne did not have the heart to persist in her disapproval.

"Very likely not! I shall write at once if I find my chamber too overcrowded with slugs."

"What a poor spirit, you are, to be sure. Write to me, indeed! I wager you will spend half the morning crawling across my estate in search of retaliatory bugs!"

"I will not take up your wager, sir, for very likely I shall lose my first quarterly pay. I find your idea inspiring!"

"Excellent, I shall look forward to a lengthy report of the term's excitements upon my return. By the by . . ."

"Yes?"

"You are not to be discomposed if you find the estate battened upon by several of my rather ramshackle acquaintances. They are dear fellows, but persist in the belief that this estate—which borders on Lord Anchorford's hunting box—is merely an extension of the same. Lord knows how they acquired such a chuckleheaded notion, but there it is. Every year I threaten to turn them out on their ears, and every year it is the same. I find I am too soft hearted by far!"

"It would appear so, my lord! How many people can one reasonably expect at any time?"

"Lord, I haven't the faintest notion. My housekeeper, Mrs. Tibbet, generally attends to their requirements. With any luck, they should not be a bother to you at all. The gentlemen tend to be a trifle foxed, but have a satisfying tendency to keep to themselves, since they are usually only accompanied by wives and do not have . . ."

He cleared his throat, aware that he was just about to make a horrible faux pas.

Anne, apprehending that he was referring to the many less respectable female diversions that London had to offer, smiled in quiet understanding.

"Just so, my lord." Her tone was an exact match of his earlier teasing banter.

"Good lord, Miss Derringer, how shocking that you are not shocked!"

"It must make a refreshing change for you, my lord, not to have to watch every sentence that slips off your tongue. It may have escaped your attention that though I am not wed, I am also not entirely a green girl."

"Thank the lord for that! However, in the matter of kisses—and though I try not to boast upon this point, I feel I ought to point out that I am a connoisseur—I find you green, Miss Derringer. Quite delightfully green."

"And I find you dreadfully improper! If you were a gentleman, you would not keep harping upon those kisses! Now go, I pray you, before I change my mind!"

The earl laughed. "You shall never change *my* mind, Miss Derringer. I shall have to spring the horses now, for you have kept me in idle dalliance far longer than I anticipated."

Anne dimpled, for it was hard to take issue with a man so brazenly impudent as this one, or hold a groat of malice when his very smile caused a fever of excitement to rage quite unaccountably within her.

She did manage to keep her countenance becomingly demure, however, as she raised a brow at the preposterous accusation.

"Idle dalliance? My lord, you wrong me!"

His laugh still rang in her ears as he disappeared in precisely the same mysterious manner in which he had arrived. It was only long after, when she was sipping a cup of chocolate in the cosy upstairs drawing room that the children *assured* her was actually the schoolroom, that she began to wonder.

What had he meant? She shall never change *his* mind? It was a puzzle, but then, everything about the last twelve hours was a puzzle. Anne set her cup down musingly. She wished her employer were not half so young or disgustingly amiable. If her wayward thoughts were to incline too often in that direction . . . but no! They would not. She set cup and saucer down with decision. As far as she was concerned, Lord Robert Carmichael was a figment of her fevered imagination.

Just as well he had chosen to fly the coop and head for the pleasures of London. It made her task so much the easier. From now on, she would don a mobcap and endeavour to play the part allotted to her with dignity, humour and yes—she would allow it—intelligence. She would earn her exorbitant wages if it was the last thing she did.

"Kitty, it is always best, when striking a pose, to endeavour to look alluring. That pout, though excellently framed, looks more devilish than charming. Here, let me show you . . ."

And so began Miss Derringer's rather exceptional duties as governess.

It might be said that the Viscount Tukebury and the older Miss Kitty Carmichael had never before found their lessons quite as unpredictable, alarming and outrageously interesting as they did now.

London was bustling with activity by the time the earl reached the refined portals of Boodles at precisely eleven o'clock. He had only partially recovered his temper by the time he was greeted reverentially at the door and divested of his cane, greatcoat and elegantly crafted beaver.

Miss Danvers had proved a trying travelling companion, for despite his foresight in travelling in separate conveyances, she had somehow contrived to weasel a lunch at the Red Fox Inn and several stops for "fresh air" out of his much put upon person. As if this was not enough, explanations to the countess Eversleigh had been harrowing.

Craven, he had toyed with the idea of simply unloading Miss Danvers and her multitudinous parcels and carrying cases. Then, with a sigh, the gentleman had come to the fore, and he had helped her down obligingly, winced a little at her simpers, and handed his card on to the butler.

The dowager countess had obviously not been overawed by his crest, for she left him kicking his heels in the blue salon for well over half an hour. This incivility alone would not have bothered him overmuch, but his sense of grievance could not help mounting as he was forced to alternately listen to Miss Danvers's strictures on decorum while watching her bat excessively short eyelashes in his direction.

The grandfather clock chimed the quarter hour with regularity as his poor horses were forced to pace about the courtyard, harnessed, still, to their coaches.

Finally—finally—the dowager duchess had made her entrance. She suffered the earl to clench her hand in his and nodded distantly at his elegant bow. Then her eyes fixed on poor Miss Danvers, and even the earl—for all his sufferings—had it in him to feel sorry for her.

A lesser woman might have quailed under the glare, but it was fortunate, indeed, that Miss Danvers was made of hardy stuff. She simpered ingratiatingly at the dowager and commented how awed she was to fall under her provenance.

The dowager's beady eyes passed from her, then back to the earl.

"Who *is* this woman?"

The earl was forced to explain, his long and careful dialogue interrupted at times by the simpering interpolations of Miss Danvers, who searched her enormous reticule for the various tomes of references she invariably carried upon her person.

The countess waved them away irritably, then pointed, once again, at Lord Carmichael.

"Who did you say she was?" With a sigh, the earl be-

gan again, only suspecting on his third retelling that the Dowager Countess Eversleigh might be a trifle deaf.

When her hearing aid was finally procured, he managed an abbreviated account into the long horn and cursed himself for a fool to get involved in the unlikely imbroglio. Only the thought of Miss Derringer's piercing, pleading tourmaline eyes kept him from making an ignoble exit down the dull marble stairs.

Finally, it was done. Miss Danvers's luggage was safely bestowed on the second lackey in the servants' quarters, and the earl was free to make his escape.

Staines was a good way away from his bachelor establishment in Mayfair, judiciously across from Grosvenor Square and overlooking several of the outstanding gardens that gave colour to the city, even in the duller, more lackluster months. So it was much later, indeed, that he made his weary entrance forcing—unbeknown to him—a footman, a valet, a housekeeper and a bevy of underservants from their beds.

By ten the next morning he had recovered sufficiently to partake of a mild repast, scan the *Morning Post* for any items of interest—there were none—and head on to his club.

Boodles was quietly active, for the season was about to begin and many other entertainments that were undoubtedly occupying the minds of member's spouses and hopeful offspring. Lord Robert Carmichael, however, had other matters on his mind.

"Morning, Edgemere!"

"Morning, Rutherford! I hear you won your wager."

"On Black Bess? But naturally. I've set my sights on another filly, however."

"Truly?"

"Yes, and not of the equine type." Lord Justin Rutherford looked too smug for Robert to misunderstand his meaning.

"Another opera dancer?"

"Spare me, Robert! I have had my fill of them. No, this one is an *actress*."

Lord Carmichael's eyes twinkled, but his voice was solemn as he judiciously agreed that that made all the difference. Heartened, Rutherford rather generously admitted that Miss Martin had a friend with ravishing guinea gold hair.

"Care to make her acquaintance?"

The Earl of Edgemere regretfully declined, for there were other matters requiring his attention.

"Justin?"

"Yes?"

"Do you still have contacts in the home office?"

"By God, Robert, you know I do! Why the interest?"

Carefully, Lord Edgemere explained. He was so unusually delicate about the query that Lord Rutherford's lazy interest was piqued.

When a simple ribbing caused his good friend to make a curt and quite unnecessary reply, his suspicions were confirmed. Miss Derringer—whoever she was—had better have a spotless record. Whilst Robert was as notorious as he for delighting in the muslin set, he had never before shown any matrimonial interest in the female sex.

The sharp set of his jaw and the uncommonly reticent manner of his speech confirmed Lord Rutherford's worst fears. Robert, at last, was hooked. He only hoped that this Miss Derringer—Anne, was it?—lived up to expectation. The name rang a faint but familiar bell in his head. Robert was right. There *was* something. . . .

The offices of Messrs. Wiley and Clark were bustling but surprisingly clean given their location just two streets down from the dockyard. The Thames was notoriously murky on this side of town, but none of the grimier aspects of the city were evident in the Spartan but elegantly furnished rooms.

The senior of the two men seated at an oak table almost the length of the second chamber looked up from his books and eyed his partner with interest.

"Any news, yet, Ethan?"

His inquiry was met with a shake of chestnut curls and a grimace at the large, hand-inscribed books in front of him.

"None, I am afraid. I have contacted the other beneficiaries, but the two remaining parties remain elusive. So far, the inquiries have not been exhaustive, but I might say they have been reasonably efficient. Any further search would involve a capital loss to the firm unless the investigation is offset by the sums held in trust."

Old Mr. Wiley set down his monocle and sighed. "I am not certain I can authorize such a step."

"But the parties can surely not object—"

"My dear Ethan, when you have been around as long as I have, you will learn not to make such foolish and ingenuous assumptions. Greed is limitless and rears its head in the most unlikely of places. No doubt Lord Featherstone and Miss . . . Derringer, was it? . . . ought to be grateful for the intelligence we bring. It is a guinea to a groat, however, that if we use some of the capital to *locate* them, one or other will lay a complaint against us to the authorities. It may not be fair, it may not be natural, but by *godfathers,* it is life."

The younger man still appeared troubled. "What shall I do, then?"

"Reinvest the capital. The money was earned on change; it is reasonable to assume the investors would keep it there. Merchant shipping is a good line; record the details carefully and buy in again."

"And the interested parties?"

"To *hang* with the interested parties! If they did not

respond to the advertisements in the *Morning Post*, it is not our fault. We still have our contacts in place at Whitehall. If they can help, so much the better. If not, well, no one can say that as a company we have not acted in the best interest of all concerned."

Mr. Clark sighed. Lord Featherstone he knew nothing about, but Miss Derringer . . . *she* was a different story. Above his touch, of course, but nevertheless not so stiff as to hold him in contempt.

They had spent a memorable hour together when Miss Derringer had recklessly placed all of her competence on change. He remembered advising her to go with a safer option, but she had smiled, simply shaking her glorious raven head. Her eyes had glowed bright as emeralds and she had had a reckless air about her. The air, Ethan knew, of a gambler.

He was not to know the despair that had driven her to him, or the do or die attitude that had caused her to be so unthrifty. Anne had decided that either way, with the competence or without, she would be doomed to a life of humble servitude. Betting on the *Polaris* was a whimsical way of casting caution to the winds. She had known, he knew, the risks. Unlike most gamblers, she had seemed not to care. When the *Polaris* had been sunk, she had nodded fatalistically and thanked him in quiet tones. It was what she had expected.

Now, it seemed, that communication had been false. It was the sister ship, the *Astor*, that had been caught on the rocky shores of the Eastern Hebrides. *Polaris* was late docking because it had been trading, quite profitably, in spices, tea and silk. Miss Derringer's competence had not grown into a fortune, but it had certainly trebled in the year or so that the *Polaris* had been trading.

Mr. Clark tapped his fingers on the table. He wished Miss Derringer had not been so precipitate in leaving Lady Somerford's, her last known address. Inquiries had led him nowhere. There was nothing, he knew, that he could do about the situation. He ticked a column in his ledger, then shut the book with a sigh.

Mr. Wiley chuckled. "Here's a thought, Ethan! You could locate Miss Derringer, then *marry* the wench!"

Not for the first time, Mr. Clark reflected on the bad taste of his partner. Still, he was a kindly man, so he managed a faint grin and endeavoured to ignore the thrust of the poor humour. Perhaps in his afternoon off he would make some investigations of his own. After all, people could not simply vanish into thin air. Or could they? Interesting thought.

Mr. Wiley held out the basket of delectable-smelling buns from Gunther's. A luxury, but it was his sixtieth birthday. Ethan bit into the sweet delicacy with unfeigned enjoyment. For the moment, the business of locating Lord Featherstone and the mysterious Miss Derringer was entirely set aside.

Seven

The night was adrift with stars. Anne looked out of her window in amazed wonderment. This was the first evening, since her fateful appointment as governess, that she had had the leisure to peer out of the tall lattice windows and thoroughly scrutinise the sky. She was right. The stars of the country seemed brighter and more numerous than those of the city. For an instant, she felt a pang, for the sky that she knew so well, the black velvet that had become her intimate friend, seemed suddenly vaster, a trifle aloof from the easy familiarity with which she had become accustomed.

But then, staring steadily, she located her old friend Polaris . . . then the blazing light of Venus, Arcturus, Sirius, Canopus, Rigel, Procyon. . . . She relaxed and allowed the known to guide her to the myriad unknown. The naked eye could not lead her to the farthest planet known to man, Uranus, nor could it reveal to her its two recently discovered satellites, Ariel and Umbriel. With diligence, however, she could make out Saturn's rings, the red glow of Mars, the constellations and clusters and trails of nebulae. . . . She felt the heady thrill of the adventurer, the explorer into the unknown, the unchartered. It was waiting for her, this night sky. Sometimes she felt its presence as a living thing. She moved from the window and retrieved her notebook where it was still tucked away at the bottom of her portmanteau. She need have no fear now of being labeled a bluestocking. There could be nothing more fitting, after all, for a governess.

Throwing a serviceable cape over her shoulders, she tiptoed downstairs with a newly lit taper and tried the door of the sewing room. It was locked and looked unlikely ever to open, judging by its age, lack of oiling and dust upon the handle. Annoyed, she walked down to the west wing. There she found a much more promising exit. The door, whilst locked, appeared to be in good repair. It would be a small matter of retrieving the key in the morning. For the moment, however, short of waking the house staff, there appeared to be no way outside.

Unless. . . . She remembered that Carmichael Crescent lived up to its name in that it was shaped in a semicircle. If it was symmetrical, as she suspected, there would be a balcony on the other side. If she could not stroll through the gardens, then stepping out onto the first-story balcony might serve her purpose just as well.

It was a good ten minutes later that Anne rounded the curve of the east wing and found her way into the room she suspected might serve her purpose. When she did, she blushed, for it had that distinctively masculine smell of leather and apple blossom that was never far from her unmaidenly thoughts. There was no question that this was his room, for the shelves were lined with books of masculine appeal and the far corner harboured the most enormous globe Anne had ever laid eyes on, set in beechwood and highly polished.

When she stepped closer, the corners of her lips tilted upward, for the globe was celestial rather than terrestrial, a further indication that my lord's mind wondered in close synchrony with her own. He had not lied, then. Nor, she realized, had he boasted when he spoke of his two-inch telescope. There it was, enticingly beyond her reach. It was in a glass cabinet crafted, almost certainly, specifically for the purpose.

She wondered if there was a key somewhere at hand. Never in her life had she had the opportunity . . . but no! He had promised to show her, and at the earliest opportunity she would tax him with that promise. It would not be fitting to go through his private drawers.

With a sigh, the very proper Miss Derringer realized that if she were not to be plunged into darkness by her flickering candle, she had best return to her chamber. Still, there would be other nights, and yes, the door eased open onto the balcony. She decided to use this wing rather than the more circumspect wing on the other side. Somehow, the room reminded her, touchingly, of Robert, Lord Edgemere.

The heavens seemed limitless. Anne suppressed her growing eagerness. Tomorrow, she would bring several precautionary tapers and resume her study of the firmament. It could only enhance her authority on the subject, and *that,* she reasoned, was the responsibility of an excellent governess.

Smiling a little, she made her stealthy way back to bed. It would have surprised her a little had she known she was not the only one roaming the enormous house that night. Tom and Kitty had been adventuring, too.

"Yawning your heads off at ten o'clock? I believe you must be sickening for something!"

Tom grinned a little, but Kitty had the grace to look uncomfortable.

"Shall we begin again? Tom, you may read from the top. Kitty, you may correct his pronunciation. That way, I shall know that you are *both* paying attention!"

"Miss Derringer, it is such a dismal thing to do, Latin proverbs at this hour. I am positive Robert would not wish it."

"Just as you are positive that this, and not that poky little chamber across the passage, is the schoolroom?"

Kitty giggled. "It is much more comfortable!"

"Granted, you little minx! Now read those proverbs before you drive me to an apoplexy."

Tom made a face that was exactly mirrored by his sister. Despite the grimaces, Anne thought there could not be a pleasanter looking pair of copper-curled scamps in all the world.

"If you get all ten correct, you shall have a reward."

"Reward?"

It was Miss Derringer's turn to grin. "We shall play truant and fish at Tom's creek. I have ordered up a picnic hamper, so desist, I beg you, from yawning, and get on with the wretched lessons!"

It did not need much more encouragement. The proverbs were dealt with in a satisfyingly short time, an excellent indication that the children had good brains if only they were extended a little. Anne tucked this newly gleaned information away for another day, then jauntily reached for her chip straw and borrowed parasol.

"Thank you, Kitty. The fringes are delightful, and the colour is exactly my favourite shade!"

"They match your eyes perfectly, Miss Derringer! Keep it. I dare swear I have *twenty* such parasols! Robert is forever buying them—to hear him, you would think I had a dozen freckles at the very least!"

"With your skin colouring you have to be careful, Kitty. Lord Edgemere sounds like the best of brothers to care about such trifles. Besides, I can see a good couple of sun spots peeking out from the bridge of your nose. Remind me to make up some of my elder flower water solution. Used with Venice soap, oil of rhodium and half an ounce of lemon juice, it is a truly excellent remedy. I know, for I used to run to the same problem myself."

"Now you are bamming us! Your skin is creamy smooth."

Anne smiled. "Perhaps because I am diligent in my use of a bonnet and parasol."

"Do you *always* have the last word, Miss Derringer?"

"Very nearly! It is satisfying, is it not?"

The days passed more quickly than Anne could have imagined. The mornings were far fuller than she had anticipated, for Mrs. Tibbet had taken to consulting her on household matters, reasoning that two heads were better than one, especially if the other was another female's.

What Jefferson, the gardener, and Carlson, the head groom, had to say about this state of affairs shall not be discussed here. Suffice it to say that a new regimen was instituted where all servants were required to bathe at least twice a week and were provided with crisp new liveries made up, in the evenings, by both Anne and the faithful Tibbet.

Between horse riding, fishing, star gazing and traditional lessons, the children were generally—but not quite—too tired for any real mischief. Anne had only the occasional frog in a tea cup and apple pie in bed to contend with. Since she was more than capable of dealing with such calamities whilst maintaining her endless good humour, the first month came and went with a remarkable rapidity.

Anne had never known such happiness. Even when she was eligible Miss Derringer of Woodham Place, comfortable in the first circles of society, she had never known such peace. As her fortune had been whittled away by a derelict father and equally spendthrift brother, she had endured two sorry seasons of ignominy, forced to hide her bookishness and her bright interest in the classics, in mathematics, in astronomy. She had been dressed in hideous pink confections cast off from her cousins, the Ladies Somerford and Apperton.

To hide her confusion she had adopted the pose of the ice maiden, making herself unapproachable even to the kindliest of suitors. Being a wallflower, she found, was preferable to the other type of attention she was prone to receive. Even with noble bloodlines—Anne was distant cousin to the Marquis of Gilroy—young men were prone to think dowerless ladies more inclined to certain liberties. She was not, of course. Her virtue earned her disapprobation and censure all round.

Funny to think Lord Edgemere was the man that finally provoked her wanton impulses. He, who had no need to dally with young improvidents. He could have the pick of the ton at his feet if he wished.

Anne thought, rather glumly, that he probably did. Then she caught herself up short. There would be no more of this maudlin daydreaming. She was as far beneath Lord Carmichael's touch as that pleasant gentleman at Wiley and Clark's had been below hers. That had not stopped her being polite to him, just as it had not stopped Robert—she must stop thinking of him as that—being pleasantly attentive to her.

Pleasantly attentive? He had been more than that, surely! Anne felt that strange warmth stealing over her body again. Lord Edgemere had been teasing, incorrigible, deliberately provocative. She could not deny it. He had been attractive despite his reprehensible ways.

And what she was to do with a sensual predilection way out of kilter with her normally stern, puritanical thoughts, she could not imagine. Admiring Lord Edgemere was like throwing a cap at windmills—she was not such a gapseed as to believe his flirtatious manner signified anything but an absurd propensity to levity. No doubt she was an amusing pastime. Certainly, he was curiously amusing—but no. It was dangerous for her thoughts to trail down that all too well worn path.

Anne glanced at the children. For once, they appeared to be concentrating on the lessons she had set them. Tom was musing on the life cycle of a frog and whether toads, like lizards, could endlessly regrow their tails. His study, thanks to some resourceful fishing by his governess, was practical as well as theoretical. He was therefore enjoying himself with unremitting relish. Anne smiled and thanked the heavens she was not born a tadpole.

Kitty was engaged in translating some fairly eyebrow raising French texts. The delectable novels had not previously been introduced into respectable schoolrooms. Again, delectable cherry lips widened in silent laughter. By the end of the week, Miss Carmichael's French would be flawless, even if her hazel eyes were slightly more saucer round than usual. There was nothing, Anne knew, so efficacious as a Gothic horror for bringing on a sudden dose of literacy.

Her gaze moved to the window, and she sighed. Her limbs were unusually mobile, her hands restless as she paced the cosy chamber the young Carmichaels had adopted as their own. She wondered if she might creep stealthily from the "schoolroom" and harness one of the horses the earl had obligingly stabled for their use. A little exercise might eradicate the salacious images that seemed burned into her wandering thoughts.

Images, always, of a blond Adonis. Handsome, strong, golden-haired and impossibly amusing. She thought of his mouth, his muscled arms entangled round her waist. . . .

"Miss Derringer, you look ill!"

"I am fine, Kitty, just a little out of sorts."

"You are pale and peakish! Perhaps you will swoon!"

"Stuff and nonsense! It is those ridiculous novels I loaned to you! Swoon, indeed!"

Tom looked up from his dissection. "Kitty's in the right of it, Miss Derringer! You look like a regular porridge brain."

Anne's lips could not help curving slightly. "I thank you for the compliment, young man!"

"It is not a compliment! It is the truth!"

"I see we shall have to have lessons in etiquette shortly. Tom, one never, never, *never* casts aspersions on a young lady's looks."

"Oh, I know *that.* But you are not young, Miss Derringer!"

"A flush hit, Tom! I concede it and concur with your wisdom. Perhaps you young varmints can be trusted not to leave your seats until I return?"

"Shall you be sick?" The hopeful tone was unmistakable.

"I am devastated to disappoint you, young man, but no, I shan't. My constitution is distressingly hardy. I shall merely take a brisk walk around the topiary gardens and hope to revive my sagging spirits."

"Oh! How perfectly tame! *I* should saddle Dartford and—"

"Have me dismissed without a character! Vile boy, Lord Edgemere would be *livid* if you attempted Dartford without permission. He is frisky even for the stable hands."

"I could manage him, though!"

"Don't be such a gudgeon, Tom! I wager all my allowance you could not get close enough to touch the reins!"

"Done!" Tom's hand shot out and grabbed his sister's in a boyish grip that was too exuberant by far.

"I forbid it!"

Anne endeavoured, through her headache, to control the pitch of her voice. She therefore appeared blithely untroubled, though her heart missed a beat at the sheer foolhardiness of what she was hearing.

Tom and Kitty dropped their hands and surveyed her with close absorption.

"Forbid it?"

"Absolutely." She held her breath and prayed her tone was suitably stern. Apparently it was, for they nodded and returned, at length, to their absorbing pastimes.

"I shall take my walk and shake the beastly cobwebs from my brain By the by, children, never say 'beastly.' It is a most reprehensible term and one you have never—*definitely* never—heard issue from the lips of your governess."

They giggled and promised to "be good," but Anne was not so green as to place much reliance on this gratifying indication of good will. She was dying to get out, however, so she gathered up her shawl and the apple green parasol and left the room quickly.

The topiary gardens were a splendid testament to Nash's careful design. They overlooked the formal rose gardens whilst retaining a unique character of their own. The hedges, trimmed with frivolous disregard for symmetry and an almost whimsical humour, appealed to Anne's sense of the ridiculous. As she admired some of the more absurd creations, she felt her ill humour vanishing, though the strange, deliciously light headed sensation brought on by errant daydreams remained with her.

She plucked a few of the primroses permitted to grow wild. Their colours were vivid and delightfully sunny. Tucking them into her modest, square-necked bodice, she looked up at the rows of windows towering in pleasing arches several floors up. Somewhere, the remains of poor Mr. toad lay scattered on a table near the beguiling Gothic fantasy. Poor Kitty! She would no doubt be in spasms of anxiety for the next week at least.

Northanger Abbey would be an excellent antidote, if

the earl's library were to house such modern and frivolous texts. Anne thought it would. Lord Edgemere, she suspected, had eclectic and civilised tastes. He also had the necessary sense of humour. She sighed. Her thoughts, it seemed, were destined to stray to the forbidden. No matter how much she scolded herself, she could not erase the annoying image of Lord Robert Carmichael from her mind.

Not for the first time, she wished her employer was kindly, round, humourless and in his dotage. He had no right to be so handsome, virile and unusually beguiling. Crossly, she stamped her foot on the beautifully kept lawns. She felt a little stab of pain where there was still a weakness in her ankle, but she was glad of it. At least the twinge diverted her thoughts.

And where were Kitty and Tom? She counted across and calculated that the large window on the second floor was probably the schoolroom more likely than not. Impulsively, she moved to the water fountain and chose herself a pebble. She aimed and unerringly hit the shaded, stained glass pane. There was no response.

"Playing truant, Miss Derringer?"

She swung round. There he was, amiably leaning against a beech tree and surveying her with eyes flecked with hazel that were quite improperly appreciative.

"Lord Edgemere! I was not expecting you!"

"For shame, Miss Derringer! Could you not have been waiting, in breathless anticipation, for my tread upon the footpath? Much more dramatic, I feel, and far more interesting!"

"Do you always talk such flummery?"

"Only when I mean it." He took two steps closer, and already she could feel the heat rising to her cheeks and her errant pulses begin their inevitable race to her throat, her wrists. . . .

Anne stepped back. "You promised."

"I promised not to compromise you. I did not promise not to talk to you in my own gardens."

"Then find, I beg you, a more edifying topic of conversation!"

"Very well, Miss Derringer, though I might say that you are unique among your sex if you find flirtation to be unedifying."

"So I have been told. How delightful of you, my lord, to remind me I am an unnatural female!"

"You delight in twisting my words."

"You delight in cutting up my peace!"

"Do I? I shall take that as encouragement." The earl smiled benignly and quite ignored the glare Anne bestowed upon his elegantly clad person.

"You would take anything as encouragement!"

"Very likely. I am especially happy to note that you desire to communicate with me in the most satisfyingly clandestine manner. The next time you throw a pebble at my window, however, do ensure I am within!"

Anne stared at him, open-mouthed. Lord Edgemere regarded her thoughtfully. Her lips were hopelessly kissable. He closed his eyes against the temptation, then continued his lazy, teasing tone.

"A moonlight rap would suffice most delightfully, though I implore you not to use too much force. Your aim, I note, is remarkably accurate—for a female—but a smashed window at midnight is something my valet cannot bring himself to approve of."

"Stop bamming me sir! That is the schoolroom window! I counted the panes most carefully."

Lord Carmichael feigned disappointment. "How very lowering. I felt certain I must always be uppermost in your thoughts! Perhaps I should remind you, however, that the gardens have an eastern aspect."

"Oh! That means . . ."

"Exactly! For someone with such an excellent wit and keen knowledge of the terrestrial globe . . ."

Anne laughed. "Very well, sir! I admit I was foolish beyond pardon! But what, if I might inquire, brings you home so soon? I had thought your business in London most pressing."

"It is, but there seems to be no end to the debate over the corn bill. Since I have stated my piece most strongly, I thought, in all conscience, I might make a brief visit home." He neglected to mention that the pleasures of London seemed suddenly, unaccountably, to have palled. Even the prettiest opera dancer of the Palace Royal had failed to tempt. And it had not been for want of trying! Robert almost grinned at her audaciousness. He had pressed a sovereign into her hand, of course, but he had declined the very kind suggestions she had put to him.

Somehow, the image of his dark-haired, slightly bluestocking, impossibly irresistible and altogether too virtuous employee kept taking the edge off his masculine appetites. On second thought, she had not taken the edge off. Rather, she had roused them to a frenzy, but had quite unwittingly made it impossible for them to be assuaged.

The ride home to Kingsbury had probably been record breaking, but there! Robert had not had the whit to time it, for his attentions were wandering abysmally astray. He gazed now at the object of his desires. She seemed unaware of the havoc she was wreaking, twining one of his prized yellow primroses. And didn't she know that tucking them into her bodice wis liable to drive a man crazy? Evidently not, for she seemed wholly absorbed in plucking the petals from them, one by one.

He resumed his teasing tone, for it was his best defense against other, less acceptable impulses.

"I am filled with misgiving, Miss Derringer! Usually by the second week of my absence I am delivered of several heavily crossed missives."

"From the governesses?"

"Exactly so! I am generally apprised of every misdemeanor, every truancy, every unsuitable term that has sullied the ears . . ."

"Good heavens! I hope you frank them, for the postage must be perfectly horrendous!"

"Then, they are as horrible as their reputation?"

"Oh, quite! They are also darlings of the first order. We do very well, indeed."

"Miss Derringer, I could kiss you!"

"So you always mention!"

She tried to keep her tone demure and faintly ironic, but her soft flush and bright eyes told another tale.

Robert's eyes softened. She was not, then, entirely insusceptible. Whilst the knowledge buoyed him, it also made him more cognizant of his responsibilities. She could not, in her position, afford to have her reputation trifled with. Reluctantly, he revised his intentions, but the militant twinkle in his eye remained, just the same.

". . . And shall no doubt continue to do so! It is your fault, you know, for being so remarkably adorable."

Anne scowled, for if she did not, she knew she would disgrace herself by falling quite wantonly into his arms.

"There. That is much better! Glaring will no doubt exercise a suitably dampening effect upon my ardour." The earl grinned engagingly. "Come, don't pull caps with me. We can cry friends, can we not, and stroll down to the river? I have to return tomorrow, so we might as well make the best use of the time."

The invitation was tempting, but Anne shook her head. "Desert the children and make off with the brother? My lord, you shock me!" She dropped the primrose and bent for the parasol. "We shall repair indoors, and I shall make them respectable. Then, after a circumspect half hour at least, they shall no doubt tumble down the stairs, undo all the good I have managed to contrive and talk ten to the dozen until you wish yourself back in London."

His lordship pushed back his tousled, slightly windswept hair and grimaced. "What an appalling plan! I suppose there is no alternative?" Almost as if he could not help himself, his eyes gleamed provocatively.

"None at all, you wretched man!"

"Very well, I shall walk down to the rose garden and nip through the maze so that I can enter my home through the front entrance."

Anne eyed him suspiciously, for though his *words* sounded reasonable, his *eyes* gave him away. They were alight with laughter.

She nodded, unable to quite fathom the source of his wicked amusement.

"Good day, then, my lord."

"Anne . . ."

"I apprehend you to mean *Miss Derringer*."

"Good lord, you are stubborn! Miss Derringer, then! If I should happen to get *lost* in my maze, can I depend upon your good will to find me? It is prodigiously puzzling, you know!"

Anne was not deceived for a minute. She smiled sweetly, however, and declared that of *course* he could depend on her to rescue him. She would send Tom in *at once* to fetch him out.

The earl acknowledged defeat. Anne felt exultant at her small victory and curtsied saucily as she stepped up the lawns toward the huge, stuccoed building that was Carmichael Crescent. Though she never turned her head once, her impeccably straight back tingled. Lord Edgemere, she knew, was watching most disgracefully.

Eight

Ethan Clark knew enough to try the back entrance. If he were to sound the knocker of the great hall, he would have been summarily dismissed from his purpose. Even so, the servants' entrance was a fairly stately affair, guarded by a dragon of a cook garbed in black worsted with a muslin apron. It was finely tucked in the Swiss style, but Ethan was happily oblivious to this important point.

When he inquired after Miss Anne Derringer, the cook's eyes grew wide, and she stepped aside, slightly, to allow the slim man entrance. Perhaps she was taken by the gleam of his topboots, or the elegant starching of his shirt points which, whilst not fashionable, were nonetheless silk and therefore slightly above her touch.

"Miss Derringer? She be the one what's come down i' the world. Used to be a lady, she did. Dined upstairs and all."

Ethan feigned polite interest in Miss Derringer's eating habits. He was rewarded for his patience by an invitation to "step in for a mite," a proceeding that he gladly undertook, for it was chilly outside and he had neglected to bring his greatcoat.

A rather pretty housemaid smiled at him as he entered the servants' hall. The dragon—or Mistress Partridge, as she preferred to be known—instantly dismissed her, exclaiming that she was a pert young thing and if it hadn't been for Betty's being laid up with the chilblains, she would never have been so fortunate as to be engaged.

Mr. Clark felt rather sorry for her, but since the object of his pity seemed accustomed to Mistress Partridge's outbursts, he did not waste time trying to reason with the dragon. Instead, he ignored the saucy minx's rather obvious wink and deferred most admirably to cook's strictures on household economy and the trials of keeping the establishment "as fine as nine pence" with a ramshackle staff such as she had to contend with.

Out of the corner of his eye, Ethan could discern a fellow he would have placed in just such a category. Brawny, unkempt and decidedly odorous, he occupied the only Windsor armchair in the room, allowing the under butler and two livened manservants the pleasure of the same cushionless, straightback chairs that he was presently enduring. Mistress Partridge rapped out a few orders, poured some fresh tea from the teapot—Ethan could not fault this—and settled herself into the hammock chair that was acknowledged, by the household, to be indisputably her own.

"Mr. Clark, 'ere—'e be interested in Miss Anne's doings. A likely lass she was—nuffin' beneath 'er, if I may say so, though she be a lady born."

"Ha! She ain't no lady *now,* if yer take my meanin'!"

"Watch yer mouf, Samson! We 'ave company." The dragon smiled at Mr. Clark most ingratiatingly and pressed a slightly scorched macaroon upon him.

"Do you have her forwarding address? The last I heard she was residing here, with Lady Somcrford."

"Ha!" came the interpolation from the Windsor chair. "She weren't no more *'residin'* than actin' unpaid housemaid!"

"Hush, Samson! Miss Derringer was worth three of yer! Very refined, she was, but not above sharin' some very 'andy 'ouse 'old tips, she weren't. It was *she* wot told me of restorin' with a lick o' French polish and a camel's 'air brush. And blue vitriol pulverized in a cauldron of boilin' water? That was 'er again."

It was the first housemaid's turn to enter into Anne's praises. She had entered by the kitchen door, just in time to note the dapper Mr. Clark. She tidied her apron and tripped in merrily.

"Be that Miss Derringer you be speakin' of?"

Mrs. Partridge nodded austerely. Lucy was a good housemaid, even if a trifle forward at times.

"Oh Miss Derringer was regular wunnerful, she was! I used to suffer most terrible from spots, and she recommended watercress to me. I been eatin' it every mornin' for me breakfast, and even Sam—the footman from Lord Inglesides—says he never saw the like! A regular miracle. *And* she taught me about Canada balsam in the linin' of 'is 'ats."

This last was a mystery to Mr. Clark, who unfortunately knew nothing of the finer intricacies of waterproofing felt headgear. He understood, however, that the housemaid was in raptures over Miss Derringer's sage advice, even going so far as to pass on a hint regarding the prevention of premature balding. Mr. Clark's lips twitched, though he remained studiously polite and thanked—Lucy, was it?—with due gravity. Now, he felt, it was time to edge round to the purpose of his visit, since they seemed, sadly, to have digressed.

"Does anyone know what has *become* of Miss Derringer?"

"Last I knew she was 'eaded for Lady Eversleigh. A regular old tartar she is, and so I told 'er, but Miss Anne, she only shook 'er 'ead and smiled sadly. Reckon as she 'ad no choice. But there, I was never a one to gossip about me betters!"

Mr. Clark nodded solemnly and agreed that common tattling was reprehensible. Then he leaned forward, engagingly, and asked in a delightfully confidential manner, whether—just between them, of course—Miss Derringer had ever arrived at Lady Eversleigh's.

"Best ask Samson that. 'Ere, Samson! You drove Miss Derringer down to Staines. I remember she gave yer a sovereign for yer trouble. Paid yer in advance, too, which was mighty fine of 'er if I say so meself!"

The coachman shuffled slightly in his chair.

"What of it? It is all spent now, and nothin' to show for it, I might add, but a bloody bad 'ead. Knocked up from blue ruin I was for a week!"

"And whose fault was *that,* Samson Weatherby? You were lucky Lord Somerford was away, else he would have cast you off without a bleedin' character!"

"Shut yer mouf, woman!"

"We 'ave company, Samson!"

"I don't give nothin' for yer namby-pamby company. 'E don't 'ave a 'andy bunch of fives, and that is all *I* consider when there be company!"

Mr. Ethan Clark, of the refined company of Messrs. Wiley and Clark, allowed this piece of interesting information to formulate in his head. When he unraveled the mystifying utterance, he was given to understand that the coachman Samson had insulted his manhood gravely. Though he was a slender personage, and rather gentle by nature, there were certain constructions upon his character that he simply could not allow. This was one of them.

He stood up, and politely indicated the courtyard through the open window.

"Care to test that theory?"

"Huh?" Samson did not immediately understand, for Ethan's tenor was mild and ironic rather than belligerent and threatening, the tones to which Samson was more *immediately* accustomed.

" 'e wants a bout of fisticuffs wif you!" Lucy was the first to interpret.

The dragon was shocked. "Not in the servant's parlour, 'e don't!"

Mr. Clark grinned and bowed, glad to be out of the rickety, hard chair at last. "Of course not, Mistress Partridge! I wouldn't *dream* of offending your sensibilities! I am certain, however, that you would wish me to defend my honour?"

Defend his honour? He sounded like a regular gentleman, he did! Mistress Partridge simpered a little and admitted that she had no objection to a bout of fisticuffs on the cobblestones outside.

Samson, who was rather slow, only now divined the trim young man's intention. His eyes gleamed menacingly, for he was always game for a fight, especially when the odds were quite distinctly in his favour.

" 'Ow about a bet on it, then? Care to lay out ye lard as fast as ye tongue?" He sneered a little as he eyed his victim. Mr. Clark stood his ground and nodded.

"Very well, I shall wager a quarter on the outcome."

"Well breeched, are yer? It is done!"

"Samson, yer cannot agree when yer *know* yer haven't a farthing, never mind a quarter, to spare!"

"Shut yer silly gap, Lucy! It is a done deal. I'll finish the lad off in a second flat."

Mr. Clark stepped into the fray. "I'll see the colour of your blunt or I'll not play."

"Welching, are yer?" Samson glared at him and sneered.

"Not welching, merely protecting my interests. Can you match my quarter or not?"

"I'll match yer 'ead against that wall, I will!"

"I take it from your delightful response that the wager is off."

Samson saw a quarter drifting from his grasp. He was fly enough to pull his punches when he had to.

"Wait!"

"What?"

"Before I mulch yer into a pulp, I'll match ye wager."

"Excellent. You have the coinage, then."

"No! I have somethin' yer want more."

"And what may that be?" Mr. Clark sounded bored, as if he was tired of the whole trumped-up argument.

"Information on that there Derringer woman. *Blessed* if I'll call 'er a lady!" Samson's voice was defiant, but Ethan could not care a hatpin. He had almost given up hope of tracing Miss Derringer, but this bully seemed to be the unexpected chance he had been hoping for. He kept his voice calm, though his excitement would, to the discerning, have been clearly palpable.

"Not a very equal offer, but I accept nonetheless. Let us step outside, mister coachman, and see who is the better man!"

Lady Somerford rang the bell, and nothing happened. She rang again, and *again* there was no response. She made a mental note to inform the butler at once, just as soon as she could find him.

She would have been astonished to know that there was a good reason for the tardiness of her house staff. All her servants were outside, enjoying the spectacle of a lifetime. A prize mill in the staid, terribly British cobbled courtyard of Somerford Mansions.

The chandler, the chimney sweep, the knife grinder and the two rather intrigued tradesmen had also seen fit to tarry a little and watch. It was just as well she was seated in the canary yellow drawing room, surrounded by edifying albums of samplers and dried flowers. Had she been positioned at any of her numerous windows, she would undoubtedly have succumbed to a serious fit of the spasms.

Mrs. Tibbet had outdone herself. The table was overflowing with floral arrangements in vase-shaped trumpets of sparkling crystal. Fern fronds offered soft, verdant backgrounds to brighter-coloured blooms, and the silver salvers gleamed upon the table. They were filled to the brim with interesting delicacies like scalloped veal, larded sweetbreads, fricasseed partridge, raised perigord pies, new potatoes and spinach, a side of turkey and the promise, on the polished oak sideboard, of a final remove of honeycomb, lemon pudding, jam tartlets and a thick, golden custard that was the housekeeper's quite famous—and most decidedly secret—recipe.

Miss Derringer was particularly pleased, for she had contrived to keep Kitty's burnished copper curls in check with a length of delightful, merry, but nonetheless perfectly respectable ribbon. Tom's face was no longer grimy, and he had agreed to change into a crisp linen shirt and knee breeches for the occasion. Robert had affected shock and had teased the children mercilessly all through dinner, keeping his eyes very virtuously focused on the flickering candle rather than on the temptations beyond it. He wished, for a moment, that Miss Derringer would leave off her crisp white mobcap or perhaps furnish herself with a slightly less severe wardrobe, but then brought himself up short.

She had been destined, he remembered, for Lady Eversleigh. That fine lady would have approved of nothing beyond drab colours and dull necklines. Anne, with her radiance and wit, must have truly been at her last stand to countenance such a dreary life for herself. And she had done it without complaint, with stoic calm and an admirable determination that brooked no argument. Lord Carmichael could not help admiring her. He cursed the fact that he had employed her, for that circumstance must naturally cast a reserve between them. He could not simply marry her out of hand, for she would never agree. The stinging slap upon his person was surely testament to that.

If he could court her, convince her that being penniless was no obstacle to a respectable marriage . . . . He sighed. He could not. She was too damnably upright to concede. Still, perhaps he could—should—convince her of his sincerity. Robert drew in his breath. The thought was a revelation to him, for though he could not deny the magnetism that drew him to Miss Derringer like a moth to a candle, he had not before formulated it in such concrete terms. Yet, there she was, mildly quoting unmaidenly Latin to Tom and causing a disreputable grin of comprehension to cross his face . . . oh, he *did* love her!

"Learning your Latin proverbs, Tom?"

Out of the corner of his eye he saw her blush. No doubt he was not meant to have overhead that particular phrase. Still, she did no more than straighten her back slightly, more rigidly than it was already held, and reach for a serving of fritters. He turned his attention, again, to Thomas.

"I should send you to Kestridge, after all! You shall do very well, now, I am certain!"

A look of alarm crossed his sibling's face until the penny dropped that he was a victim, once again, of his brother's unsporting tongue. A severe pummelling ensued, during which a straight-faced butler just managed to prevent a salver of lobster sauce from oversetting all over Kitty's newest and most modish evening gown.

Amid the ensuing shrieks, Anne's voice of calm prevailed.

"Have done, Tom! My lord, I shall not be so brass-faced as to reprimand you in your own dining room, but I shall, perhaps, venture to mention that antics like common brawling are best left to after dinner, when the ladies have retired."

Kitty shot her a piercing glance and giggled. She *liked* being classed as a lady and hearing her dear, adorable, bullying brother being politely ticked off for impropriety.

It made a delightful change and one which she highly commended. When she ventured to say so, she received a pinch on her cheek for her trouble. A darkling glance was cast Miss Derringer's way, but the smile that accompanied it entirely eradicated any alarm she might have suffered.

Smoothly, the earl allowed his wineglass to be refilled and directed the conversation toward Miss Derringer. He asked her whether she had found the stars to be satisfactory, since Carmichael Crescent was such a satisfying distance from London. She blushed with pleasure, pleased and a little surprised that the earl had remembered her interest. It was a fortunate choice of topic, for her face lit up and she described, in surprising detail, the sightings she had been fortunate enough to view.

"Have you seen the planets?"

"Most, my lord, although not, unfortunately, our newest planet."

"Georgus Sidum?"

Anne smiled. "I believe they are calling it Uranus, now, my lord."

"So they are! You keep up extraordinarily well with the Royal Astronomical Society."

"I try to read their transactions, although they are not always easy to come by." Anne neglected to say *especially* if you were a young lady eager to avoid the debilitating label of "bluestocking."

The earl, however, believed he understood. He nodded his head absently and flicked a sweetmeat across the table. It was neatly caught by Tom.

"Shall I show you my telescope?"

Anne blushed. How could she say that she had already seen it and that it was the most wonderful instrument she had ever laid eyes upon? She had no business, she knew, entering the earl's private apartments, much less the inner sanctum of his library. And yet, she had. Night after star-filled night.

"I would love to, my lord." Perhaps, later, she would be able to tell him the truth.

He nodded. "Excellent. After dinner, then."

He was rewarded with such a breathtaking smile that he could not help but add the words in a low, somewhat teasing, somewhat caressing tone, "When it is quite dark."

Anne felt the crimson rise to her cheeks. She could not scold him for such blatant innuendo in front of the children, so she addressed herself almost entirely to her lemon pudding for the remainder of the evening.

Her indignation did not abate, however, when she heard a faint, masculine chuckle escape his lips. She could almost feel his breath upon her nape, for he was seated to her left and she had studiously turned her head toward the floral arrangement on her right. All her senses tingled, and she wondered, for an instant, whether he suffered the same agonies. She hoped he did.

Tom and Kitty noticed none of the subtle tensions that beset their elders. It was between a third helping of custard and jam tartlet that Tom commented on the commotion outside. Kitty ran to the window and flung open the drapes in a most disreputable way.

"Look! It is a high perch phaeton and a chaise and a . . ."

"Where?" Tom didn't wait for her to finish, but jumped down from his seat in a manner that made poor Miss Anne cringe. The earl must think little of her ability to teach common table etiquette!

"Oh, no!"

"What?" the earl inquired.

"It is Lord Willoughby Rothbart and Lady Caroline!"

"Bother!" Kitty pulled a nasty tongue, and Tom emulated her with the unique gusto of his age. The earl frowned, but did not admonish them as perhaps he ought to have. The names meant little to Anne, so she turned inquiring eyes to the earl. He did not seem unduly pleased, but managed to hide his annoyance admirably. It was left to her to wonder if she had imagined the infinitesimal pause that had followed the announcement.

"Is there anyone else?" his lordship asked.

"*Scores* of people!" Tom announced this with relish. The earl sighed.

"It must be the hunting party for Lord Anchorford's. I had forgotten it was that time of year again."

"Children, I believe it is time we retired."

"No!" the earl objected.

Anne turned inquiring eyes upon her employer.

For once, he seemed uncertain. "That is . . . I bid you a very good night, Miss Derringer. Kitty, Tom." He took their hands briefly, then turned from the room.

Anne blinked. What had she done? The earl seemed suddenly so shuttered, so terribly formal. She swallowed and picked up Kitty's little posy. Both children appeared unusually subdued. They trailed after her up the winding stairs that led to the nursery chambers. Somehow, the night seemed entirely dimmed.

Nine

Although he was panting heavily and sporting a bloody nose that threatened to ruin forever his smart neckerchief and elegant shirt points, Mr. Clark could not help smiling. He felt singularly at peace with the world, for not only had all his assiduous training at Gentleman Jackson's paid off, but he had also planted a facer on Samson the coachman that would likely as not leave him with a black eye for weeks.

Further, that gentleman was now lying face first in the cobbles and moaning pitifully. Mr. Clark was not a vengeful man, but he had not liked Samson from the start and could not help but feel that the man had got what was coming to him. Evidently, the chandler, the tailor and at least two unidentified onlookers felt the same, for they were clapping and cheering in a most satisfactory manner.

Mr. Clark grinned and wondered, fleetingly, what his staid and cautious partner, Mr. Wiley, would think if he were to see him now. But he wasn't going to, of course, so on this basis Ethan smilingly accepted the offer of a round of ale up at the White Hart. Before this momentous occasion, however, he had business with Mr. Samson.

It was the small matter of Miss Derringer's whereabouts, she being nowhere next or nigh Staines. Ethan's reliable sources had already checked.

Samson sat up in the dust and glared belligerently at

Ethan, though his countenance held a grudging, if reluctant, respect.

"Never would 'ave thought yer lily white mawleys would stand up to a drubbing!"

"I live by my wits, but it is always good to have a handy bunch of fives."

Samson nodded in agreement, then scowled.

"I suppose you want to know about that . . . that . . ."

"Lady." Ethan stressed the word and stared hard at his adversary.

Samson, tired of the spectacle and of the dust rubbing into his swelling eye, capitulated. "Oh, orl right, *lady,* then!"

"That is better! Do you have her address?"

Samson snorted. "Am I 'er keeper? Orl I can tell yer is, I dropped 'er off three miles from Kingsbury."

"Why, Samson, yer lazy good for nothing . . ."

The dragon approached him threateningly. Ethan almost felt sorry for the coachman, but his concern was more with Miss Derringer.

"Before the toll or after the toll?"

"Dunno." Samson twitched his shoulders.

"Samson, there is black puddin' for dinner tonight and I *swear* yer shall 'ave not a morsel if yer don't tell this 'ere gennelman all that yer ken."

Ethan secretly blessed Mistress Parson, for her threat seemed to be having the desired effect. Samson's mouth was opening. He scowled and dusted himself off. The butler and the liveried servants drifted back into the house. Now that the mill was over, there was no point making a spectacle of themselves. If the master should appear. . . .

"Dropped 'er off a little way back from Kingsbury on a dirt track. 'Andy little shortcut it be if yer know what yer doin'."

"Is it on a map?"

"Warrant not. Private property, yer see."

Ethan's heart sank, and his hand fisted into a ball. He would like to cut out Samson's liver. Miss Derringer had been a delightful young lady. The thought that harm might have come to her . . . that she might have been arrested for trespass. . . .

"Do you know whose property she was abandoned upon?" He tried to keep his voice calm.

"Think I'm green be'ind me ears? Of *course* I know what land it was!"

"Whose, then?"

"Some big toff. Lord Carmichael or whatever."

"Thank you." Ethan released the man's shirt buttons. He doffed his cap at Mistress Partridge, smiled engagingly at both the upper *and* the lower housemaids, stanched his blood heroically with an ice white handkerchief and bade them all good day.

Anne watched from her window as several carriages stopped by the courtyard. She released her hair from its decorous prison and brushed it soundly. Who were they, she wondered, and why had the children scowled so fiercely? She had not liked to press them into confidences, for the earl's guests were, after all, his business. Still, she could not help feeling a slight stab of disappointment. She would have to wait for another time to view, at last, the modern, deliciously intriguing telescope that sat so invitingly in its cabinet. That was *all* she was disappointed about, she told herself crossly.

She had no desire for midnight trysts with Lord Carmichael. He might cause her pulses to race mercilessly and her instincts to turn against her in the most deplorably wanton of ways, but she was still a lady born. Young ladies did not yearn to be kissed with passion and to be held, trembling, in fiercely tight arms. They did not throw caution to the winds and. . . .

Good God! She was behaving like a veritable schoolgirl! The very proper Miss Derringer pulled herself up short. Tom and Kitty, she hoped, were sleeping like babies. She blew her candle and shut her ears to the revelry below stairs.

It was midnight—past that, if the darkness was anything to go by. Anne woke up with a start. Something had disturbed her. Was it footsteps? Perhaps it was a stray valet or maidservant. Judging by the carriage loads that had arrived today, the house would be full of them by morning. It was fortunate that house guests tended to bring their own staff. Mrs. Tibbet would be quite overset, otherwise. At all events, she would have her work cut out with the extra guests to feed, linen to provide for. . . . Anne would see what she could do to help in the morning.

She tried to sleep again, but she was tense and unusually jumpy. Too many thoughts crowded her head at once. She needed to clear it, so she could think straight in the morning. Perhaps a breath of fresh air. . . . Her eyes, by now, were accustomed to the dark, so she did not need a candle to light her way to the window. She pulled the drapes and gazed at the wilderness of stars. There was something about them that fascinated her, compelled her to do more than just blink and acknowledge their existence. They called to her, called and cajoled. They invited her to partake of their glitter, to plumb their depths, to understand their light, their distance, their greatness. The night sky had always acted as a restorative to her soul. Her spirit drew thirstily on its magnitude and retained, in a small way, some of the sparkle.

She threw a dressing gown about her. The house was quiet. She must have been mistaken about the footsteps, for there was not a single creaking floorboard. Her ears were sharp, so she was confident she was not mistaken.

She lit a taper using the tinderbox by the hearth. The room flickered to light, casting strange shadows that reflected her sultry mood. She crept from the room and shut the door quietly behind her. The path she would take was well known to her, for she had used it time and time before.

The earl's library was in total darkness. She knew that, because there was no telltale light beneath the crack in the door. Relieved, Anne pushed open the now familiar door. Lord Carmichael, she reasoned, was now as soundly asleep as the rest of the household. She walked over to his desk and lit another, longer, candle with the flame of her taper. It was wax, so she could rely on its gentle half light for some hours.

Briefly, she looked at the cabinet. The telescope was still there, nestled snugly in its glassy cocoon. She sighed at the temptation as she had on every night she had visited this chamber.

Then she eased open the door and walked outside. The fresh air struck her like a splash of cold water. It was a shock, but refreshing to her strangely deflated nerves. She pulled the gown about her a little more closely, then looked up at the world's greatest wonder. In the constellation of Leo, there was a comet, bright and unmistakable. It blazed a trail of fire that seemed, to Anne, like a faint haze of dust. She knew it was brilliant beyond imagination, hot beyond belief, fathomless yet indisputably real, as predictable as the sun's rising and setting. It had an orbit that was definable and calculable. It was the incarnation of rational and scientific thought, yet it inspired in a qualitative rather than quantitative manner. She settled to watching it, wishing she had remembered her log book. The last few nights had been cloudy, and though she had been expecting it, she had not yet been granted the felicity of seeing it.

"Celeste."

Anne swung round. Lord Carmichael had been watching her. In that sudden, breathtaking instant, she knew it. How long had she been star gazing? She knew not, but it was true the sky was lighter than she remembered.

"My lord . . ."

"Don't you think, in these circumstances, *Robert* would be more appropriate?"

Anne tried to still the beating of her heart. It was hard to answer when he was watching her so closely, and with such obvious amusement. Why did he stare so hard at her lips? And why, when she took two steps backward, did he follow her, so that she was almost leaning against the rails of his balcony? There, that was better; his eyes had left her mouth. Perhaps she could, in a moment, breathe again . . . but no, now he was staring at her gown. Even in the flickering candlelight she could see the blaze in his eyes . . . good God, she had to do something. . . .

"Robert."

He smiled. "Better, much, much better. And I shall call you . . ."

"*Not* Anne!" Too late, she remembered propriety. He smiled indulgently.

"No?"

"No!"

"Then, I shall call you, my dear Celeste."

Anne was confused. "Beg pardon?"

"I shall call you Celeste, for your eyes shimmer like stars and your heart is as bold and as bright as the firmament."

Anne could not speak. He drew her hair to him in long, silky strands, so she was forced to step forward, closer to him than was perhaps entirely sensible. He smiled mysteriously and placed his finger on her chin. Then he tilted it upward and looked into the tourmaline eyes made dark by the night. "Do you still claim such a knowledge of the celestial globe?"

She nodded.

"Share it with me." His whispered words aroused such a passion in her that she mistook his sense and wrapped her arms around his taut, deliciously well proportioned back. She heard an intake of breath, and then his mouth was upon hers, teasing, passionate and everything her imagination might have desired but dared not dream, even to herself.

"Celeste, Celeste . . ." The words were whispered endearments on her throat, her neck, her chaste dressing gown with its chintz trim and its high neck ruffles. He struggled with it, moaned slightly, then pushed her away.

She staggered a little against the rail, her eyes wide and uncertain.

"You torture me, you enchanting little witch! I wish I had never given you my promise. But I have, so I shall play the gentleman and spare you the trouble of slapping me."

Through her daze of physical passion, Anne understood. She nodded her head dumbly, feeling foolish and more than a little contrite that it was *he,* not she, who had called a halt to the madness.

"I shall be gone tomorrow, so you shall not be troubled by my attention again."

Anne was always honest. "My lord, you must know that I appear to have lost all sense of virtuous propriety. Though I am troubled, I have to admit that it is not by your attentions!"

At this, he cocked his head to one side reflectively. Then he eyed her again, the telltale hint of laughter lightening his brow. The sky was pinkening up at every moment, so she could see his square jaw and soft curls just brushing his shoulders. The golden hair glinted tantalizingly close, and she could feel his eyes upon her blushing cheeks. For, although she knew full well she was behaving like a hoyden, she still felt unaccountably shy.

"Honest to a fault, my little Celeste! And I shall have to bear this confession in mind, for though I return to London tomorrow, you may be perfectly certain my return shall be swift and sweet."

"Your lordship!"

"So formal, again?"

She nodded. "I may have perversely enjoyed your attentions—no doubt they are well tested—but I nonetheless remain a virtuous woman. I cannot think your imminent return can bode well for either one of us, so I beg you to stay away. If you do not, I shall have to terminate this position."

"You are an uncompromising woman, Celeste."

"I have two wills to fight, my lord—yours and my own."

"Have you ever considered what it would be like *not* to fight?"

"That is like saying have you ever thought of behaving dishonourably? I am certain, my lord, that you would not countenance such a thing."

He laughed. "Not, I have to admit, until I encountered *you,* Miss Derringer! Very well, I shall stay away. When I return, you may be satisfied that this engagement, at least, is terminated."

Anne nodded. He was being scrupulously fair. It was quite ridiculous that her heart should feel so heavy or her hands reach out so instinctively to keep him with her.

He sensed her movement, for his arms suddenly became entangled in hers; then his fingers were about her waist with his face, inscrutably, in her long, untrammelled hair. He kissed her lightly, lingeringly, then watched the candle finally extinguish in her hand.

"It is late. Or rather, it is early. If you do not wish to

be wholly compromised, Miss Derringer, you had best return to your quarters. It will not do for you to be . . . bother!"

"What is it?"

"Hush!"

Anne heard it clearly. The door to the library was opening. She, like the earl, felt sick. If she were to be found with him at this time, she would be ruined. She wrapped the gown tightly about her as if the flimsy thing would afford her protection. It would not. Nothing could, and in that split instant, they both knew it.

Robert pushed her against the rails once more. This time, though his muscles were taut with tension, it had little to do with desire. She felt his urgency, however, and obediently retreated.

"Stay here!" The words were more gestured than spoken, but Anne understood. Her whole life depended upon it, for what possible use either as companion or governess could a fallen woman ever be? None at all. She thought this calmly, rather than hysterically as might, perhaps, have been expected.

It was almost in a detached manner that she watched the handsome lines of Robert's back retreat into the house. Who could be entering the library at that hour? An overzealous housemaid? *Surely* not one of the hoards of houseguests that seemed suddenly to have descended upon them?

But yes! It was a woman's voice. Most likely the Lady Caroline of whom Kitty spoke, for insofar as Anne was aware, she was the only woman to make up the hunting party.

"Robert, darling! I have searched for you simply *everywhere!*"

Anne felt sick. The simpering intimacy of the tone could not be mistaken.

She could not hear Lord Carmichael's reply, for it was

in very low tones that he spoke. Anne despised the compromising position she was in. It seemed hardly fair to be so imminently on the brink of scandal. She and the earl had wasted such a great deal of time engaged in the virtuous task of *resisting* each other's charms.

Now she was forced into the untenable position of eavesdropper, and she squirmed at the very thought. Especially when she caught sight of Lady Caroline through the glass. She was a picture of glorious curls piled high, golden like Robert and ravishingly beautiful. Anne could not see much, for the woman's back was turned to the window, but she could see that the creamy flesh of her shoulders was displayed bounteously in a bodice that was both strapless and fashionably low cut at the back. My lady's evening gown was obviously of the first stare, for Anne fleetingly noted that it was spangled in gold and edged in a floss silk that shimmered as Lady Caroline moved. Although Miss Derringer could not make out the full elegance of her form, she had no doubt that the low, rounded cut of the gown would set off the stranger's features to perfection. Lady Caroline was obviously blessed with a beguilingly feminine form, something that Anne had not previously too keenly felt the lack of. Now, with her statuesque height and slender waist, she felt rather like a waif than the desirable siren Lady Caroline appeared to be.

She closed her eyes as the lady flagrantly disobeyed propriety and began playing intimately with his lordship's shirt ruffles. Anne felt hot from shock and shame. How wicked of her to have been entertaining wanton desires! Clearly, Robert was meant for another. Lady Caroline would not have been so forward if she was unsure of her welcome. Surely, too, she would not have searched for Robert *anywhere* at that hour unless they had an understanding. How could she have been so blind? And the children? Their reactions should have told her that Lady

Caroline was more than a passing guest. Their dislike had been palpable.

Oh, what a coil! Should she come out and declare herself? Anne thought not. Apart from her own ruin, it would bring shame on Lord Edgemere and hurt the innocent victim in all this, Lady Caroline. No, it would be her penance to wait patiently on the balcony and pray for a swift escape.

"Caroline, I thought I made my intentions clear!"

"Indeed you did, Robert! You promised to marry me and marry me you shall!"

"I was in my cups, Lady Dashford, and well you know it!"

"What odds? You offered and I accepted. That is all there is to it."

"I offered after you'd plied me with enough blue ruin and cherry brandy to sink a galleon!"

"Let us not quibble, Robert. You shall have your freedom when we are married, and before that . . . well, you shall have your usual rewards."

The words were hideously intimate, and Anne felt routed to the spot. So! Lady Caroline was no victim! The thought simultaneously heartened and sickened her. Whatever she was, she was cunning and vile, and Lord Carmichael had bedded her. Would he try to do the same with her? Anne shivered.

"I do not want your favours, Lady Caroline! You were spoiled goods before ever I touched you and you know it! By God, if I hadn't been such an innocent little greenhorn at the time . . ."

"But you were, weren't you, Robert?"

The voice was honey sweet, but Anne recoiled at the undercurrents.

"Yes, more is the pity! But I shall not pay forever for that sin, Caroline! I agreed to marry you out of compassion, but I have learned, recently, that compassion is not a good enough bedfellow for marriage."

"And what is?" The words grated harshly on Anne's untrained ears.

"Respect, boundless admiration, passion—and yes, dammit, *love* is the proper basis for the wedded state!"

"Oh stop reading penny novels, Robert! You may be experienced with women, but you and I both know such talk is for sapheads!"

"Perhaps I shall surprise you, Caroline!"

"Do whatever you like so long as the Carmichael ruby is on my finger."

Anne had to stop herself from gasping. The woman was as cold as the ice maiden *she* had always been accused of!

The Earl of Edgemere sighed. "I am ringing the bell, Caroline. A servant should be here within three minutes. If you wish to preserve your reputation, you will be gone by then."

Caroline laughed. "Don't be such a goose, Robert! It is all the same to me. If you compromise me, we shall have to be married."

"By God you are callous! I shall call your bluff, ma'am, and *then* you shall be in the suds."

Anne knew a crazy moment of wishing to step into the fray and declare *her* claims on the earl. He could not, surely, be forced to marry *two* women whose reputations had been ruined by spending the night with him! She resisted the impulse, however, for she was a sensible person and not given to histrionic outbursts. Besides, embroiling Lord Carmichael in a further distasteful scene was not to her liking.

"Caroline, *listen* to me! I have no intention of making you my countess. You may, however, have free rein of this place in my absence—as you always do. Further, I shall make you an allowance. I am trying to be both generous and fair. Though it was not I who ruined or deflowered you, I did take advantage of your bounteous charms. I am willing to pay for that youthful mistake, but it would be wise, I suggest, not to ask more than I can give."

There was a faint silence as Caroline looked at him speculatively. Anne could not divine her expression, for her face was turned in profile. Lord Carmichael's handsome, aquiline features appeared impassive. Anne's eyes, accustomed to the dark, fancied they could detect a small pulse throbbing in his neck. It may, however, have been a trick of the shadows and flickering dawn candlelight.

"Shall I have the diamond necklace at Christopher's?"

"Tomorrow, if it will make you cease with this nonsense!"

"Very well, Lord Edgemere, you may rest easy. I shall leave you to your lackey and your port and whatever *else* you do in here. What is that strange-fangled thing in the cabinet? It looks at odds with the decor in the room. If I were you, I would have it removed."

She placed a leisurely kiss on Lord Carmichael's lips. Though he did not respond, she appeared satisfied with her night's work, for she laughed.

"Robert?"

"Yes, Lady Dashford?"

"So formal? For shame! I am glad you call my charms . . . uh . . . bounteous."

She kissed her fingers mockingly and finally—finally—made an exit There was a moment's acute and dreadfully embarrassing silence. Robert waited until he was certain there would be no further interruptions. Anne, now shivering, whether with cold or from a multitude of unspoken emotions, remained motionless outside. She did not move until the curtains parted and she was led, gently, into the warmth.

"Miss Derringer!"

She noted his use of her proper title with misgiving

allied with respect. There would be no more "Celeste" and improper but rather comforting "Anne." From now on, she would be plain "Miss Derringer." It was as it should be, but still, there felt a dreadful void in her heart that somehow words could not fill.

"Say nothing, Lord Carmichael. I think enough has been said for one evening. The sun is rising and I really should not be in this wing. Should *never* have been. For my part, I apologize."

"Do not apologize for something you know is not wrong."

"Do I?" Anne shook her head sadly. "I wish I did."

"Will you not hear me out?"

"Not now, Lord Edgemere. You owe me neither apology nor explanation. Tomorrow you shall be in London purchasing jewels, and I shall resume my life as usual."

"Purchasing jewels?" Robert looked bewildered. Anne was silent.

"Oh! The diamonds for that . . . that . . . Miss Derringer, can you not believe that any feelings I may have harboured for Lady Caroline were extinguished a long time ago?"

"I believe it, Lord Carmichael. What I do *not* believe is that it is any of my business. We are worlds apart, and if it is not Lady Caroline you are betrothed to, it shall be another. That is the way."

"What if the other has raven's hair and ravishing eyes of tourmaline green?"

"I would say it was a remarkable coincidence but nothing more."

"Come, come, Miss Derringer! You know there is nobody on this earth but yourself of whom I can possibly be speaking. Your combination is quite unique."

"Then you either have a sadly flattering tongue, or your wits are wandering!"

"Do you not imagine you are beautiful?"

"Hardly so, but we digress from the point!" Anne waved her hand impatiently.

"That being?"

"That being that *whichever* lady you choose to share your life with, it cannot be me."

"Perhaps I am obtuse. I thought we were discussing the finer points of precisely the opposite."

"Are you proposing, Lord Carmichael?"

"No, but . . ."

"Precisely. Now, if I may venture past you? I should hate, after all this, to be discovered by your lackey."

"Anne . . ."

"Good night, your lordship."

"Stay a bit. We have much to speak of, and I shall behave, I promise you, quite impeccably."

He was so serious and so contrite that Anne felt her firm resolve wavering. He was dressed, even at that hour, quite faultlessly in a ruby frock coat with brass buttons. His waistcoat, severely cut and trimmed only with the veriest hint of darker ribbon, was matched by a pair of breeches that only the most daring—or foolhardy—of men would have the audacity to effect. My lord, however, needed have no qualms. The skin-tight unmentionables were breathtaking to behold, for the eighth Earl Edgemere had the felicity of a perfect, positively *indecently* unsettling physique. The ensemble was set off by a pair of topboots artfully folded down mid-calf, which, intentionally or not, only accentuated the muscled thighs above.

This, ultimately, was his undoing, for he was *too* handsome. *Far* too masculine for Anne's disordered sensibilities to tolerate with any degree of equanimity. "Do not ask that of me, Lord Carmichael! *You* may behave, but *I* am sadly lost to all propriety! Since I have no burning desire to lose either my virtue or my self-restraint at this early hour, I shall bid you, finally, farewell."

Robert bowed silently. He could not speak, though

Anne was entrancing and he wished, so much, so much, to take her in his arms and kiss away her cares. But she was not ready for it, and he . . . he had some business to attend to.

"You shall remain at Carmichael Crescent?"

"As long as the children need me and you stay as far away in London as possible."

"What if I can't stay away?"

Anne smiled regretfully. Then, my lord, I shall resign my post as governess."

Robert stared at her hard. "You'd do that?"

"I'd do that."

For an instant, their eyes met, and Anne felt his stare burning into hers like charcoal embers from a blazing fire. He touched her lute string sleeve lightly, but it was as if she had been burned. Robert must have felt the same, for he recoiled almost instantly and retrieved his gloves from the table.

"Go, then. It is nearly light."

Anne nodded and opened the door. The vast corridors loomed ahead. It was a long way to traverse in flimsy slippers of Oriental satin. She was, she knew, lamentably and most indecorously clad.

For a moment, the twinkle reappeared in the earl's lazy, hazel eyes.

"I should have bought you the half boots as I promised!"

"And have me tramp thunderously along your elegant parquet flooring? Another time, I thank you."

"I shall deem that as a promise!"

Anne made no comment, though her humour was somewhat restored. His voice softened gently.

"Shall you manage, sweet Celeste?"

She bit back a sudden, troublesome tear and nodded. It was the least she could do.

Ten

Lord Carmichael left early that morning, too early, in fact, to properly greet the guests that had so unexpectedly arrived the previous day. Anne had no time to feel the pangs she anticipated, for the house was buzzing with activity and several of the men had already cantered off in the direction of Lord Anchorford's. Mrs. Tibbet, to Anne's complete astonishment, was in her element.

"Oh, Miss Anne," she said, eyes shining, "I do so *love* to have regular menus to plan and the fine china taken out and the silver to shine . . ."

It seemed that Lord Edgemere had not exaggerated when he had stated that the land agent had orders to finance such impromptu parties. No expense was spared in hiring extra milk, parlour and scullery maids. Even the stables were not forgotten, with additional grooms, coachmen and ostlers being rustled up for the occasion.

An inspection of the larder revealed an interesting array of brandied fruits, jellied custards, fresh-picked strawberries and clotted cream in large containers. Hanging from the tiled ceiling were various meats— Anne thought she detected a venison, a selection of pheasant, several sides of beef and some cured ham and bacon. On the slate shelves stood cheeses of varying descriptions. Double Gloucester, Port du Salut, York cream, Cheshire, Stilton and what looked like an enormous cheddar loaf. She was much struck by the mingling of aromas—all pleasant—that whet her appetite and fixed her interest in the large breads that were baking in the kitchens.

Two scullery maids were up to their elbows in flour whilst several of the lower housemaids had been seconded to strain the liquor of oysters for the buttered lobster sauce. A few unfortunates were tammying endlessly for anything from gravy for the gravy boat to a delicate negus composed of water, orange juice and sugar, into which was skillfully added perfumed cakes and several drops of rose water.

Anne felt both slothful and aghast. "It is a miracle, Mrs. Tibbet! How in the heavens have you managed so quickly?"

"Got the gardeners up at the crack of dawn, I did! Been picking strawberries and grapes and what have you from the hothouses. The rest of us . . . we been workin' all night, we have."

"All night?" Anne could not help colouring, for if all the staff had been up at that hour, she had had a lucky escape, indeed.

Mrs. Tibbet looked at her keenly. "Don't like to criticise, me luv, but you have those nasty dark circles under yer eyes this morning. How 'bout you be givin' those wee rascals a break and takin' a nap?"

It was a mark of the exceptional accord that had sprung up between the two women that the housekeeper felt she could talk so comfortably with a "lady of quality." For, as she told her intimates, "If that there Miss Derringer ain't a lady born and bred," she would "eat me best cotton shift and to hang with the consequences."

Anne laughed. "Good gracious, no! Desert the ranks before the first battle? Never! The children shall have a valuable lesson in household husbandry this morning. Kitty can air the sheets, and Tom can help remove the holland covers from all the furniture in the north wing."

"Miss Anne!" Mrs. Tibbet was shocked. "That be no work for gentry folk! The master . . ."

"Will approve heartily, I am certain!"

There was a moment's hesitation as Mrs. Tibbet fleetingly wondered whether the governess had run mad. Then, as if some new thought had occurred to her, she looked sharply at the deluded Miss Derringer. The scrutiny lasted some half minute, so Anne was singularly inclined to either laugh or protest, but she did neither. At last, shrewd grey eyes met fine green ones.

"Aye." Mrs. Tibbet nodded. "So *that's* the way the wind blows. Reckon as not you know the master's mind better than all of us. *Let* the children dust and sweep."

Anne did not know whether to be relieved or distinctly nervous. Since there was now a quite definite commotion above stairs and the bells seemed incessantly to be ringing, she decided not to waste further time on the matter. She afforded the housekeeper a gentle, if somewhat harassed, smile, then proceeded upstairs to face whatever might await.

The breakfast room was abuzz with faces. For the most part, Anne did not recognize the guests, though one or two stood out in her memory from the seasons she had suffered through in London. Her hand quivered a little on the doorjamb; then remembering both her breeding and her newly acquired demotion to the ranks of upper servant, she held her head aloft and curtsied quietly but politely to the room in general.

She was met with several curt nods, one or two quizzing glasses and a general atmosphere of disinterest. Since she cared not a rap for such a reception—why should she?—she moved to take her place up with her charges. Kitty was already tucking heartily into a breakfast of kippers, eggs and anchovies, whilst Tom seemed to be playing with his boiled brains, rather than consuming them, as was, perhaps, the idea.

Anne chuckled. "Good morning, my angels! I wonder if it is at all the thing for us to be eating down here?"

Kitty swallowed with relish. "Why shouldn't it be?"

"You are far from out, Katherine, and these young men . . ."

". . . are old and disgusting enough to be my grandfathers!"

"Kitty!" It was hard to admonish the outrageous creature when the gist of her words was horribly true.

Tom pushed his plate away and declared that brains were not all they were cracked up to be. Anne had to concur gravely.

"I hope that woman does not come in to dine; my appetite is quite ruined as it is." Tom scowled fiercely and buried his head in his bowl. Anne was not left to wonder about whom he meant, though she did wonder if she would be forced to suffer Lady Caroline's condescension. She was not left wondering long, for with an air for the dramatic, Lady Caroline sailed in and took her place up at the head of the table. She was wearing a daring ankle-length morning dress of white sarcenet with a crimson sash and a demitrain to match. Her feet, of course, were daintily encased in a pair of Grecian sandals, the very epitome of elegant perfection. Anne wondered how long it had taken her dresser to achieve the perfect golden ringlets that framed her pretty oval face.

"Cat!" she admonished herself. It was hateful of her to be jealous, but just thinking that she and Lord Edgemere had enjoyed an intimate . . . but no! It would not do to reflect upon such a subject.

The gentlemen rose at once to greet her, and the high, tinkling laughter grated on Anne's sensitive ears. She had just identified a waft of Lady Caroline's exotic perfume—a pungent confection of orchid and tea roses, she conjectured—when there was a loud scream.

"Good heavens, what is the matter?" Anne wondered.

Kitty started to giggle, and Tom, suspiciously straight-faced, stared out of the window.

"There is a mouse in my reticule! Oh, my God, I shall swoon!" And swoon she did, neatly into the arms of Lord Dell, who was most conveniently situated to her right. The offending creature looked more startled, if possible, than the injured party. It scuttled across the table at breakneck speed, never once stopping to nibble on some of the finer examples of Mrs. Tibbet's repast.

Anne glared at the youngsters, for the culprits did not leave much to the imagination. Then she marched up to Lady Dashford, inquired whether anyone had smelling salts—none had—and so, as a precautionary measure, poured a jug of deliciously cold water over the dramatically unconscious countenance. This instantly revived the golden-headed beauty, but did nothing for the state of her temper.

"What in tarnation . . ." She opened her eyes and wiped the drenched ringlets off her face. Then, catching sight of a rival beauty—for, though Anne had ceased seeing it, a beauty she undeniably was—she gave a little gasp and sat bolt upright in her seat.

"Who the devil are *you?"*

Anne would not normally have answered. She did not care to be addressed in that particular tone. She did, however, remember her station, so swallowed a vast quantity of her pride and made a suitable bob. "I am Anne Derringer, madam . . ."

"And who invited you?" Lady Caroline took a sweeping glance at the rather worn blue dimity with its outmoded petticoat front and the simple, unadorned mobcap that Lord Edgemere abhorred and Anne alone deemed appropriate.

"I believe Lord Edgemere did, ma'am. I am the governess."

"And do you think it is quite proper to be dining below

stairs? I am sure his lordship will think it most strange in you! I shall tell him at the first opportunity!"

Anne's eyes flashed, but she lowered her gaze and was silent. This action infuriated Lady Caroline all the more, for it afforded her the lowering opportunity of viewing the darkest, longest and altogether most sultry lashes she had ever seen. That they adorned Miss Derringer's and not her own sweet face seemed heinously unfair. This crime, coupled with the fact that it was obviously the Edgemere brats who had disturbed her peace, made her more wrathful than ever.

"Are they in your charge?" She pointed at the pair of mirthful siblings who found the sight of Lady Caroline, drenched to the bone, too amusing not to laugh.

Anne nodded, gesturing to them slightly.

"I trust you will see to it that they are well punished for their antics."

"Indeed, I shall, your ladyship. As a penance both Kitty and Thomas shall offer you their profoundest apologies."

The double meaning—that apologizing to her was a penance—was not lost to the sharp-witted Caroline.

She frowned, but concentrated on the now scowling children.

"My dear Miss . . . Derringer, was it? I hope you mean to do more than simply make them apologize! If you prefer, I shall attend to their punishment myself."

Anne forced her eyes upward. They met Caroline's coldly. "What would you have them do? Scrub the floors?"

"Don't be ridiculous, woman! Peers of the realm do not undertake menial tasks!"

"What, then? A spell in the corner?" Anne just managed to keep the scorn from her tone. The gentlemen with quizzing glasses were eyeing her avidly, and a third, she noticed, was leaning interestedly upon a door frame. He seemed vaguely familiar, but faced with the situation before her, Miss Derringer could be forgiven for not quite placing him.

"They shall each receive a well-deserved thrashing. I assure you, Miss Derringer, it will be a week at least before either can take their place at a table, never mind try any more ridiculous tricks."

Kitty gasped, and Tom stopped smiling. Two pairs of beseeching eyes were turned on Anne. Lady Caroline shot each of them a satisfied glance, then smiled at her audience.

"I am perfectly certain that if my *dear* Robert were here, he would agree entirely. A little painful discipline is essential to the moral fortitude of young ones. Indeed, I have heard him threaten the whip on several instances during my little visits to this estate. I speak the truth, Thomas, do I not?"

"Yes, but he is only teasing. He never *means* it!"

"Tush, child! You are merely being cowardly to avoid a well-deserved whipping. You may both repair to your chambers until—"

"Excuse me, ma'am, the children are in my charge. They shall do as *I* say." Interested eyes focused, for the first time, almost entirely on the unspeakably forward governess. If the situation had been any different, Anne, naturally retiring, would have wished to sink through the floor. Now, however, her demeanor was rigid with controlled fury.

There was a faint titter and a curl of the lips from Lady Caroline. "And what do you say?"

Anne ignored her coldly. "Tom and Kitty, make your apologies. We have wasted too much time on this nonsense already. In the future, we shall dine in the nursery. The company, I feel, is less offensive."

There was an outraged gasp from the crowd. The golden-haired sylph looked daggers at the beleaguered Miss Derringer.

"I shall ensure your dismissal without a character for that!"

Anne nodded. "So be it, ma'am. I take my orders from Lord Edgemere. If that is his will, I shall leave upon the instant."

"I shall write to him, then. He shall be home this evening, for he is engaged today on a most *interesting* enterprise." Anne thought of the diamonds and was uncomfortable. She doubted whether the eighth earl would wish his parting gift to be made public knowledge.

Caroline, however, seemed set on baiting her. She was threatened, perhaps, by the trim, statuesque figure that comported herself with such careless grace. Governesses were meant to be colourless creatures that faded, at all times, into the background. They did not challenge their betters or selfishly turn all the heads in the room.

Lord Willoughby Rothbart—Anne recalled one of the gentlemen from her debacle in London—was regarding her with the interest of a seasoned connoisseur. No doubt Lady Caroline resented his defection as much as *she* did. But enough of this appalling scene! She must stand on her dignity and escort her charges from the room. Eating below stairs had been, as she feared, a dreadful mistake.

Miss Derringer bestowed an all inclusive curtsy on those gathered, secured a mumbled apology from the miscreants and schooled herself to depart sedately from the room. She was shaking inside, hating, hating, *hating* the beautiful Lady Dashford. To think that woman had ambitions of becoming the countess Edgemere! No wonder the children were in a taking.

She turned to leave. The children, for once, were following meekly behind her. Now, if the gentleman in the tasselled Hessians and the padded red riding coat would just desist from leaning against the door frame . . . oh, God! Anne herself felt close to a faint. No wonder he had disturbed her consciousness earlier.

The man, with his distinctive dark moustaches and faint, almost imperceptible swagger, was none other than Sir Archibald Dalrymple. He smiled mockingly and removed the olive silk top hat from his head. Anne was not deceived. Sir Archibald, kind enough once to make her an offer, was likely, after this spectacle, to make her quite another. He was, after all, a notorious rake. It was all Miss Derringer needed to complete her morning. She bit her lip, then looked away. Perhaps the cut direct would work its silent message. In the meanwhile, she would heed Lady Caroline's ill-conceived advice and stay well away from the strange assortment of house party guests.

Eleven

The offices of Messrs. Wiley and Clark were satisfactorily bustling. Mr. Wiley was engaged in calculating several very pleasing profit margins, whilst his partner, the younger and slightly more debonair Mr. Clark, entertained some rich and potentially viable clients in the inner chamber.

His heart was not in it, though, for Tuesday was his half day and he was planning, when the interview ended, to make an impromptu trip out of London.

At almost precisely the moment he contemplated this proposition, Lord Robert Carmichael, the eighth Earl Edgemere and a man very much in Ethan's thoughts, paced the Aubusson rug of his town lodging and glanced lingeringly at the two pieces of correspondence that had obligingly come to hand that day. Forgotten on his desk lay a small velvet pouch. To the collector, it contained two pieces of interest. A necklace of finest blue white diamonds and a ring. Strangely, it was the ring that was the greater of the two prizes. It was set with a flawless ruby the size of a wren's egg. Unfortunately, being a family heirloom, it was not for sale. It was the betrothal ring of the seventh Countess Carmichael and the six countesses before her.

Robert ignored these articles and contemplated the marble bust of Minerva, goddess of learning. Both letters had been a revelation to him. One had satisfied curiosity, and the other had opened his eyes to the bleakness of that which could have been his future. How he could ever have been beguiled by Caroline's fulsome flattery and equally fulsome figure? It was pointless thinking on past pleasures. They were well and truly over, especially since he was in receipt of this latest outrage. He looked at the letter again, though by now he knew it off pat. Breach of promise. Breach of promise! He was outraged.

The woman really stooped to the depths. For all he knew, he had never even *proposed* that night. He was forced to believe her word, for there had not been a sober thought in his head at the time. Now he suspected she may have been dealing in false coin, but there was no way of proving it. If she took her allegations to the world, she would probably find enough sympathizers in the haut ton to get away with it. There were many who envied the young Lord Carmichael his rank, his position and yes, his palpably athletic good looks.

A court of law would throw it out, out of hand—there had been no exchange of rings, no formal declarations, no banns posted. But he had been seen languishing after her on several occasions. At all the fashionable squeezes he had begged for a second waltz, sat several of the dances out when she was unavailable, called a gentleman to account when he had had the temerity to solicit her hand three times—quite beyond what was permissible, of course. Good lord, what a halfling he had been!

There would have been no question of his intentions had she been virtuous. Had she been virtuous, however, he would never have been in this coil. It was she who had taken a late night hack to his apartments and offered herself to him quite brazenly. It was only later—very much later—that he had realized he was not the first to benefit from such favours. Yet, in the eyes of society, Lady Caroline Dashford was all that was amiable, charming and proper.

No less than two patronesses of Almacks had offered her vouchers and introduced her to personages as high as the Prince of Wales, the Duke of Cumberland and even the rather bluff Lord Arthur Wellesley, Duke of Wellington. It would be her word against his, and despite the people who would undoubtedly support him, his name would forever be besmirched. He would be labeled as a "jilt" behind fans. Quite intolerable. Particularly now that he was, quite seriously, considering the matrimonial state.

He would be a cad, though, if he offered for Miss Derringer under such a cloud. People would naturally regard her with suspicion and active distrust, attributing the earl's supposed change of heart to *her,* rather than to the brazen lies Caroline was ready to disseminate. And if he gave her the wretched diamonds he had purchased from Christopher's that morning? She would use them against him for certain. As *proof* of breach, or, realizing that he was susceptible to the *threat* of breach, as the first in a long list of such expensive demands. Her requirements would quite probably be endless.

The second letter caused his brow to clear and a little smile to play about his mouth. The inquiries at Whitehall, though tedious, had borne fruit. His curiosity about his intriguing governess was both piqued and satisfied. She was, as he had always recognized, a true lady of quality. It was fortunate that she had been educated at Miss Mannering's Seminary for young ladies; however, her father and her brother, for all their noble birth, could hardly have been accounted in that category.

The Honourable Sir Marlborough Derringer had, by all accounts, frittered away a countryseat, a remarkably well endowed stable, a respectable fortune and several rather lavish country homes into the bargain. This he had done not by any particular genius or wit, but by his remarkable skill at losing every wager he was inclined to take, his inclination for trumperies and opera dancers and his singular lack of interest in the management of his estate. He had died, as he lived, at the losing end of an argument.

He had challenged Sir Archibald Dalrymple to a duel over the cut of his Carrick coat, averring that the garment was obviously not in Weston's style. It had, he announced, far too many capes for either comfort or fashion. Sir Archibald might have permitted the issue of comfort to pass. But fashion? He was a notable arbiter and would not stomach the insult. Two days later, Sir Marlborough was dead. It was an unfortunate circumstance, for Sir Archibald, a notoriously erratic shot, had been aiming merely for the foot.

Anne's situation was in no way improved by this development, for whilst her brother was not as palpably foolish as her father, he was decidedly more calculating. He had recalled her from London mid-season and introduced her to Sir Archibald, who was inclined, after the incident, to harbour some slight remorse. As soon as he laid eyes on the untried beauty, however, the lecherous rake had intimated he would do her the favour of marriage. He had hinted, even, that some of the family's more pressing debts of honour would be scotched.

Anne had been horrified and steadfast in her refusal. Her brother had washed his hands of her and passed her on to her cousin, Lady Somerford. There, at least, she would not be a burden on his rapidly diminishing finances. According to his sources, Anne had had at least one further concrete offer of marriage and several other rather more dubious offers. She had accepted none, however, and settled, as many of her class did, to a life of untrammelled but genteel drudgery. The rest was history, but for the information now in Lord Carmichael's possession. He looked it over curiously.

What could have possessed his love to throw away her small competence on such a harebrained venture? Not gambling, exactly, but speculating on 'change was nonetheless notoriously risky. Somehow, though he knew she had strength of character, a steely resolve, a quirkish sense of humour and an almost fatalistic sense of truth, he did not think Anne was irresponsibly impulsive. *Not* unless there was some other reason driving her actions. He looked again at his papers.

Ah! His brow cleared. The wretched ship was called *Polaris*. That would have accounted for it. He smiled tenderly. Their first child would have to be called Ariel or Umbriel after the moons of Uranus. She would never be satisfied, else.

But now . . . should he tell her? Of *course* he should. But if he did, she would cry off from her engagement as governess. There could be no reason for her to continue working if her miserable forty pounds a year was no longer at stake. She was almost an heiress. The thought was too dreadful to contemplate.

If he were free, he would tell her, then simultaneously offer her the protection of his name. But that would not do either. Not now, when there was a breach of promise suit hanging over his golden head.

What, then? What? What? What? Again, the poor Aubusson carpet was in danger of being paced to threads. My lord was so lost in thought he did not hear the hall clock chiming the hour or even the low murmur of voices in the front receiving room. Oscar, the town butler, always attended to such matters anyway.

Lessons were fitful, Kitty tearful and Tom more than a trifle gloomy at the prospect of being cooped up all day. In truth, Anne herself was more inclined to gaze wistfully out the window than concentrate on the dreary conjugations she had been determined to get over with that week.

Mrs. Tibbet didn't help. Anne's plans to aid her with

the chores were scoffed at summarily, although there *was* a grateful twinkle to be detected behind her spritely grey eyes. She assured Anne, however, that household matters were in fine fettle. This Miss Derringer had no difficulty believing, for the crescent positively sparkled and in every corner there were huge baskets and epergnes. These were filled with ferns, poppies and a brilliant array of English country roses. The air was scented and sweet, mingled only with the clean smell of soaps, carbolic, starch and crisp, well-aired linen.

How the bevy of maids attended to all these matters, Anne could not imagine, for, like a truly well run household, they were almost never seen, though their presence lingered refreshingly in the neatness of the anterooms and in the dust-free marbles and in the Sevres china that was scattered artfully on shelves and occasional tables. The billiard rooms had been opened and aired; the cellars, by all accounts, were being well utilized, some of my lord's finest burgundy, hock and claret being sampled well into the early hours.

Now, at last, Anne could see the last of the riders set off on their trail across country to Lord Anchorford's estate. Just why he could not accommodate the party remained a mystery to Miss Derringer, who privately thought the absent earl much put upon by his guests. Still, he was obviously generous to a fault, and Anne, already beset by a very soft spot for the errant earl, could not find it in her heart to berate him for such a truly honourable shortcoming.

Perhaps, now that Carmichael Crescent was free again, she could venture into the gardens with the children. They could fish by the stream and supplement the evening's menu with a nice basketful of trout. Not that it needed supplementing, of course, but the activity itself would most likely be beneficial. She drew away from the window and shut the festoon blinds with a flourish.

"Tres bien, mes infants! Close your books. That is enough dreary work for one day. All the hard work vanishes, I promise you, when you travel to Paris. Perhaps you shall, some day, now that the war is over."

Her words were quite lost to her charges, who slammed the offending books closed and clamoured to alternately cat call and hug her. An unexpected lump rose to her throat. She loved them, these little scamps. The thought was a revelation to her, for up until now, she had thought mostly—and on similar terms, though she would have been loath to admit it—of their debonair half brother.

She patted Kitty's bouncy, irrepressible copper-coloured curls and laughed. Tom stepped back and grinned saucily. "Shall we fish?"

"You shall fish. I, however, shall be very ladylike and take up my pastels. How long do you think you rapscallions need to get ready?"

"We are ready now!"

"Gracious, Tom! Not even I would be so foolhardy as to recommend you take up fishing in your present attire! Go change, I beg you, and be brief! Kitty, do not forget a parasol and some of that excellent *unction de maintenon* I made up for you yesterday. *That* should keep the freckles from your face!"

"Miss Derringer, it shall be an *age* before we are ready!"

"Nonsense, not if you run, slide down the front banister and cross quickly over to the south side. You should be in your chambers in an instant!"

Tom giggled. Kitty chuckled merrily, the sudden smile miraculously removing faint shadows from her face.

"You really know nothing about governessing, do you?"

"Not a jot!" Miss Derringer was strangely cheerful for such an appalling admission. "Perhaps you shall instruct me as we go. You, after all, have had the benefit of several governesses."

"All of them singularly trying!"

Anne's eyes twinkled. "I wonder? Was it not you, my sweet ones, who were so singularly trying?"

"Only because they had no notion how to go on! You, on the other hand . . ."

". . . have every notion! And my notion is that if we do not hurry, the day will be over before we set out. I must beg a lunch basket from Mrs. Tibbet, grab a bonnet and then we shall make haste. Shall we meet over by the stream? Tom, can you fetch my easel? Thank you." Miss Derringer, energized by this sudden change of curriculum, winked at her charges and set off primly down the marble corridors. She had no premonition whatsoever of what was next to occur.

Lady Caroline Dashford surveyed the pretty blue chamber with an eagle eye. It was hung with azure cretonnes offset by cheery, daffodil-coloured muslin blinds. Her nightstand was of cherry oak, but the bedstead was of the very height of fashion—iron emblazoned with balls and rails. Lady Caroline, however, thought she might prefer brass.

Her stockinged feet slid over the Kidderminster rug noiselessly. She approved of *that,* for it was the very height of exquisite taste and luxury. Perhaps, when she was countess, she would have it removed to her own quarters. Mind you, more likely than not, she would merely procure another such a one. Certainly, the walls would be rehung with patterned silk, and the beds—well, unless they were four-poster or brass at the very least, they would be relegated to the nursery or servants' quarters.

With a little smile, she contemplated life as the newest Lady Edgemere.

It was all so simple. Just as soon as that sapskull Robert handed over the diamond necklet, she would wear it downstairs to dinner and coyly announce that they had a declaration to make. Robert could hardly cry off with half the eyes of the ton staring at him—and at the lavish gift he had just bestowed upon her. She felt, rather smugly, that she had been sufficiently careful with her reputation for no suspicion to attach to her baser motives. Robert would be in a spot, and there was only one way out of it. Marriage, she had come to see, had its advantages. Despite the evidence of her looking glass, she knew, with more than faint dismay, that she was not getting any younger. It was imperative that she land her fish now, before it was too late.

And that vile governess . . . for all her modest attire she did not trust her an inch. Robert had been behaving unaccountably strange lately. She must have a care.

To this end, she threw down her curling papers and called in her dresser.

"Jane!"

It did not take long for the excellent Jane to appear from the dressing room, where she had been repairing a tear to one of the modish bombazine walking dresses she had sole charge of.

"Ma'am?" She bobbed a curtsy and waited on her mistress's pleasure.

"Jane, I wish you to dress my hair in a psyche knot. I believe the curls will show to great effect over my new poke bonnet."

"The azure straw?"

"Whichever else? Hurry, the men shall return soon, and I wish to appear at the best advantage."

"You always do, ma'am!"

Lady Caroline sank into the settle with an air of supreme satisfaction. "I do, don't I, my dear? If you manage the ringlets tolerably, you shall have my batiste gown with the mameluke sleeves. The colour, I find, is a trifle outmoded. Besides, that *detestable* governess was wearing something of that nature this morning."

The maid did not point out that a faded dimity did not in any way compare with an exquisite chintz morning gown designed by Madame Fanchon. Lady Caroline's loss was, after all, to be *her* gain. She pulled all the pins from madam's hair and began brushing vigorously.

It was not her fault that Lady Caroline, at that moment, should choose to take her somewhat into her confidence. Neither was it her fault that she allowed the curling papers a little extra time in the bright, guinea gold hair. After all, anything that affected Lady Caroline's stature must, necessarily, affect her own. With a prim smile, she fluttered over to the duchess and collected a handful of plumes.

"Now, ma'am, if I might make so bold, who is ye fortunate suitor? I believe in me excitement I may 'ave missed 'is name." She glanced slyly at Lady Caroline. "Like as not, ma'am, there be *many* as what would wish to shower you wiv diamonds and what not. You are like a honey pot and them gennelmen so many bees!"

Lady Caroline preened. It was true, what the maid said. She could snap her fingers and have any number of gentlemen purchase trinkets and baubles. Indeed, she had many an interesting piece to show for it. What she did not have, however, was a ring. Since Lord Edgemere was so obliging as to be the wealthiest and highest ranking among her intimates, it was only fitting that he should provide it. Besides, there was no denying his other charms. . . .

"Jane, you should know I do not gossip with the lower orders."

"Yes, ma'am." Jane lowered her eyes modestly and picked out a Japanese feather. No one would say her mistress was not the very height of vogue. Lady Caroline, encouraged by the youthful effect, relented somewhat. It would not do to be *too* harsh on the girl. She was, after all, a genius with curling papers. Besides, she didn't count. She was simply a servant.

"I shall tell you this, Jane. He is quite the handsomest man of my acquaintance." There! That could not have been plainer. Lord Carmichael, with his muscular, trim and quite overpoweringly masculine physique was obviously the gentleman to whom she obliquely, in a strictly ladylike manner, referred. As for his adorable, guinea gold curls that so exactly, to a shade, matched her own . . . she sighed. He was a fine specimen.

The maidservant's eyes gleamed knowingly. The handsomest man of her acquaintance? She thought instantly of the rakish Sir Archibald Dalrymple. He had stolen a kiss in the courtyard once, and the very memory still made her wish to swoon. Yes, he was very dashing, bold Sir Archibald. And his dress sense! Superlative beyond belief. She couldn't wait to be dismissed to the kitchens. It would be a fine thing to tell Jeeves. Jeeves was not bad himself *and* liable to be butler one of these days! Thank goodness Lady Caroline had had the notion to part with the batiste. Jeeves, she knew, would admire the mameluke sleeves.

Twelve

"Miss Anne, may I talk with you?"

"Of course, Mrs. Tibbet! Do you need help, after all? I thought, when I saw the table menus . . ."

"No, Miss Anne! Don't you go worrying yourself about those! It is all under control, it is, except for the fennel which Morton *swears* he planted but which is now nowhere to be found. Like as not it was the marjoram he planted, for we have that bountiful. I shall have to send Bertha down to Lord Anchorford's. Like as not the under gardener is probably not so half witted as our addlepated young Morton. A right dressing down I gave him. How, I ask you, am I to make a perigord pie without fennel? It is beyond comprehension."

Miss Derringer knew better than to suggest a perigord could probably manage without the sprinkling of herbs. Mrs. Tibbet, when it came to household matters of great import, was fastidious to a fault. She therefore frowned sympathetically, agreed that Morton was more dim than wiled, and waited, patiently, for Mrs. Tibbet to reveal what was on her mind.

"There is a gentleman below stairs asking after you.

"Beg pardon?" Whatever Anne expected, it was not this. Mrs. Tibbet looked at her closely. She had her own suspicions about the state of Anne's heart. But now, with a gentleman calling . . . She shook her head. "Usually the staff only receive callers on their half days, but I reckon that you, Miss Derringer, are different. I took the liberty of inviting him to the small parlour, for though he is not a *gentleman* if you understand my meanin', he is nevertheless a very pleasant spoken fellow and rather above the likes of Jeeves and Morton and what have you."

Anne was now more bewildered than ever. Who, in the world, could be calling on her? Who in the world even knew where she was? She had, of course, written to Lady Somerford, but receiving no reply had assumed the connection cut. Who, then?

When applied to, Mrs. Tibbet shook her head and stated that she was none the wiser, for though the gentleman had been kind enough to show her a card, she had never had a formal education and so could not, unfortunately, read. She reddened at this admission, and Anne resolved at once to offer her some tuition. She did not voice the thought, however, but nodded in a mystified manner and allowed Mrs. Tibbet to lead the way. Carmichael Crescent was so large that she could not yet trust herself not to get lost, especially with the amount of small parlours the establishment housed.

The man who paced the room anxiously beamed when he turned around and caught sight of her standing a little hesitantly in the doorway. Then he strode forward and took her hand so warmly that Mrs. Tibbet could be forgiven entirely for mistaking the circumstances. As it was, she looked intently at Anne, who smiled and introduced her to "Mr. . . . Clark, was it? from Messrs. Wiley and Clark." The formal address and the gentle way in which Anne extricated her gloved hand quelled Mrs. Tibbet's half-formulated surmises. She bobbed politely, then excused herself, listing a dozen things at least that required her immediate attention. Then, carefully allowing the requisite three inches of open door—Anne was amused to see she was still being treated as a lady rather than an upper servant—Mrs. Tibbet took her leave.

After gazing at Anne for a moment—for all his boyish detective work, he had quite forgotten how beautiful she was—Ethan Clark stepped forward and handed her a package.

Anne raised her brows.

"Whatever is this, Mr. Clark? Surely not an early Christmas present in June?"

"I hope it will be welcome *whatever* the month, Miss Derringer! It was a regular song and dance I had to find you. Still, if you find the contents to your liking, I shall be well satisfied."

"Mr. Clark, you are mystifying me! Whatever can . . . oh!"

Anne startled as a handful of banknotes fell to the ground.

"What in the *heavens* is this?"

"Heavens is right, Miss Derringer. That star, Polaris, you were telling me about. Well, it came in."

"The star came in?" Anne looked at Mr. Clark solicitously. Was he quite well? Was he headed, sadly, for Bedlam? She shook her head and retrieved some of the notes.

Mr. Clark saw her reticence and chuckled. "Jove, I am a gabster! Not the star, the *ship!*"

"Mr. Clark, the ship was sunk. Whatever are you talking about?"

"It was not the *Polaris,* but the *Astor* that sunk off the Eastern Hebrides. The *Polaris* came off unscathed and docked in Dover all right and tight."

"Then . . ." Anne paled.

"Then, you are rich, Miss Derringer."

Anne closed her eyes. She felt herself trembling, but ignored the sensation. She was made of sterner stuff.

"Mr. Clark, exactly how much of a fortune do I possess?"

"I believe the total to be in excess of thirty thousand pounds, ma'am. The balance is being held in trust at

Messrs. Wiley and Clark. My partner, Mr. Wiley, suggests you reinvest in some other merchant shipping." He did not say that his partner had given up searching for her and had already exercised this option.

He merely smiled and offered Miss Derringer one of his impeccably clean, carefully monogrammed linen handkerchiefs.

"You must think me a watering pot, Mr. Clark! Though pleasant, I find this news nonetheless a shock."

"People have swooned for much less a reason, Miss Derringer. I hope, though, that the news is not too late."

"Too late?" For an instant, Anne was puzzled. Then she smiled." "Oh! You mean, I collect, my reduced circumstances. Mr. Clark, you may not believe it, but I have truly been happier as a governess than as an idle lady of quality."

"You are fortunate, then. The life of an upper servant can, I believe, become precarious."

Anne's eyes sparkled as she recalled just *how* precarious it could be. Lord Edgemere was a hard master to work for. Not because he was unduly harsh, but because he was so excessively . . . what was the word she was seeking? Magnetic? Attractive was too tame an appellation. She would have to mull it over in the privacy of her chamber. But not now! Already, Mr. Clark was regarding her faint blush with interest.

She decided to turn the subject to lighter matters and was just commenting on the delightful spell of warm weather when Mrs. Tibbet made a cautious return.

"Jason has just watered your horses, sir. I suspect, from the look of you, to stop with us a mite? that you have travelled far today. Would you like to stop with us a mite? Though we are at sixes and sevens with our houseguests, I have a leftover joint of beef and a trussed turkey going abegging."

"How very kind! I would love that, though I fear I

must look horribly unkempt for you to notice my travel-stained state!"

"Tush! It is no more than can be expected with the country road such as it is! Did you come by the pike?"

So followed a pleasant and desultory discussion of which, it must be said, Anne heard nothing.

Presently, however, she remembered her charges and gasped in dismay.

"Tom and Kitty! I have abandoned them by the stream!"

"Where like as not they are getting into a great lot of mischief but none that you need worrit your pretty little 'ead, over, Miss Anne! Besides, his lordship is more like to laugh than turn you off if ever he found out!"

Mr. Clark laughed conspiratorially at the notion of Miss Derringer being dismissed. "Do not alarm yourself, Mrs. Tibbet! Miss Derringer will not have to concern herself with such things anymore. You shall not, *shall* you, Miss Derringer?"

Mr. Clark's tone was playful as he turned to her. Anne dropped the parasol she had hastily retrieved from the occasional table. The gentleman was right! With her fortune, she had no business in the kitchen when she was a lady born. She had no business, in fact, hiring herself out as a mere upper servant. She would have to leave and leave at once! Neither Lord Edgemere's *nor* her reputation could stand the scandal if she stayed.

And yet . . . how could she desert her charges? Though she had only been with them a short time, she knew that it would tug at her heartstrings to leave them to the tender mercies of Lady Caroline and the like. Besides, she was positive that they felt an equally strong attachment to her. It would be cruel. In her—rightly or wrongly—were pinned their hopes, trust and childish needs. She was not such a cad as to dismiss that out of hand. As for Lord Edgemere . . . the desolation of not seeing him on such intimate terms again pained her so greatly she had to close her long, hopelessly dark lashes to the thought. The best she could hope for, in the future, would be a distant bow and faint moue of recognition. He might favour her with a dance, but never again a starry night alone with nothing but the stars and a two-inch telescope for company. She hadn't even had that promised pleasure to treasure up in her memories. But her reputation! it was unthinkable, *unthinkable* to remain.

Mr. Clark was looking at her fixedly, and Mrs. Tibbet, though politely patient, was cocking an inquisitive eyebrow in her direction. Anne's feelings were tumultuous and must have been expressed in her eyes, when she opened them, for both guest and housekeeper simultaneously moved forward to support her. Ethan opened the small arch window and let in some of the fresh afternoon air.

"Miss Anne . . . a little water, perhaps? Or some of the lemon cordial . . ."

"No, thank you. I shall be quite all right. It is unlike me to succumb to such a silly fit of the flutters."

"You have every call to. Miss Derringer, my apologies. I believe I was too precipitate. Believe me, it was only my delight at your changed circumstances that—"

Anne held up one slender, though quite properly gloved, hand. "Mr. Clark, you have no call to apologize. You have done me a great service this day, far above your call of duty. It was I, after all, who was so scatter brained as to not leave a forwarding address."

"And why should you, when you believed yourself penniless beyond hope?"

Comprehension was beginning to dawn as the housekeeper looked from one to the other.

"Miss Anne! You don't mean . . ."

"That I am no longer in reduced circumstances? Mrs.

Tibbet, I have to tell you that Mr. Clark has just brought me excellent tidings in that regard."

"Then, we must celebrate at once! That is . . ." Mrs. Tibbet looked suddenly hesitant and a little sad.

"That is?" Anne was forced to prompt her, for she had let her sentence die mid-utterance.

"Oh, Miss Anne! I am afraid we are no longer good enough company. It is not fitting! You shall take your place above stairs and—"

Anne voiced the thought that was uppermost in every one's mind. "Mrs. Tibbet, there *is* no place for me above stairs! I am no relation of Lord Edgemere's, and therefore it would be most unfitting for me to remain under his protection another day. As for your company not being good enough, why, I am most hurt! That you can hold me in so little esteem as to think good fortune makes me desert my friends . . ."

"I think no such thing!" The housekeeper looked indignant despite the consternation on her expressive features. However unpalatable the truth, Miss Anne must leave at once. All very well for brazen hussies like Lady Caroline, sponsored by the Countess Lieven, to use hunting parties as a convenient excuse to put up at Carmichael Crescent. For the less well-placed Miss Derringer, it would be fatal, *quite* beyond the pale.

And what a crying shame that was, especially since Mrs. Tibbet fancied herself a closet matchmaker. Whatever the world thought, she still harboured the niggling suspicion that Lord Edgemere was not sufficiently epris to offer for Lady Caroline.

Laws a mercy! The very thought churned her stomach. It would be wonderful to have a mistress at Carmichael Crescent again. And one the likes of Miss Derringer, a lady born, not that dreadful Dashford woman, with her airs and graces.

"Mrs. Tibbet, I wonder . . ." An outrageous idea was

germinating in Anne's head. Still, she had been outrageous before. Permitting Lord Edgemere to persist in his ridiculous misapprehension had been outrageous. Throwing her cap at windmills and placing all of her competence on *Polaris* had been equally so. Surely stretching the truth a little . . . just a little, would be permissible.

Anne did not labour the point, for she had a quite dreadful inner conscience that would undoubtedly be shocked. Blithely, she ignored its irksome twinges and plunged herself headlong into trouble.

"Is it possible, Mrs. Tibbet, to keep this news quiet for a while? Just until I see the children settled or have a chance to speak with the earl myself? I could continue to governess as usual and no one need be any the wiser!"

Ethan frowned. There was paperwork . . . but bother it! Why *shouldn't* Miss Derringer continue to teach if she wanted to? It was a scandal that a good mind should be wasted just because it belonged to a lady of quality. Mr. Wiley, he knew, would be happy to see the funds reinvested rather than retired into her keeping. *He* would not mind the small deception. To be certain, Ethan resolved not to tell him of this visit. It was, after all, his half day.

He nodded a little at the housekeeper. Taking her cue, with relief, from a gentleman of the world, Mrs. Tibbet smiled.

"Bless you, dear! Of course I shall 'old me peace! I am not such a jaw-me-dead some others what I can name!" She glared balefully at the door, for the under butler was carrying a salver of fruit through to the kitchens. Jeeves, she knew, was a regular gabster.

Lord Edgemere ordered his carriage sent round. There was still time, he judged, to stop by Lord Anchorford's and speak to a few interesting individuals before springing the team and making Carmichael Crescent by nightfall. It was not what he had planned, but then life was never a smooth path. Tonight, he would give Lady Caroline something to think about, and if it wasn't a stinging good spanking applied to her curvaceous little derriere, he was probably a better man than he gave himself credit for.

By God, he was angry! Breach of promise, indeed. In all conscience, he had no recollection of offering for her. Even if he *had,* a decent woman would have permitted him to cry off without having him branded a cad in the process. He sighed. By this stage he should have realized Lady Caroline was *not* a decent woman. Moreover, she was not only not decent, but she was downright dangerous.

He signed one of his papers, skillfully adjusted his cravat into a highly stylized cascade and took up his cane. Lady Caroline and Sir Archibald Dalryrmple had better look to their laurels. He had a score to settle with both.

The kitchens were abuzz with the talk. Jeeves, glad of the attention, expounded at length. What he did not precisely know, he embroidered. After all, a little attention to detail was all that was needed to grant him pride of place at table, with a delicious ladle full of Mrs. Tibbet's best turtle soup to aid digestion and unseal his long, slightly wooden lips.

Mrs. Tibbet, a small, satisfied smile hovering on her own homely lips, allowed this unprecedented scene to continue. There was no love lost between her and Jeeves, but tonight he earned his keep. No one would be thinking of Miss Anne when it was the scandalous Lady Dashford who was uppermost in everyone's thoughts. And Sir Archibald, the sly dog! There were ribald bets placed on who visited whose chamber on this particular house visit.

Miss Anne, when applied to, continued filling her picnic hamper with an assortment of fruit, light cheddars and thick slices of ham. The latter she wrapped carefully as she pressed her lips together and declined to comment. She wished, however, that just half of the rumours were true. Unfortunately, she knew that Jeeves, for all his knowing airs, was talking nothing but a load of unadulterated codswallop. Lady Caroline would not jeopardise an elevation of rank simply for the sake of a clandestine roll in the hay. More was the pity!

Something as scandalous as this rumour would scotch any claims she might be making on the present earl. Besides, if Sir Archibald's roving interest was fixed on Lady Caroline, Anne could breathe easy. She would not have to suffer the importunities she feared. Rather guiltily, Miss Derringer let the servants' gossip take its course.

Thirteen

Lord Anchorford's hunting box was a festive affair, festooned with ribbons and little coloured gaslights. As the Earl of Edgemere reined in, he caught the smooth rustle of silks and the bright damasks as the extensive gardens were utilized by the ladies of the party. Not that there would be many, strictly speaking, to fall into that category. Lord Anchorford's "ladies" were generally high fliers rather than high sticklers.

Robert grinned and winked at a pert little thing who glanced rather boldly at him as he dismounted. If Miss Derringer had not already wreaked havoc with his desires, he was perfectly certain he might have spent a creditable evening with the lass. Certainly, her silvery gauze overlay was all that one might wish for, especially since it appeared that her petticoats had been dampened and there did not, from his experienced vantage, appear to be much in the way of corsetry to hamper any masculine curiosity.

From within, he was shocked to hear the stentorian tones of Lady Anchorford and Miss Delia Wratcham, her trusted companion. The presence of Miss Wratcham was a particular shock. She, Robert knew, merited the distinction of having the sharpest, most tattle bearing tongue of all her generation.

Gracious heavens! Surely Charlie was not so addlepated as to mix the company? He was just pondering on the unsolicitous circumstance when Lord Anchorford himself approached him on the wide, cobbled footpath.

"Robert! I am in the devil of a hobble!"

"So I infer, if that is your lady I hear within!"

"It is, and not only that, she has brought the whole dashed family down!"

"Never mind the family—was that Miss Wratcham I heard?"

His lordship permitted himself a sigh of unutterable wretchedness. He nodded and rolled doleful eyes heavenward.

Lord Carmichael raised quizzical, masculine blond brows at this obvious calamity. His lips twitched, however, and his hazel eyes harboured a slight, almost imperceptible, twinkle. He and Lord Charles Anchorford went back a long way.

"Charlie, mincing your beaver is not going to help the situation, unless, of course, your case is so bad that you actually wish your valet to kill you?"

"What?" Lord Anchorford looked at his close friend as though he had run mad. "Oh, my hat! I'd forgotten I was holding it."

"So I infer by its current reprehensible state. My advice is to discard it at once. Here, you may have mine."

Robert whisked the dashing, velvet-brimmed top hat from his head and tossed it to his friend.

It was caught, but only absently, and without any palpable enthusiasm.

"See here, Robert! How the lord can a person think when his best friend persists in talking like a milliner?"

"Very true. My apologies, Charlie, but one should always, I feel, have a certain sensibility for priorities." The teasing note altered as he realized Anchorford's very real distress.

"Is there anywhere we can talk?"

"There is the library, but I had the notion of turning it into a gaming room . . ."

"Poor Charlie! You really *are* in a hobble!"

"That is what I said! See here, Robert . . ."

"Why does my heart sink when I hear those words in that particular tone? You are up to something, my dear Charles! Whatever may it be?"

"Nothing of any consequence, Edgemere! I merely implied—only implied, mind—that the guests were up from Carmichael Crescent."

There was a stunned silence. "Let me understand this, my dear friend, and esteemed neighbour! *I* house the excess of your party—none, I might add, in any way felicitous—"

"Balderdash! What of Lady Caroline?

Robert stared at him hard. "I repeat, *none* of them in any way felicitous . . ."

"By George, Robert, you must be blind! Lady Caroline is a regular pattern card of perfection. Her angel gold hair, her cherry lips, her sparkling white teeth, not to mention her fulsome cleavage and—"

"Careful, Charles! You are like to bore me to death. Besides, when you wish to turn out sonnets, get some help. Your similes are hackneyed."

Lord Anchorford glared at his best friend and staunchest ally. Then he threw aside both hats with a carelessness that would have brought down the wrath of heaven from at least two trusted manservants, and laughed uproariously.

"Beg pardon, Robert! I am overset!"

"So I understand. Now begin again. Lady Anchorford believes me so debauched as to house ten opera dancers and at least two other bits of muslin."

"Exactly. It is no more than the tiniest stretch of truth, Robert, for you are not *unknown* to the muslin set."

"Indeed, I should hope not!"

"So you see, switching the composition of our guests was not such a great tarradiddle . . ."

"Mmm . . . was your good lady satisfied?"

"Well, she is off to bed with a hot posset from the shock, and then I have convinced her to return, forthwith, to London. Miss Wratcham is administering sal volatile and looks depressingly cheerful."

"Well, of course! Think of all the scandal mongering she can spread!"

His lordship, the fourth Viscount Anchorford, lifted his hands in despair. "What can I do to stop her? Thank goodness the stables are extensive enough to allow for a change of fresh horses. Tomorrow, they shall be off."

"Not so fast, my fellow. I think I can solve your difficulties and perhaps my own at the same time."

"Robert, you are a savior!"

"Before you ruin your doeskins by slobbering over me, I should mention there is a catch."

"A catch?" Charles sounded alarmed.

"Indeed, yes. It is the *muslin* set that is to return tomorrow. Right now, I have urgent need of a few well born ladies. Come, walk with me and I shall tell you all . . ."

It was easy for Robert to slip, unseen, onto his estate. He wished, for tonight, at least, to avoid Lady Caroline's poisonous tongue. It was almost dark when the horses were finally tethered, the coachman tipped, the grooms alerted to their new charges and the first available drain pipe shinned with effortless ease and supreme disregard for the handsome riding coat of powder blue that was so artfully coupled with darker stockinet breeches. The Hessians still sparkled, despite the dust of dirt tracks and busy city roads. He eased a window open and noted, with annoyance, that it was stiff and creaked.

Uttering a small oath, he edged the pane upward,

tensed a little, then eased his deliciously muscled legs inward.

They were viewed making their entrance by an amused, prim and altogether discomposed young governess who wickedly resisted the proper etiquette of averting her eyes.

There! He was in, and Miss Derringer was not sure whether it was her heart or his feet that had caused the definite thud her ears detected. Whatever the case, she now folded her arms sternly and demanded to know the cause of the invasion.

Robert drew in his breath. Seated there, at the little table with nothing but the flickering taper of a candle to guide her way through the paperwork before her, was the woman of his dreams.

She had thrown off her mobcap and it lay, forlorn, like a discarded dish rag on the empty chair beside her. She had obviously been thinking, for he could see faint shadows where her hands had cupped her chin. Several of her pins were coming loose about her forehead, telltale signs that she had been absently playing with her long, lustrous tendrils.

He could smell her, deliciously clean and hinting, a little, of rose water and something curiously elusive. Whatever it was, it was beguiling. Robert was hard pressed not to take the few steps that breached the distance between them. Instead, he stood like a naughty schoolboy, caught out in some iniquitous act.

"Is this the schoolroom? It was dark, and I must have miscalculated . . ."

He enjoyed the relish with which she chuckled. "Indeed, sir? Then, you are well and truly hoist by your own petard! Who was it who was badgering me, not so long ago, about the same mistake?"

"Touché, Miss Derringer! Like a gentleman, I concede

defeat! Whilst I am mortified to have made so palpable an error, I nonetheless cannot regret its results."

His meaning was obvious, and Anne felt the heat rising to her cheeks. Also, there was that curious warmth again . . . damnation! Did Lord Edgemere *have* to be so unbearably attractive?"

She reached for the mobcap but he was swifter. His wrist held hers, and again, she had the sensation of burning. "Leave it! It is a dreadful confection that has no business in your hair!"

"It has *every* business! It reminds you, I hope, that I am not to be trifled with . . ."

Robert's eyes darkened all of a sudden, and he dropped her hand. "I should hope, Miss Derringer, that you know I do not *trifle* with you. I am a gentleman of my word."

"Then, why have you come back?" The words suddenly were an anguished whisper.

Robert watched her, motionless. She was so startlingly beautiful, so unconscious of the dark, fluttering eyelashes and the searing tourmaline eyes. Even with the heavy calico skirts and the modest bodice of finer chemise, her figure was as tantalizing as if she were wearing the sheerest silk or chintz. She carried herself with blithe disregard for her extraordinary beauty, but no man—certainly not one as experienced as he—could be deceived. Miss Derringer was a diamond of the first water. If she had failed to take in her first two seasons, the blame must be laid squarely at her father and brother's door. Were they not such a squandering, philanderous bunch of hen-witted jaw-me-deads, Anne would have been well settled by now. He supposed he should be grateful to them—*and* the jealous tabbies who labeled her a bluestocking—that she wasn't.

Now! *Now* was the time to apprise her of her changed fortune. Now, when she suffered the indignities of being labeled an upper servant and of spending night after night alone either in the confines of this schoolroom, or blanketed by myriad silent stars. For all their dazzling light, there was not one among them that could offer her human warmth or companionship or comfort. Robert hesitated. If he told her, he would set her free. He was not sure he could bear that. And yet . . . he was a man of honour. He *must* tell her! He cleared his throat and took both of her hands in his. He was conscious, as he drew her up, that her mouth was but inches away from his own. It was novel but not unpleasurable, to have a woman almost match him in height.

"If I said that I am a man of my word, that you are released from your engagement . . ."

There was a knock on the door. Robert ignored it, but Anne, conscious of her position, stepped back, disentangling herself from the intimacy of their stance. She swallowed. "That will be one of the underservants to sweep out the hearth. You should leave, my lord."

Robert placed his fingers, very gently, on the corner of her mouth.

"This time, Celeste, I believe I shall." Then, with a swift bow, he was gone almost before the handle turned.

The following morning was fine, and the male guests were in high fettle to be off over the commons to Lord Anchorford's. The grouse was prodigious, and there was some talk of bagging larger game like venison.

Guns were loaded upon packhorses and sent on ahead, although many a gentleman still sported fishing rods. Lord Charles was blessed with a diligent gamekeeper, making his well-stocked streams an excellent choice for those with a less bloodthirsty turn of mind.

Lady Caroline, dressed in scarlet, was ready for the hunt. She nibbled delicately on a wafer of toast and allowed Lord Willoughby Rothbart to vie with Sir Archibald Dalrymple on the question of whether she would take tea, or something a little stronger.

In the event, she smiled charmingly at Sir Archibald—he was the handsomer, if lesser ranking, of the two—and admitted that some of the steaming, creamy, deliciously potent Irish coffee would be delightful.

She was surprised to find, upon her return to the morning room, that a card had been delivered from Lady Anchorford. She ripped open the seal and scanned the contents quickly. So! A flattering invitation to take up residence at the hunting box. It did not quite suit Caroline's purposes, but whilst Lord Robert was away, there was no reason she supposed, to kick her heels at Carmichael Crescent. There would be time enough, after all, when she was married.

Besides—her eyes gleamed—a little light flirtation with Sir Archibald Dalrymple and the noble Lord Rothbart could be pleasant. They positively haunted the Anchorford estate. All things being equal, she thought she would accept. Besides, Miss Delia Wratcham was a cousin to the Marquis of Illswater. It would be *fatal* not to cultivate the connection.

It seemed that Lady Caroline was not the only one in for a surprise that day. Mrs. Tibbet was positively bursting from ill-suppressed excitement and wasted not a moment to draw Anne away from the prying ears of the lower servants and into the upper servants' parlour. There, after fussing over a cushion clean and soft enough for Anne's back—Anne had to remind her sternly that in the eyes of the world she was still a servant and unless Mrs. Tibbet wished to set the kitchens by their ears, she would continue treating her as one—she expounded at length, in tones of great excitement, something that sounded completely obscure to the normally astute Miss Derringer.

Finally, however, when the words stopped tumbling from Mrs. Tibbet's mouth like a veritable waterfall, and when Jeeves had made a surly entrance muttering something about "jollification" and "extra work for them but what has mouths to feed," she started to make sense of the puzzle. Lord Edgemere, it seemed, was to hold a ball. Not, in London terms, anything like a "crush" or a "squeeze"—for that he would need a hostess—but something quite creditably formal and indisputably select. The thing that sent Mrs. Tibbet's mind atizz was that the notice was so short—only thirty-six hours. The upper housemaid, however, was more intrigued, when apprised of the situation, that the ball was to take place at *all*.

It was the first of its kind since Lord Edgemere's mother, the seventh countess, had been the belle of all London. So followed a lot of reminiscing that gave Anne to understand that the seventh countess, like her son after her, was much beloved of the household. They hardly noticed when she slipped from her chair quietly and made her way to the topiary gardens. There, she could almost feel his presence. What had he meant, when he had started to question her? What exactly had he said? She closed her lustrous eyes and concentrated. "If I said I am a man of my word, that you are released from your engagement . . ."

So. He wanted her to leave. Perhaps it was better that way, for the attraction was becoming quite unbearable. She could have sworn, however, that he felt it, too. It was all so perplexing!

Lord Anchorford's library was unrecognizable. The heavy beechwood furniture had been pushed back against the walls to make place for the billiard and card tables that had been carted in from his town house. The chintz drapes were drawn, and the walls had been hung with damask silk in bold, fleur de lis patterns. The drapery entirely covered the encyclopaedias, almanacs and scholarly works—leather-bound—of his father before him.

Most noticeable was the smell of smoke that twined through the room and encrusted itself in the Kidderminster carpets and velvet furnishings that the room temporarily housed. This was not surprising, since Lord Anchorford was excessively generous with his beautifully fashioned cigars. He was also a noted collector of snuff boxes, and since each box contained quantities of high grade tobacco and were displayed open, for easy consumption, it was not surprising that the library was now smelling—as well as *looking*—like a common gaming hell.

It was dark, and the select dinner hosted by her ladyship was long since served. The hunting box was illuminated prettily inside and out with scores of candles in long, elaborate holders. These were complemented by the gaslamps which emitted a delicate, slightly ethereal hue.

The conversation among the ladies was polite and desultory, for Lady Anchorford had not had a great deal of time to prepare for the occasion. The gathering would have been livelier had she invited her dear acquaintance Lady Codswall or even the Salinger sisters. Still, the presence of Miss Wratcham and the Ladies Elizabeth and Mary Bellafonte lent the evening a degree of refinement. All three were kin of dukes and marquises. Lady Anchorford sighed in satisfaction at the social coup.

Then there was Lady Caroline Dashford. She offered poise and beauty, but really Lady Anchorford could not help thinking, for all her angel ringlets, she was something of a cold fish. She wondered, for an instant, how much longer the men would linger in the library. They had surely been a prodigiously long time over their port! Still, men would be men. . . .

"Miss Hampstead, would you care to favour us with a

song? Lady Elizabeth might wish to accompany you." And so the evening progressed.

"What is up, Robert? You have been buying up that Dalrymple fellow's vowels all evening. I wager they are not worth the paper they are written on, for he has been dipping deep."

Lord Edgemere smiled in satisfaction. He bowed to an acquaintance and turned to his dear, thick-witted friend Lord Charles Anchorford.

"Excellent! It is as I hoped."

"But why? You shall lose on the transaction."

"Do I ever lose?"

"You have the devil's own luck if *that* is what you mean!"

"It is. Now cease worrying over me like some addlepated sheep. Go and fetch Sir Archibald for me and tell him I have a proposition."

Lord Charles set down his glass and looked at the clock. "Gracious! Lady A will hang, draw and quarter me if I don't return with the gentlemen."

"Then, that is your fate, Charlie, for I must speak with Sir Archibald! I wish to challenge him to a game of faro."

"Faro? You should rather choose commerce or vingt-et-un. You are too skilled simply for a game of chance."

Lord Edgemere sighed as he wiped off a speck of invisible dirt from the chitterlings of his fine lawn shirt.

"Do as I say, Charles! And if you are so worried about the ladies, draw them in."

"To the gaming room? Robert, have you lost your senses?"

"The library, Charles, the library! And when you tell them *this* is at stake, I warrant that they shall cast aside all objections!"

With a flourish, Robert pulled out the blue-white diamonds. They were no longer in their pouch, so he allowed them to drop down the length of his dove grey gloves and flicker tantalizingly as he turned them over in the light of a hundred candles.

Fourteen

The chatter in the room ceased as several gentlemen noticed the gesture and sauntered over to see what sport was up. Sir Archibald, a little green from his recent excesses, and more than a trifle aware that his losses were greater than his winnings, stared harder than most.

Lord Anchorford slipped out to invite the ladies to view the spectacle. His exit was unnoticed by all but the central protagonist, Lord Robert Carmichael. He now placed the necklace on the makeshift faro table and gestured lightly to Sir Archibald.

"Dalrymple!"

"M . . . my lord?" Archibald was prone to an unfortunate stutter when agitated.

"You seem dazzled by these beauties! Would you care to stake a claim on them?"

Dalrymple hesitated. The diamonds would be precisely what he needed to hold off the duns, cover his immediate debts and retrieve his credit at Weston. On the other hand, he did not need to do too much thinking to know he was too far dipped to be able to cover the dibs. He looked uncertainly around the room. He owed too much! Not even that idiot *Crawley* would be so obliging as to stand buff. But the diamonds. . . . Oh! How they sparkled and danced to the light! He stepped forward and fingered them longingly.

The door opened behind him, and the ladies crowded

into the much beleaguered room. Lord Anchorford hurried solicitously to close his snuff boxes and extinguish some of the half-smoking cigars that had been discarded around the room. Lady Anchorford suffered a brief spasm over the state of one of the burnished leather chaise longues, but then even her attention turned to the scene that was unfolding.

Behind her, Lady Caroline gasped at the sight. The diamonds! Those were *her* diamonds! Lord Edgemere had pledged them to her! They could not be mistaken, for even in the tapering light she could recognize the clasp. Besides, the quality . . . the quality was impeccable.

She opened her lips to object, then shut them again tightly. Lady Elizabeth and Miss Wratcham would think it very strange in her to be claiming valuable trinkets whilst she was still in the unwedded state. She was too clever and too careful with her reputation to fall into that trap. She smiled in amusement. So *that* was Edgemere's game! He hoped to expose her for a grasping little tramp. Well, he could stake the diamonds. Her reputation would remain as pure as snow.

"Well?" Lord Edgemere allowed a hint of impatience to tinge his tone. Dalrymple, fearing that the chance of a lifetime would be whisked away in front of his very eyes, nodded. "I accept, Lord Edgemere, and stake my land upon it."

Edgemere's eyes glittered. He had banked on Dalrymple being a cad, and he had been correct. Sir Archibald's land was entailed to the hilt—the commonest gabster knew it. Still, it served his purpose to have Sir Archibald accept his challenge.

He nodded off-handedly and drew out the faro box and a dice. "We shall dice to determine first call. Lord Melford, would you care to deal?"

The game did not take long. Lord Edgemere was declared the winner. To everyone's shocked surprise—no more Sir Archibald's, who looked fit to swoon—he called again. "I am in a frivolous mood, Sir Archibald! What say you to double or nothing? If I win, I shall take your country seat as well as the land. If I lose . . . well, there are always these." He pointed to the sparkling stones once more. Dalrymple choked. As it was, he was ruined. Ruined, ruined, quite ruined! When Edgemere heard the land he had staked was entailed . . . it would be a debtor's prison for him! Defaulting on a debt of honour . . . that he could have sunk so low!

A half-uttered moan issued from his lips. The perspiration poured mercilessly from his forehead and down onto his drooping shirt points. Not even the handkerchief he absentmindedly daubed himself with quite served its purpose. He was ruined, ruined. The thought caught at him like an icy wind. And still the diamonds sparkled. The ladies were crowding around, admiring them.

They could *still* be his . . . the more he thought about it, the more positive he became that his luck would turn. *Must* turn. Besides, he had nothing more to lose.

"Accepted, Lord Edgemere!"

Robert set down the glass he had taken up and bowed. "Very well, Dalrymple! It is your turn, I believe, to call."

Sir Archibald stuttered through the order of cards. Lord Melford sprung the little machine, and to Dalrymple's profound relief, the black spades appeared as if by answer to prayer.

Lord Edgemere raised his delectable blond lashes just slightly. His lips quirked a little, but all eyes were focused on the diamonds. These he lifted gently, allowing them to dangle, for an instant, in the air.

"Was it best of three, Dalrymple?"

"No it dashed well wasn't!"

"Then, I suppose I must declare you the winner." He turned to Lord Charles on his left and sighed in a bored, rather disinterested fashion. "A pity, I feel, Anchorford.

The design of the clasp is quite exquisite." He wound the whole into his palm and placed the clasp briefly under one of the candelabras. "Unique, quite unique!"

Miss Wratcham stepped forward to look. So, too, did Lady Elizabeth. Lord Edgemere permitted them for a moment, then he slid the whole across the table to Dalrymple.

"They are yours, dear fellow. Enjoy them with my compliments." Then, with a sublime disregard for his loss, he bowed over the plump Miss Chartley's fingers and offered her his arm.

Lady Caroline stepped twice on her partner's foot before excusing herself with a throbbing headache. She was furious that the earl had outmanoeuvred her. His trap to discredit her had failed dismally, but she had lost the diamonds in front of her eyes. Never before had her velvet tunic felt so tight, or the pearl beads embroidered daintily on their little silk disks looked quite as tawdry. Pearls were all very fine, but diamonds! Diamonds were what she coveted—what she had *always* coveted and what she had just lost. She would find Lord Robert and call him to account.

He would buy her a better set or she would instantly sue for breach. She wished she could force a proposal from his lips, but that, she knew, was pipe dreams. He would have to be tricked into that, and for such a trick to hold water, she needed the diamonds.

She turned from her course just as soon as the liveried footman closed the door. Unlike the rest of the guests, who seemed set for many more hours of pleasant carousing, Lord Carmichael would be heading for home. He had said so, after losing the fateful turn of cards. Caroline sneered inwardly. Yes, he may pretend to poised indifference, but she knew better! Why else would he leave so hastily, if not to lick his wounds in private? Well, she would add salt to them. It was no more than he deserved, after all.

If she waited for him close to the stables, she would be well-placed to steal a word. It was annoying, though, creeping about in velvet slippers and wielding a swansdown fan. There was nowhere to put it, however, so she resigned herself to her fate and waited patiently. She chose, for her rendezvous, a spot closer to the house than to the stables. It would be no good at all if she got her gown muddied, even if she *did* manage to get up to her chamber undetected. Her dresser, she knew, was a prodigious gossip.

The time seemed to drag interminably. She strained her ears for footsteps in either direction but, apart from several false alarms, heard nothing but the gentle sound of hooves and the odd snore from an errant stable boy. She was just pondering whether to return to the hunting box or continue her uncomfortable vigil, when her long wait was finally rewarded.

"Lord Carmichael!" She hissed the words as soon as she saw his unmistakably elegant calves—clad in the finest clocked stockings—make their appearance on the track. Robert stopped and allowed one of his famous lazy smiles to cross his face.

"Now, why am I not surprised to find you here?"

"Perhaps because you know I have a score to settle with you! You've treated me very shabbily, my lord." Lady Caroline pouted and peeked up at him through her lashes. Perhaps cajolery was better than anger.

Lord Robert bowed. "No more than you, my angel! But what is it that you want? Perhaps, as we ponder the point, we should kiss and make up?"

Lady Caroline would have been glad to oblige if there had been a suitable audience to the spectacle. *Then* Lord Robert might be forced to come up to the mark. She looked round and cursed. There was no one in sight. Drat the man! He had never been serious anyway; she could tell from the cynical curl of his annoyingly handsome lips. He was playing a deep game, for he nevertheless advanced determinedly toward her. She stepped back coldly.

"Perhaps, my lord, you might cease taking this all so lightly!"

"I never take kisses lightly. But then, I *never* kiss where there is no inclination. Shall I make you inclined?" For an instant, his eyes sparked and Caroline felt the familiar magnetic power toying with her inclinations. She wished she hadn't been so fast as to damp her underskirts, for her voluptuous form seemed to leave little to my lord's imagination. In the past, he had stripped her naked. Now he did so with the veriest flicker of amused eyes. By God, she could feel the contempt! Caroline drew her breath in shock.

My lord turned his gaze to the intricate silver interleafed on the top of his cane. This he twirled absently before searing her, once more, with hazel brown eyes. "Make you inclined? No, I think, perhaps, not. I shall therefore retrieve my noble offer and ask, again, what it is that you want of me?"

"I hate you, Lord Robert Carmichael!"

"Very possibly, my dear. I am not, myself, overfond of you. Entrapment does not rank among my pet likes. It still begs the question, however, of what you are doing, lying in wait for me."

"I am *not* lying in wait!"

"What odds? Standing in wait, then. By the by, your hem is getting muddied."

Lady Caroline picked up her skirts crossly. Why did the man always seem to place her at such a decided disadvantage? It was hard to press home a point with threats when a victim did nothing but smile politely as one vainly wrestled with a swansdown fan and skirts more suited to the ballroom than the barn.

"I want the diamonds!"

"You shall *have* them!"

"What?" Lady Dashford had been prepared for a fight. She had not been prepared for such ready capitulation. She therefore sharpened her tone and badgered Lord Edgemere on the state of his addled wits.

"The diamonds are no longer yours to *give,* my lord. The whole dashed world and his wife were privy to your gambling fever!"

"Tut, tut! Do you doubt me? And tut tut again! Your language is execrable!"

The Earl of Edgemere took the liberty of enjoying himself thoroughly. Lady Caroline threw him a poisonous look, then stepped back into the shadows. She thought she heard someone coming. It was a false alarm, but one that made her more anxious than ever to have done with the interview.

"Lord Robert, you shall tell me what you mean!"

"Mean?" His hooded lashes looked innocent, but Lady Caroline was not fooled.

"I want the diamonds!"

"So you have said. *These,* I infer?" Out of his impeccably tailored waistcoat, the diamonds were drawn forth.

Lady Dashford's hands trembled. "It was all a silly mistake, then? You did not lose the necklace?"

"Oh, but I *did!* But I also confronted Sir Archibald with all his vowels—I hold the bank, you see—and so he quite saw that redeeming the debts was a matter of honour he could not, in all conscience, ignore. So! A little lively swap and lo, the diamonds are mine again!"

"You are a devil, Lord Robert!"

"Mmm . . . but not without a heart. I promised Sir Archibald that none would be any the wiser. As far as society is concerned, the gems are his. Tomorrow, he will be able to take out a loan on the strength of the collateral. After that . . . well, after that it shall be put about that he sold the necklace."

"To you."

"To me."

"For me!"

His lordship sighed. "Yes, for you, my dear Lady Caroline!"

"Lord Robert, I did you an injustice!"

"Do not be too hasty, Lady Caroline. Perhaps I play a deeper game than you think."

"What do I care? So long as these dear, dear diamonds shall be mine!"

"They *shall* be, Lady Caroline."

"When?"

"Perhaps on the night of my ball." His voice grew stern, and the soft silk of his hair shimmered slightly in the moonlight. "But there is an end to the matter, Caroline! You shall stop hounding me and accept, at last, that you shall not be the next Countess Edgemere."

Lady Caroline looked sharply at the earl. His jaw was firm and his eyes crushingly direct. She decided, therefore, to be conciliatory, curtsying in as beguiling a fashion as she knew how. "Agreed, your lordship."

Lord Edgemere held her glance for a moment or so, then nodded.

"Very well, Lady Dashford, it is agreed."

The arrangement was sealed on a slight, somewhat merry bow, before his lordship resumed his midnight amble to the stables.

Lady Caroline looked after his straight, imposing back for a moment. A wicked smile played on the corners of her lips.

"Oh, *Robert!* For all your worldly charm, you are still a mere greenhorn!" She snapped the swansdown shut with a click. "No one will believe, when I appear with your diamonds, that I am not betrothed. You *shall* marry me, Lord Robert, like it or no. For a man of breeding and conscience, there is no other course."

She would have been discomforted, indeed, to learn she had just fallen, quite splendidly, into the trap of Lord Edgemere's careful crafting.

When he sprung it, there might, indeed, be a wedding. But whose?

The eighth Earl Edgemere's groom was surprised to hear his master whistle rather jauntily all the dark way home.

It was too late for Robert to hope Anne would be star gazing. Nevertheless, in the forlorn hope that she was, he ceased his restless attempt at sleep and stepped up to the library. There were no welcoming tapers, no revealing little flickers of light. He opened the door and set his *own* candle down on the mantel. Well past one o'clock. A good night's work if everything went according to plan.

Strange how the room seemed so hollow without Miss Derringer. It seemed to echo with creaks and groan from the load of half-read books upon the shelf. To rectify matters, a little, the earl decided to take down his Byron. He was in the mood for something to balm his soul. It did not take long to flick through the familiar pages, nodding a little here, memorising a little there. Ah . . . Robert smiled with pleasure. He had not been mistaken. The words he had been seeking jumped off the page as if crying for deserved attention.

You walk in beauty like the night
Of cloudless climes and starry skies;
And all that's best of dark and bright
Meet in your aspect and your eyes.

Byron must have known such a one as Anne. His words whispered of truth, of immortal clarity. If my lord had not known better, he would have guessed that the poet had met Miss Derringer during one of her notorious seasons. After all, she had bright eyes and a mane of hair as pitch as midnight itself. It was only its lustre that granted it its sheen and likened its movement to the sparkle of so many stars on the celestial horizon.

Celeste, ah, Celeste! It belonged to her now, this library with its masculine smell of leather and the scent of pages well worn or waiting.

Waiting to be opened by slender, appreciative hands. Waiting to be granted life by the lady society had carelessly branded a bluestocking and he—he had branded as life's sparkling joy.

He poured himself a brandy from the decanter and settled back on his chair. He tried not to think of his comely little governess, tucked up in crisp, well-aired sheets. She was dreaming, perhaps . . . he did not dare invade the privacy of those dreams.

He sighed and allowed the book to drop from his lap. No doubt he wasn't the only person lost to repose tonight. She might be sleeping, but Sir Archibald would be *seething*. He had not been pleased to be confronted with the total of his carelessly penned vowels. For an instant, Robert had feared the Manton's pistols that he sported upon his person.

Dalrymple was several thousand pounds freer of debt, but *that* was unlikely to weigh with him. It was the diamonds he would regret, their brilliant coming and their equally brilliant going. Then the instant passed. Sir Archibald would have to be crazed to challenge him, publicly, to a duel. He would have no wish for the world to learn of how pressing his debts were, or how ready his immediate need for cash. Besides, the vowels in Robert's possession were all debts of honour.

They had been called in, and refusing to cover them was social suicide of the deathliest form. No, Lord Robert had been safe from the pistols. He had slipped the gems into his waistcoat quietly and promised to say nothing of the matter. The relief on Dalrymple's ashen face had been instantly palpable. No doubt he had already secured some loans on the strength of his possession. If he did not hastily procure more tomorrow, Robert would miss his guess. The strength of his plan depended on Dalrymple illegally embroiling himself in this type of shameless transaction. Odds were, he would. And if not?

Robert chuckled. If not, Caroline would have secured for herself a very expensive parting gift. No doubt, she, too, was awake, scheming, the little hussy, to cast her coils about him even tighter. Well, she could scheme. With a small smile, he toasted Lord Anchorford's unexpected guest, the good Lady Caroline Dashford. His *own* houseguest, Sir Archibald Dalrymple, he saluted with two large gulps of finest Madeira. The brandy had not been enough. It took *more* to toast the toadies of the world, the careless takers who thought nothing for consequences.

Fifteen

Sir Archibald Dalrymple was doing more than not sleeping. He was plotting dire and unmerciful revenge. He patted the mounds of vowels in his pockets and threw them on the table beside his bed bitterly. So! Lord Edgemere sought to play May games with him. Host or no host, he would be made to pay.

For an instant, Dalrymple relived the moment when the necklace, in all its shimmering glory, was placed in his hand. Oh, the exultation! He could read chagrin on faces the likes of Morrison and Cambridge. Stuck up old toffee noses! It was *he,* the honourable Archibald Dalrymple, who had plucked the nest egg from their noses.

He glanced sourly at his handwriting, scrawled untidily across the mass of screwed up paper. Can he have pledged so much? He supposed so. There was Latham and Cedric, and . . . but good God, how was *he* to know they would all sell up to Lord Edgemere? And why, for heavens sake, did the earl go to so much trouble? If he needed to hedge his bet with the diamonds, why bother to wager them at all? It was all rather a puzzle, and Dalrymple's head ached. He was not sure whether it ached from Anchorford's punch brandy, from the night's disappointment or from the shock of seeing the Derringer chit all over again.

Well, he had offered marriage, and she had taken off like a bolt of lightning for the Somerford woman. Now he would offer something else. A carte blanche to a mere governess must be regarded as a windfall. He sneered a little and made a series of lewd remarks that mercifully went unheard but for a few barn owls at the open window.

But first! He would retrieve those diamonds by hook or by crook. All the world knew them to be his, and he would prefer to keep it that way. He would set fire to the abominable vowels. That way, there would be no proof that the motley collection ever existed. If Lord Edgemere proclaimed the necklace to be stolen, the world would think he was indulging in a fit of pique over its loss. It would be hard pressed, certainly, to believe that the necklace had passed back into his possession then out of it again in a mere matter of hours.

Good! Time was on his side, but he would have to act now. Feverishly, Dalrymple lifted each bit of paper and cast it into the embers on the hearth. They failed to ignite, although little drifts of smoke curled at the edges, blackening them, and promising, by slight smoulders of red, to blaze at their own lazy leisure.

Dalrymple did not have the luxury of waiting. He grabbed an iron poker and stoked up the fire until, in a rush of flames, the last vestiges of his gaming debts were engulfed forever. He nodded sourly. *There* was an end to that! And now, to regain his lost fortune.

But how? Whilst the household was usefully occupied in slumber, he could not very well creep about it in the hope of stumbling upon the loot. He must think the thing through carefully. The last he had seen, Lord Edgemere had placed the necklace into the pocket of his deplorably raffish waistcoat. How *could* the man have such elegant taste?

He, himself was wearing the most modish creation, padded skillfully to bolster his shoulders and striped in the handsomest golds and lilacs. Did anyone notice? Not a one. Yet, when Lord *Edgemere* entered the room, all eyes turned. It was most provoking! Sir Archibald scowled and kicked the tasselled Axminster with his unslippered foot. Yes, the diamonds had definitely been slipped carelessly into the pocket. What might have happened from there?

Lord Carmichael would have returned home, bathed—drat the man, he was the type who insisted on cleanliness above perfumes and other more civilised devices—and headed on for bed. At this very moment, he was probably lost in sleep. But what of the waistcoat? Had he thrown it unceremoniously on a chair? Would his valet have stayed up to attend to the matter? Very possibly, but then, my lord would first have removed the diamonds. Or would he have?

Very perplexing. Sir Archibald fingered his curling moustaches absently. If Carmichael had removed the necklace, it was probably sitting in a drawer in his library. My lord was prodigiously fond of that dreary room. On the other hand, it was more probable that he would have headed straight up for bed and left the tedious business of stowing the thing until morning. He would not, after all, have expected them to be thieved under his very nose. Especially when the world and his wife thought they were no longer his to stow.

Dalrymple eased into the wing chair situated by the window and mused. My lord's apartments were on the second floor, along with his precious bookroom. Either way, he would have to head off in that direction. If necessary, he would check both, though he hoped, for once, that his luck would be in. He would start with the chamber, for Lord Robert was just the sappy type to permit his valet to shirk his duties and sleep until morning. In that case, the waistcoat might just, with a stroke of luck, be dangling inelegantly from his chair.

He uncrossed his legs, threw a dressing gown about his person—a glorious sapphire brocade, emblazoned with buttons of the first stare—and lit a wax candle from the fire now raging in the hearth.

Then he crept out stealthily, his nightcap just catching on the door handle. With a muttered curse, he pulled the thing from his head, turned it about crossly, then jammed it on again. Then he left his door ajar just a crack.

Miss Derringer opened the window and allowed a cool rush of night air to linger over her face. The stars were more glorious than anything she could have imagined. It was the perfect night for star gazing. Again, she thought longingly of the Herschel telescope stowed safely away in the glass cabinet. If only she could use it, just once, to glimpse the outer vistas of that which she had only imagined before!

She was rich enough to commission her own; but Sir William was an old and frail man now, and though his son was becoming just as great an astronomer, she did not think he had the time to produce the precision, hand-crafted instruments that were his father's especial gift. Maybe . . . she would set inquiries in train. Strange to think she was wealthy enough to indulge her interests in this way! Still, she doubted whether she would feel the same about her own instrument as she did about Lord Edgemere's. The telescope was a symbol, for her, of combined passions, interests, aspirations. . . .

She sighed. She would have to leave tomorrow. Lord Edgemere had started to indicate this was his desire, and it was not fair—never mind downright foolhardy—to press on with her charade. She was not a penniless upper servant, no matter how much she wished to be!

Anne's delicious sense of humour could not allow this thought to pass without an exasperated chuckle. Strange how odd life was. She had thought the world was coming to an end when she had sent herself into service. Now she was loath to remove, once more, to the fashionable world. Why? Because, scandalously, she would rather be in Lord Edgemere's keeping than not. She would rather be prattling proverbs and participles than batting her eyelashes and allowing herself to be whisked across a ballroom by the likes of Lord Willoughby Rothbart and the mincing, brainless fop, Sir Archibald Dalrymple.

Better to be a wallflower, or the ice maiden . . . but no! She wished for neither, yet both were to be her destiny. She sighed. Perhaps it would have been better if Mr. Clark had never been so good as to inform her of her change in fortune. Now, she supposed, she would be at the mercy of fortune hunters. At least she need never worry that Lord Edgemere was one of those detestable creatures! He made her small fortune look paltry!

Which reminded her . . . it would be dangerous to think of the earl in those terms. No doubt, when she was no longer living under his roof, in his employ, the attraction on his part would cease. Gracious heavens, he would never consider *marrying* her! Look at how appalled he had been when Lady Caroline had ventured to shackle him! And she refused—utterly refused—to be placed in the same category as Lady Caroline.

She would pen a note and leave it for him in the book room. If he discovered her altered position, it would be just like him to fathom she was compromised. Anne had no desire to have to convince Lord Robert that she was not ruined. Some temptations were best left alone.

Now she left the window and the shooting stars that left a blazing trail across the skies and sat down to sketch a missive to her lord. The room was dark, so she boldly, wastefully, lit several tapers at once and set them in the wooden candelabra set aside for her use. She had no qualms, for Lord Robert's spirit, like his pocket, was admirably generous.

If a few tears stained the missive, she was not so foolhardy as to leave them to dampen the crisp, cream sheets. Instead, she rubbed at them carefully with her handkerchief and blotted the inky letters neatly with the little muslin square. After all, she reasoned, she could always buy another. It would not do for her work to be either illegible or tearful. Either way, it would reflect detrimentally upon her character. Somehow, even though she was bidding farewell, she still found it necessary to retain the eighth Earl Edgemere's high esteem.

Task done—she had only written the sketchiest of explanations—she folded the letter and tucked it into her chemise. Then she scribbled a longer, more tearful, letter to her charges. This she planted next to her bed. They would be bound to search her rooms, the rascals!

She tucked her feet into Kitty's delectable outcasts—little satin things with ludicrous spangles that the staid Miss Derringer would never *dream* of purchasing, but nonetheless rather enjoyed wearing—and headed, for the last time, toward the second floor.

The door was locked. Drat! Sir Archibald set down his candle and tried the handle again. Locked, if his name was not Sir Archibald Latham Arthur Dalrymple! But how could this be? If the earl was within, sleeping, he would surely not lock the heavy oak door? How, then, was his valet to enter in the morning to open the drapes and hand him his copy of the *Morning Post* or the equally essential *Gazette?* No, Sir Archibald was certain Lord Robert was not the type to lock his door.

Not unless he was pleasuring some ladybird . . . but no! The earl was too much of a gapseed to indulge in such interesting activities. Dalrymple tried the handle again. He was so engrossed in the activity that he did not notice another, more shadowy figure appear down the hall. This time, with a creak that made him positively startle, the door gave way. He was propelled, rather unceremoniously inside.

It did not take long for his eyes to adjust to the relative darkness—the halls were well lit with a series of hanging tapers—so he moved swiftly to the bed. No doubt the earl was fast asleep, though no snores, sadly, were emanating from his person. Sir Archibald shrugged. What odds? The bed was rumpled, and he could detect some slight lump on the far end of the lavish four-poster. This was draped luxuriously in the finest Friesland velvet, in a moss green shade that even the fastidious Dalrymple could approve. He did not, however, dwell over long upon this point of fashion. Instead, his quick eye took in the washstand and the intricate chestnut dressing table inlaid with marble and harbouring, to his profound relief, my lord's discarded cravat, beaver, buckskins, enviable lawn shirt with chitterlings and yes, yes, *yes!* The Weston waistcoat of ruby serge peeked invitingly from beneath the greater frock coat. If only the necklace was still there!

Sir Archibald listened for breathing. Hearing none, he eyed the lump on the bed again. Was it Lord Robert? He thought so, but must take nothing for granted, nonetheless. There was a cupboard on the far side of the room. If there were footsteps down the corridor, he could bolt into it, though he fervently hoped that such a cramped fate was not to be his. Especially not in the sapphire brocade. The creasing would be horrendous.

Cautiously, he sidled up to the dressing table. A marble bust exactly matching the inlay stared down at him from a pedestal. He shuddered, then moved the frock coat out of the way. It glimmered, slightly, in his hand, and he could not but envy the rich quality of the materials used. This did not stop him from unceremoniously dropping the garment to the floor, along with the velvet-lined beaver and the discarded neckerchief. His hands alighted, for a moment, on the chitterlings, before reaching their final goal: the waistcoat. He could hear his heart hammering heavily in his chest and wondered whether he was in danger of revealing himself to the sleeping form. Surely Lord Robert would not sleep through the heavy pounding? Apparently he would, for he did not move an inch, and Sir Archibald breathed a little easier. He eased the waistcoat toward him and smiled as he felt the revealing bulge. Excellent! The night's work was achieved. He placed his fingers along the satin lining and drew out the pocket. Nothing but a snuff box and a discarded piece of flint! He half cursed before remembering the other side.

Feverishly, in the half darkness, he fumbled with the garment, pulling relentlessly at the lining until the second pocket was exposed. There *was* something hard! A moment more of furtive fury and the diamonds were his again. He breathed a sigh of sheer relief and was surprised to find beads of perspiration standing on his forehead. He wiped them carelessly with his nightcap. The necklace felt delightfully heavy in his hand. He watched the diamonds twinkle a little in the soft candlelight, before taking up his taper and creeping to the door.

Miss Derringer's pulses were racing. It had been a close shave, she knew. If the earl had seen her in his private quarters, he might have jumped, quite wrongly, to certain conclusions. . . .

She did not allow herself to dwell on the thought. Suffice it to say, she had been admirably self restrained and slipped gently into an alcove, waiting a good many moments—it seemed like an hour—before daring to so much as breathe again. Somehow, she knew that if she encountered the earl that evening, she would be lost.

All her admirable resolve would melt away to nothing, and she would drown in his caresses and sweet words as if there were no turning back, no harsh tomorrows, no impending ruination to have to deal with.

Part of her—an impish, quirkish, impossibly daring part—told her that just one such night spent in his lordship's bedchamber would be worth all the recriminations that would undoubtedly follow.

The other part—the sober, sensible, governess part—told her that she was behaving like an addlepated greenhorn and that if she kept her head, it did not matter at all that she had lost her heart.

Keep her head she did. She strained to hear noises in the bedchamber, imagining my lord doing his ablutions, preparing for bed . . . but look! The door handle was slowly turning once more. She sank back into the alcove, puzzled.

The man emerging seemed slighter than the earl, and though it was dark, the corridor was sufficiently lit to see that dark hair rather than entrancing blond was creeping from the nightcap. Anne gasped. This was not the earl; this was her almost husband, the Honourable—if such an appellation could be loosely applied—Sir Archibald Dalrymple. And looking very pleased with himself, too, the way, catlike, he smoothed his moustaches and stepped quietly, with unshod feet, along the plush line of Axminsters.

Anne became more aware than ever that she was clad, negligently, in little more than a shift with a warm wrap draped firmly across her slender frame. For a man of Sir Archibald's roving eye, this was tantamount to nakedness, for he would make out the full detail of her form with no trouble at all.

Oh, why, oh why, had she not dressed to make this particular excursion? Surely her *last* nocturnal encounter should have taught her the wisdom of a great deal of petticoats, an uncompromisingly high bodice and perhaps, even, a betsy ruff top to complete the ensemble?

As for flibbertygibbet slippers that were more revealing than the unclad state . . . she bit her lip in panic. She only hoped Sir Archibald would be too engrossed in what he was doing to notice her shadowy figure flattening itself frantically against Lord Carmichael's elegant panelled walls.

And what was he doing? The flash of diamonds made her catch her breath. By God, if she were not Anne Amaryllis Derringer, the man was stealing the necklace! The selfsame necklace, she warranted, as Lord Carmichael had purchased for Lady Caroline. She bit her lip at the thought and watched as he placed it stealthily in his pocket.

"Thief!" The words were out before she could stop them. She was outraged that the man could take advantage of his host. Sir Archibald was so startled that he stubbed his toe on a particularly valuable hall stand of marble before cursing and advancing toward Anne with a great deal of ill intent twisting his dark, altogether sinister lips.

"Hush, my dear Miss Derringer! There is no need, you know, to awake the entire household!"

Anne forgot her flimsy attire in her anger. Her tourmaline eyes smouldered as she regarded the man she once considered marrying with a palpable contempt.

"I beg to differ, Sir Archibald! When there is thievery abroad, the alarm should be sounded."

Dalrymple reached her just as she was opening her mouth to scream.

"Oh, no, you don't, you little vixen!" She could feel his breath, dank and tepid, upon her cheek. His hand was about her mouth, so she could taste the vile saltiness of his skin.

He swung her round. "Before I release you, I shall outline a little scenario, my dear. If you cry out, none but the servants shall hear you. The earl stayed over the night at Lord Anchorford's. He was foxed, you know."

Anne stopped struggling.

"Excellent, my dear. I see you see reason. If you cry out, nothing more shall happen than the servants being afforded the—ahh, undoubtedly interesting spectacle of you being compromised in your night shift. Whilst I don't doubt that Primrose, the serving maid would undoubtedly switch places with you, I somehow feel that you, you little ice maiden, would prefer to have your snow-white reputation kept intact."

The fury in Anne's eyes now turned to a dull fear. Sir Archibald chuckled as he removed his hand from her mouth. There would be time enough later.

"Give back the diamonds and I shall say nothing!"

"You jest, my dear!"

"I am deadly serious."

"Then, I shall return the favour. The diamonds are mine and so, my dear, at last, are you!"

"Have you taken leave of your senses, Sir Archibald?" Anne's throat was dry because she knew, only too clearly, that she was steering a dangerous course. If only Lord Carmichael was home! But he was not, and it was up to her, now, to retrieve his jewels and preserve her own virtue.

She did not notice, in her anguish, footsteps upon the far carpets. Neither, one might add, did the feverish Dalrymple. He laughed a little and took Anne into his arms. Too shocked to protest, it was exactly the sight Lord Robert came upon as he rounded the corner. He was sickened to the pit of his stomach and stood stockstill, watching the scene unfold. And to think he had nearly, *so* nearly, invited Anne to become his wife!

What were they saying? He could hear nothing but Dalrymple's low chuckle. He decided not to stay. The sight was sickening, and he loathed, above all other things, the practice of eavesdropping.

So! Miss Derringer had had a change of heart. She would, after all, be accepting Sir Archibald's kind offer. There could be no other construction, surely, upon what he had just witnessed. She had been magnificent, as always, in the simplicity of her shift. Lord Robert tried not to reflect on the glorious dark braids that gleamed with lustre, or on the rounded curves that proclaimed themselves through the flimsy nightdress. The wrap he discounted. It was already falling from her shoulders. Soon, he thought, it would be on the floor.

With a heart heavier than stone, he turned on his heel and silently walked back the way he came. There was sawdust in his throat, though his eyes, stubbornly, remained dry.

Sixteen

Anne struggled silently in the man's grasp. She fought like a tigress, for it was more than just her reputation at stake. She had not resisted Lord Edgemere so staunchly, against the will of both her inclination and his, to be ravished by a man only half his calibre.

She was breathless from the struggle, for Sir Archibald was wiry and determined. Unbeknown to her, she had the advantage, for Dalrymple was concerned about waking the earl. He suspected he was straining his good fortune to be struggling with the vixen rather than making good his escape. Still, fortune, so far, appeared to be smiling upon him. He renewed his efforts, seeking to constrain Miss Derringer to walk docilely down to the first floor, where many of the houseguests had been accommodated. He was succeeding, for despite not being as well endowed as the earl with regard to superior physique, he was a man, nonetheless.

Anne gasped in pain as he wrenched at her arms and forcibly dragged her a few steps down the hall. She twisted desperately, ducking in silent struggle. A few more moments and she would have no choice but to scream. The earl might be absent, but surely some small contingent of staff was at hand? Even the appearance of Lord Willoughby Rothbart might be welcome at this juncture. But her reputation, of course, would be in shreds. In the world of the high ton, there was no smoke without fire, and a woman caught dishabille in a sheer nightgown with *any* man, screaming or not, was doomed.

Anne drew in a breath and pushed. All of a sudden, she was stumbling, for the steely grip had wavered just a second. She did not stop to think or to allow Sir Archibald to recover the advantage. Her hands, in the dim illumination of the hall—many of the candles were now extinguishing—touched something cold. Quite without thought for the value of her employer's treasure, she pushed at the marble statue with all her strength, relying on sheer determination to make up for any feminine deficit. It worked. The statue came crashing down on Sir Archibald's head.

He jumped out of the way, but moments too late. He was struck a glancing blow, enough to shake the wits out of him and to see him crumpled like a pack of cards upon the floor. Anne gasped and knelt beside him, relief at her freedom engulfed by the horrible fear she might have done him some lasting injury.

She need not have worried. The pulses in his neck were strong, and when she tentatively removed the tasselled nightcap, there was no more damage to be seen than a rather nasty lump forming through his thinning, dark hair.

With a sigh of profound relief, Anne tried to gather her shattered wits about her. It was not easy, for there was a marble arm lying forlornly dismembered next to its classical torso. The head, sadly, was missing its aquiline nose. How ludicrous that such a thing should, after the night's events, overset her. But overset Anne it did.

As she valiantly retrieved the necklace from Dalrymple's luxurious brocade pocket and placed it next to the disfigured arm, she felt tears cloud her jewel green eyes. She dabbed at them fiercely before collapsing some way from her tormentor. Then she picked up the torso, fingered the rough, cracked marble edge, and wept.

My lord, alerted by the crash—as was half his staff—

did not trouble to move. The decanter in his hand was empty, and though events had occurred too quickly to allow him to be foxed, his natural inclinations were to stay fixed in his seat without bothering to move. What, after all, could be more momentous than the spectacle he had already witnessed.

It was the sobs that did it. At first, a small, hushed wail, then the profounder kind of choking sniffs that he had never, even as a small boy, been able to resist. That was how Kitty, with her dear, copper curls, had always managed, somehow, to cut a wheedle with him. But this! This was not Kitty! This was his Celeste, his Anne, his light, his star, his life. He forgot his hopelessness in his sudden compulsion to enfold her in his arms and kiss away the tears. Whatever the tangle between them, he would unravel it.

He was down the corridor like lightning, just in time to see Anne, wrapped like a baby in her heavy merino wrap, cradling a sadly dismembered Psyche. Behind her were a host of well-meaning minions, from the lordly Hastings, to a common serving girl beset with toothache. With an imperious wave of the hand, Lord Edgemere cleared the hall, indicating only that he wished for a quiet word with his valet. Hastings stepped forward gingerly, for he had no wish for his stockinged feet to be jabbed by shards of marble.

"Hastings, I believe I can rely on your discretion?"

"Most certainly, my lord! I shall impress discretion, too, on the rest of the staff. You may be sure that this matter shall go no further. Miss Derringer, if—"

"Do not concern yourself with Miss Derringer, Hastings! Rather, get Sir Archibald back to his chamber before the rest of the houseguests awake. Tomorrow you may serve him, in his room, a breakfast of coddled eggs and possibly a good dose of cod liver oil. I believe it does wonders for the digestion."

Hastings maintained a straight face. "I believe so, my lord. But if I might make a suggestion . . ."

"What is it, Hastings?"

"My lord despises coddled eggs. He made a particular point of it to Mrs. Tibbet . . ."

"Excellent. As I said, Hastings, just a nice selection of coddled eggs."

"Yes, your lordship."

"Hastings?"

"My lord?"

"You have not seen Miss Derringer tonight. She was vastly fatigued and enjoyed an excellent night's sleep as a consequence."

"But naturally, my lord."

"Very good, Hastings. You may go."

With a small nod, Hastings eyed Sir Archibald assessingly. Then, with nothing more than a slight intake of breath, he lifted him aloft and slumped him, protesting a little feebly, upon his broad shoulders.

"Good! The man appears to have regained consciousness."

Anne smiled a little weakly.

"Night, night, Hastings." Was there a buoyant curve to my lord's mouth? It was too dark to tell.

Lord Robert waited until there were no further footsteps on his Axminster. When the far door shut, at last, he drew in his breath and looked down at Anne. She was still clutching at the statue, but her sobs had subsided. He slid down next to her on the floor.

"Was it very expensive, my lord?"

"Oh frightfully! I procured it, you know, from Lord Elgin."

"Then, it is priceless!"

"Quite possibly. Now, my dear, can we cease talking about such paltry matters?"

Anne nodded. His lips were impossibly close, and his intimate smile was warming her quite delightfully.

"I take it Sir Archibald's suit was rejected out of hand?"

"Out of hand, my lord."

"Could you not, possibly, have resorted to a sharp slap? I believe that is efficacious upon occasion." His eyes twinkled at the memory of just such a set down.

In spite of her predicament, Anne felt the familiar twitching of her wide, sensuous lips.

"Do you, my lord? It does not, however, prevent a man from redoubling his efforts upon other occasions."

"True, it does not. You did well, upon reflection, to stun the man senseless."

Anne giggled. Somehow, when she was with this nonsensical gentleman, her prodigious heap of troubles seemed to melt away as if by magic.

He continued to tease, though there was a gleam in his eye Anne felt slightly troubling. Well, not troubling, perhaps, but dangerous. Definitely, she decided, dangerous.

"I, on the other hand, have recovered from the sting of my sharp rebuff and shall now commence redoubling my efforts."

"At the risk of another resounding slap."

"Only, I hope, if I do not please."

His eyes locked with hers, and Anne, once again, felt herself in the thrall of a gentleman. This time, however, powerful arms were not constraining her mercilessly in an ironlike vice, nor were her senses reviling any outrage to her dignity.

She was bound only by silk soft eyes and breath just moments from her own. Her dignity was not outraged; it was celebrated, with the touch of a golden finger upon her cheek and a gentle hand at the nape of her soft, swansdown neck. Her braids were uncoiling into lengths of dark, lustrous, long black curls. She knew an overpowering desire to reach out and touch the blond strands that were so tantalizingly close to her own, touch the masculine lump that protruded, ever so slightly, from his throat. He was clean shaven, yet there was a slight, inviting stubble that she would have given her fortune to explore. It was exposed, now that he had discarded his cravat in the bookroom.

She shivered at his touch, and once again, the serviceable merino threatened to slip from her shoulders.

"Leave it!" His voice sounded cracked, though imperious.

"My lord, I am practically indecent!"

"Practically beautiful."

"Only because you look at me so."

"Then, I shall always look at you so!"

His words, so much what Anne wished to hear, yet such an impossibility, recalled her to her senses.

"Lord Edgemere, it is not fitting to be cavorting with your hired help amid shards of marble. You could be injured."

"Injured be damned! And stop referring to yourself as the hired help!"

"But I am, am I not?'

"No, because you are dismissed."

"Dismissed? My lord, that is outrageous!" Anne forgot the letter of resignation sitting silently in the lining of her chemise. "You cannot simply dismiss me out of hand! What about Kitty and Tom? What about—"

"What about *what,* Miss Derringer?" Was he mocking her? She looked at him more closely. No, she did not think so. He was regarding her somberly, as though restraining himself with great effort. As indeed, had she but known it, he was.

His little Celeste offered a powerful temptation in her underclothes, however chaste the ice white chemise. He would not defile her in his own home, not now, when her heart was fully revealed to him and when the summation of his plans was about to come to fruition. He would wait, however exquisite the torture. Inflaming her indignation—even her anger—was the best way he knew of preventing what might otherwise be an intoxicating interlude that they would both, quite possibly, live to regret.

Besides, he liked to see the militant sparkle back in her eyes. He suspected it was not often that she was racked by sobs. Though she might not admit it, the Dalrymple affair had cut deep.

Anne paused and blushed. She had very nearly said, "What about us?" She must not forget that to the seasoned earl, she was no more than a pleasant interlude. However much he might protest against her calling herself the hired help, he nevertheless placed her in that category. How else could he thus summarily dismiss her?

As if reading her thoughts, the earl chuckled.

"Hoist by your own petard, my dear! It was *you* who made me promise to release you from your engagement on my return to Carmichael Crescent."

"Very true, my lord! My wits have been quite addled by this night's affair. Do you, by any chance, have another taper?"

"Beg pardon?" The earl, for once, was startled.

Anne was patient. "Another taper, my lord. There is wax dripping on the Axminsters, and there is precious little left of your overhead candles. They are all almost nothing but wick."

"How true! When dazzled by a star, one seldom notices the dark creep in."

"You have a honeyed tongue, my lord."

"One day, Anne, you shall know the truth of what you say."

Anne blushed. With those direct eyes upon her, there was no mistaking his meaning.

"Regretfully, I think not, my lord. It is better that way."

The earl grinned, undeterred by the firm words. She had said regretfully, and she had knocked the only other eligible suitor unconscious. That said something, surely, for his chances?

"Very well, little Celeste, you shall have it your way for tonight. If you come to my chamber, I shall renew your candle."

"Step into the parlour, said the spider to the fly."

"That old nursery rhyme? You wrong me, my dear! My intentions, I assure you, are of the purest. Were they not, I should have ravished you right here upon my intricately knotted carpets."

"Nevertheless, you shall *fetch* me the candle, my lord. Your chamber, though no doubt sumptuous, is not a place I wish to enter this night."

"No?" He cocked his head to one side and allowed his finger to rest, ever so gently, upon her chin.

"No! Decidedly not, my lord!"

"Mmm . . . me thinks the lady doth protest too much. However, being ever true to my rash promise, I shall obligingly fetch you out the wretched thing. If I don't hurry, we shall be plunged headlong into darkness."

"Exactly my point, your lordship."

"My given name is Robert. Since you are no longer engaged as my governess, there can be no further obstacles to its use."

"I can think of many! However, I suggest we continue the argument at a more suitable hour."

Since all her tartness had returned, his lordship felt sufficiently comfortable to leave her, for a moment, whilst he stepped forward into his inner sanctum. She had stopped shivering, the most obvious outward sign of her disquiet. At a future date, Sir Archibald Dalrymple would be called to account for that. In the meanwhile. . . .

"You will stay there until I return!"

"My, you are imperious! I shall stay merely to keep poor Psyche company."

Excellent! Her humour was returning. Lord Robert turned on his heel and made for his chamber.

In the stillness that followed, Anne closed her eyes, the better to visualize the features etched so clearly in her memory. How handsome he was! How dear to her he had become, the glorious eighth Earl Edgemere! If only he had not been quite as witty, if only he had been a smidgen less amusing, a tad—the veriest tad—less handsome! But no, circumstances, as always, conspired against her.

Lord Carmichael was a paragon, and there was no gainsaying the truth. She, Anne Derringer, was doomed to spinsterhood, for there could be no accepting anything less than what he was—perfection. Or, more rightly speaking, perfection in imperfection. My lord was never tediously correct or predictably proper. How dull he would be if he was! Anne smiled. She adored her spats with him. It honed her wits and made her tongue as razor sharp as her mind. A mind that was complemented by his. . . . She startled as a flame flickered behind her.

"You have returned!"

"Don't look so shocked, Miss Derringer of Woodham Place! I did say I'd be back directly!"

"I am not of Woodham Place anymore. My brother sold the estate to sell off some debt."

"I hear it has been sold again. Anne, if you wanted it, would you consider purchasing it?"

"On forty pounds a year? My lord, even *with* your exorbitant salary—which I shall hold you to, by the by—you must have windmills in your head!"

"Not windmills, Celeste. News."

"News?" She couldn't keep the faint tremor from her voice.

The earl resumed his seat beside her, silently cursing a splinter of marble that had made an impression on his unmentionable—but decidedly desirable—posterior end. Anne dropped her eyes, for her gaze rested overlong in that direction, and it was, she knew, quite shamelessly admiring.

The earl's eyes flickered, for a moment, then grew disquietingly sombre. He knew that he could no longer keep from Anne what was her right to know. It would be self-serving beyond all permissible reason. He only hoped that she would not pack her bags at once, now that her circumstances were so vastly altered.

"Anne, I have dismissed you from my employ for two reasons. The first—though I shoot myself in the foot to say it—is that it is no longer fitting."

Anne cast inquiring eyes at him. He concentrated on his fingernails, for the dark, tangled lashes were too intoxicating to contemplate. In a moment, she would know the truth. She would know that she was an heiress, eminently eligible, and worlds away from needing his meagre salary. She would know, not to put too fine a point upon it, that she did not need him.

He chose to cast caution to the winds. There was no point in mincing matters. "Miss Derringer, though you do not yet know it, you are an excessively wealthy woman! As a matter of fact, though you have the face of an angel, you also appear to have the luck of the very devil! You and your *dashed* stars! Who, but a dear, addlepated, hen-witted *widgeon* places their entire fortune on a merchant ship more likely to sink than not, purely on the basis of its celestial name?"

"*I* do, my lord. And I am not hen-witted! When the Astor sank . . ." She stopped, remembering that she had chosen to remain on as governess despite the impropriety. What construction would the earl put on that? Not, she hoped, the correct one.

He looked at her keenly. "Do I infer that this is not

news to you? That you, my dear Anne, are once again an impostor in my household?"

"Imposter?"

"You know very well what I mean! Passing yourself off as an upper servant when you are more eligible than Miss Fairfax and that Wratcham woman—"

"It is not what you think!"

"No?" A sudden smile lit bright eyes. "Give me leave, Anne, to hope that it *is* what I think!"

"I could not leave the children in the lurch . . ."

His eyes clouded. "No, I suppose not. Anne, can you continue the charade one day longer?"

"It is best if I leave tomorrow."

"No!" The earl grabbed her hand. For an instant, he held it within his ungloved grip. Anne had never been more aware of him than at that moment. She blushed furiously, then wriggled her fingers free.

"You are imperious, Lord Robert!" Attack was always the best manner of preserving one's dignity.

"I have a right to be! You deceived me, whatever your reasons! No . . . don't look so damnably stubborn. I shall change tack and plead instead. Please, Anne! Stay! If not for mine, then for the children's sakes!"

Anne relented. It was hard to resist someone who sent shivers deliciously down one's spine and who entreated one with eyes of hazel velvet.

"Very well, I shall stay until after the ball."

Lord Edgemere breathed a sigh of satisfied relief.

"Till after the ball, then."

Miss Derringer stood up, taking care to allow the wrap to envelop her slender, statuesque frame as perfectly as it possibly might.

Lord Edgemere, victorious, leaned back in sudden amusement. It did not matter—the soft candlelight set her feminine charms off perfectly, wrap or no wrap. His eyes darkened, but he made no attempt to forestall her any further.

As she moved, the nonsensical confection that was her slipper struck something hard. She exclaimed, bent down, and retrieved the necklace. It shimmered like thousands of tiny stars under the little orange flame.

"Good gracious, my lord! This had quite slipped my mind!"

With complete lack of consciousness, she handed Lord Edgemere the gems and muttered something highly disparaging—if not entirely ladylike—about the good Sir Archibald Dalrymple.

When she departed for her own wing, the earl was staring after her in dazed amazement. She was quite a lady, the demure Miss Derringer!

In no more than half an hour, she had confounded a thief, resisted a noxious attempt upon her virtue, held a reasoned conversation in disgracefully compromising circumstances, then forgot—*forgot,* mark you!—that a necklace of blue-white diamonds lay somewhere in the rubble of marble shards.

Lord Edgemere chuckled. Lord Elgin's Psyche had cost a cool ten thousand pounds. He could not have dreamed up a better use for it himself.

Seventeen

The day of the ball dawned grey and unpromising, causing Mrs. Tibbet to hurry about in a frenzy of anxiety, ordering the potted palms back into the main receiving room, changing menus—iced sherbets on a cold day was unthinkable—and poking her finger outside on a five-minute basis to test for rain.

The children were in high spirits, tasting here, testing there, until even the staid Augustus was forced to chase them with an umbrella, an unprecedented event that caused them to laugh uproariously and hound him all the more. Finally, Anne was applied to, for the servants were at their wits' end, what with one thing and another.

Lord Morrison's coach was too large for the stables, the coal had not yet arrived, one of Lady Dillsworthy's matched team had cast a shoe on the road from Hampton. She had sent a note begging a new conveyance. . . . The list was endless. Anne offered to help, but was assured by a chorus of upper servants—and a cheeky lower servant—that removing the Viscount Tukebury from the house would be help enough. Jeeves chipped in to mention that Miss Kitty Carmichael was none the better, so Anne was immediately apprised of the urgency of the situation.

She discovered the little varmints polishing the floors with an excessive amount of beeswax and knew at once that their industrious and innocent activities were brimful of mischief. She stepped up to little Lord Tukebury—Tom, to his intimates—and curtsied grandly.

"Put down your brushes and dance with me, my good man!"

Tom bowed in excellent imitation of Robert's polished address and took her hand.

"On second thoughts, Tom, I shall sit this one out. Dance with Kit instead."

"But . . ."

"Go on, then, I am in a fever of anticipation to see whether my charges do me credit. Governesses, you know, are always held accountable for such things."

Tom nodded importantly. "Kitty?"

"Don't be such a gudgeon, Tom! Miss Derringer is awake to all suits! She only wants to see us take a tumble on the slippery boards!"

Anne chuckled. "The game is up, I see. Come, my little chickens, you shall set these floors to rights, return the polish to poor Wiggans, who I am certain must be searching high and low for it, then meet me at the stables. It is an age since we have exercised the horses and given them their head."

This occupation seemed to be met with approval, for it did not take long for the floors to regain their quietly elegant gleam and for the trio to head out of doors, toward the large, positively bustling stables. Miss Derringer did not have a riding habit, but she did have a dark serge gown that served the purpose, though her ankles were sadly prone to exposure. Since no one of any consequence was likely to see her mount or dismount, however, this seemed of little import. Some days before, Kitty had pressed a rather grown up top hat with frivolous flowing scarves upon her person, so despite her fashionable deficits, she nonetheless contrived to look respectably elegant when confronting the head groom.

He doffed his cap gaily—everyone had a soft spot for

Miss Derringer and the young ones—and saddled the horses quickly, even though several of the houseguests were about to return from hunting and there was "a heap of work afoot, with the ball and all."

It was not long before they had carefully crossed Tom's stream and were galloping, with abandon, in the meadows. Anne would have been exultant, were it not for the fact that she knew that this was to be her last such day.

Somehow, she did not wish to spoil it by telling the youngsters, so she set aside her nagging heartache and joined in the mirthful exuberance. Finally, the horses were panting from exertion. Anne decided it was more than high time to rein in and lead them down to the stream for water. She resolutely ignored the black clouds that seemed to loom threateningly above them. A wetting would not harm the children overmuch, and for herself, she did not mind in the least. It was better than watching preparations for a ball she would have no part in, knowing that tomorrow, when the excitement was long faded, she would be gone.

London was a daunting prospect—she had no wish to contact Lady Somerford and certainly none to contact her brother. It struck her that perhaps her best option would be to take up a house in Bath. There she could quietly resume the life-style and accoutrements of a lady of substance while most fashionable eyes were still firmly focused on London. Anne found that she had little desire to cut a dash, or try her hand at a third season. Undoubtedly, now that she was wealthy, she would not have to suffer the indignities or importunities of the past, but this did not weigh with her. She found she had no taste for being courted for her fortune.

What was that? Anne was sure she could hear hooves hard against the pastures. She settled her skirts primly over her ankles, just in case. She had been caught, unawares, once too many at Tom's stream. Half of her hoped it was Lord Edgemere. The other scolded her for being such a ninnyhammer. Lord Edgemere, in residence, had a thousand things to do to entertain his houseguests. He did not go galloping like a wild thing across fields of verdant clover.

"Oh I hope it does not rain and spoil things!"

Tom clicked his tongue. "Kitty, you sound like Mrs. Tibbet!"

"Well, it's true! Our first ball and—"

Anne broke in. "Not *your* first ball, Kitty! You shall need to be some years older for *that!*"

"Oh, *bother!* I am certain Robert would not mind at all if we were to attend. He might *look* like a curmudgeonly mawworm—"

"Thank you very much, Kitty! I do not believe I recall ever having before been described in such flattering terms . . ."

"My lord!"

"Miss Derringer, your servant."

Robert leapt nimbly down from the magnificent Arab that Anne had heard a few moments before.

"Robert! *You* do not mind if Tom and I—"

"Kitty, it does no good to bob your curls at me cajolingly! I am afraid, in this instance, appearances are correct. I am a curmudgeonly mawworm. No, don't pull such disgusting faces at me. You are a long shot, my dear little sister, from being out, and until then, you shall remain in the nursery."

Tom sighed. "I knew how it would be! We never have any fun around here."

"No fun, and you playing truant with your governess? I'll have you know, little sir, I pay Miss Derringer forty pounds a year to tutor you!"

The words were severe; but his eyes caught Anne's, and there was the unmistakible twinkle in them that she had come to find quite distressingly irresistible. She was not, however, going to take his criticism—even playful—without a scathing retort of her own.

"It is you, sir, who are truant! Galloping about when there is a ball afoot and houseguests aplenty to entertain! We, on the other hand, are diligently involved with Latin proverbs. We are, are we not, Tom dearest?"

"Very true, Miss Derringer!" Thomas could be relied upon to be prompt on the uptake. "We were just learning . . . um . . . what *were* we just learning, ma'am?"

Anne looked shocked. "Carpe diem, Tom! Carpe diem! You remember, surely?"

Tom looked dishearteningly puzzled, but his deplorably handsome brother had no trouble in the translation.

"Seize the day? Well, with a picnic hamper that size I should say you will. Do you demonstrate *all* proverbs in such delightfully practical terms?"

"All *respectable* proverbs, my lord!"

Anne's tone was reproving, though a merry little dimple appeared in her cheek. His lordship, she knew, had some decidedly improper Latin proverb in mind. His lips were twitching most suspiciously, and his eyes raked hers with teasing mirth. The mirth, however, was tinged with something else. Especially when his gaze rested on the glory of her trim ankles, momentarily exposed by the overshort serge gown. It was altogether decidedly disquieting and made Anne feel vulnerable and breathless. Despite the chill as grey clouds enveloped the sky, she was enveloped in a rosy warmth that placed a blush on her cheeks and caused her to touch them consciously before pulling her skirts firmly about her.

My lord laughed. "How very disappointing!"

Anne did not know whether he was talking of the proverbs or her ankles, but was too canny to question him. Probably, by his deplorably reprehensible smile, he meant both.

"I . . ."

He stopped as another rider appeared on the horizon.

"Bother!"

"My lord?"

"It is Lady Caroline! What need has she to go haring about the countryside . . ."

Kitty tossed her copper curls crossly. "She has *every* need! She is coursing you, Robert! *You* are the rabbit!"

"Hush, child!" Anne's tone was sharp, though privately she agreed with Kitty. Lady Caroline, she thought, had no shame. She was stalking Lord Edgemere. It did not take long for her chestnut to pull up alongside the earl.

"Darling! I *thought* I spied the Arab . . ."

Lady Caroline was a breathtaking vision in a riding habit of amber velvet, trimmed with embroidered gimp and interspersed with several large pearls. She wore, on her head, a bonnet of chip straw. This was a very modish creation, streaming an amber velvet ribbon the identical shade of her habit and sporting three guinea gold feathers. These, needless to say, offset her flowing locks perfectly.

Anne, despite her own striking features and magnificent dark lashes, felt positively dowdy. Her feelings must have been mirrored in her eyes, for Lady Caroline laughed a little consciously and murmured that all could not be blessed with high good looks, and if Miss Derringer wanted, she could recommend a very good rouge pot. . . .

The governess declined politely, but was surprised to find her fingers curled in a tense grip at the impertinent condescension.

Lord Robert appeared oblivious to these feminine undercurrents, for he stroked Lady Caroline's mare absently and produced a lump of sugar.

Lady Dashford turned honeyed eyes upon his person. Indeed, he was a magnificent sight, resplendent in cream breeches that left little to the feminine imagination and a multicaped Carrick coat that though heavy and warm, nonetheless moulded to his person in such a way that it was obvious no padding had been employed in its making. The ensemble was finished by gleaming Hessians and a cravat that though loosely tied, was nonetheless the epitome of careless elegance.

Kitty cared nothing for these matters. She glared at Lady Caroline and pulled one of her deplorable faces. Tom giggled and followed suit. Miss Derringer wanted to sink through the ground, for undoubtedly she would have to admonish the youngsters for such a breach of common etiquette. She was spared the trouble by Robert, who frowned frostily and demanded that they apologize.

Grudgingly, they did, though Anne could tell from their mulish looks that they would soon be up to pranks. Lady Caroline, glad to be the focus of his attention, feigned a conciliatory manner and obligingly forgave them, though she did mutter to Robert that clearly they needed a mama. At this, Lord Edgemere was noncommittal, but his former high spirits faded into a polite but impersonal demeanor.

"Are you headed back to Lord Anchorford's, Lady Caroline?"

"Yes, I shall ride with you, Edgemere! I am *agog* with excitement! It is the night of the ball and you know that you promised—"

The earl cut in quickly. "Let us hope all your heart's desires are satisfied. I certainly hope that *mine* shall be this evening."

Anne could hear by his tone that he was sincere. She dropped her gaze and stared at her spangled serge hem. Her heart hammered quite painfully, for she had thought Edgemere's connection with Caroline quite at an end. Now she saw—or thought she saw—that she had been mistaken in this matter.

Because her lashes were cast miserably downward, she did not see the tender and meaningful glance that was cast her way. Lady Caroline did, and her beautiful lips pursed spitefully. Only a few more hours and Lord Edgemere would be trapped. As soon as the diamonds were about her neck, she would announce her engagement to all her dearest and closest friends. The diamonds would be proof—*everyone* knew them to be his. They also knew he was not the sort to trifle with ladies of quality. His gift would be a declaration in itself. Let him try to cry off *then!* It would be impossible. No gentleman of honour could show his face under such circumstances. And the little governess . . . well! It would be a pleasure to give her her marching papers.

She cooed. "Oh, Edgemere! You have such a way with words! Shall I race you back? I believe you have a gift, of sorts, for me."

"There is no need, Lady Dashford. I have pressing concerns at Carmichael Crescent. You go on, though. I collect that the gift to which you refer is already in your chamber. I bribed a lady's maid to smuggle it through the doors."

Anne felt sick. So! She had always known the diamonds were destined for Lady Caroline, but to be so brazen about it. . . .

Lady Dashford positively preened with pleasure. "Excellent! I shall do it justice, you may be certain! I have had a gold-striped organdie with delicate taffeta—"

"Spare me the details, my dear! I am certain you shall look charming! Now, if you will excuse me, ladies . . . ?" He cast an inquiring look at Anne, but she did not trust herself to meet his eye. Undaunted, he mounted his Arab with effortless grace and bade his siblings behave. Then, as quickly as he had come upon them, he was gone.

"Well!" Lady Caroline looked at Anne in satisfaction. Miss Derringer concentrated on keeping her back straight and her feet carefully tucked under her skirts. She would not have Caroline see her at any disadvantage.

"Cat got your tongue?" Now that Lord Edgemere was

no longer with them, Lady Dashford felt free to be impertinent.

"The only thing catty around here, Lady Caroline, does not, I am sad to say, walk on four legs. Now pray leave us. I have a lesson to finish."

Tom choked and Kitty snorted behind her, but Anne was too furious to notice.

"Finish it, then. Your choice of words is apt. Tonight Lord Edgemere and I announce our betrothal. I advise you to pack your miserable bags immediately. I have relatives who might possibly need some hired help and shall suggest the notion to Robert on the morrow."

Anne allowed amusement to curve her lips. It was a valiant and determined effort, for she felt the world was crashing about her ears. Betrothed! She could hardly credit it, but for the evidence of her eyes. Lord Edgemere had been singularly polite to Lady Dashford. He had promised her the diamonds and had flattered her vanity by pretty compliments. Anne suffered, for honesty compelled her to acknowledge that Lady Caroline *would* look charming.

All this flashed through her mind in less than a proud instant. It dawned on her, of course, that Lady Caroline still considered her to be no more than a destitute upper servant. She would naturally be devastated to learn of her change of fortune. It was on the tip of Anne's tongue to tell her so. But no! She would learn it soon enough, and the chagrin would be so much the worse if the earl confirmed its veracity. . . .

"Suggest away!" She smiled sweetly, though again, her fists were tightly clenched.

"Be sure I shall, you impertinent baggage! And now, if you please, I have a necklace of diamonds to attend to. *So* much more pressing! Good day, Thomas! Good day, Katherine!"

She did not wait for any particular response. Instead,

she tapped her mare expertly with the tip of her riding crop and set off at a canter toward the Anchorford estate in the far distance.

Anne didn't bother to unpack the picnic basket. It was drizzling now, and only the trio's spirits were as black as the clouds above them. Any moment, she knew, they would be soaked through to their skins.

"Can you mount, Kitty?"

"Of course I can!" The tone was unusually scornful, and Anne knew that she was upset. Tom said nothing as he lifted his foot into the saddle and waited for the others to do the same.

"Is it true? Is Robert truly going to marry that . . . that . . ."

"Let us not dwell on Lady Caroline's descriptions. For myself, I have no notion whether they are to wed or not. Why should I? I am not, as you both well know, in your brother's confidence."

"Oh, but we had quite thought—"

Hush, Tom!" Kitty poked him in the back with her parasol.

The conversation did not progress much further, for the heavens opened and the thorough wetting that they had anticipated came to pass. By the time they arrived at the back door of Carmichael Crescent—Anne would not have dreamed of traipsing through the front, soaked and muddied as they were—there was nothing to be heard but the odd splash and grumble as a particularly large droplet lodged itself somewhere uncomfortable. So much for Miss Derringer's elegant attire! The flowing scarves were as drenched as her gown. Not that she minded overmuch—the day matched her mood perfectly.

The party handed their horses on to the grooms and trailed through the kitchens, where Mrs. Tibbet was frantically ordering the decorations to be salvaged from the rain and deciding whether the increased number of people likely to be indoors rendered opening the second ballroom an essential.

Anne, when applied to, nodded. She was glad to see that even when her heart was aching, her common sense, at least, prevailed.

"Set the supper room up between the two so there is a good ebb and flow. The dowagers can seat themselves quite comfortably in one while the orchestra and dancers occupy the main ballroom as planned. You still have the card and smoking rooms, so it should not be too dreadful a squeeze! Besides, I understand Lord Edgemere has only invited a select few. It is not as if we are expecting the whole of London!"

"At Lord Carmichael's first ball? You'd better believe it, Miss Derringer! By the by"—Mrs. Tibbet leaned closer to Anne and muttered conspiratorially—"do you attend? There is no reason, after all, why you should not."

Anne wanted to wring her hands in despair and cry that there was *every* reason. Instead, she replied coolly that she had a headache and could think of nothing better for the evening than a hot posset and light supper tray in the nursery.

Mrs. Tibbet took time from her own troubles to note the drawn features and the frown that worried at her creamy brow. If she suspected she knew at least some of the cause, she was far too polite to speak of it. Instead, she discreetly mentioned that my lord was "pacing up and down the gallery as though he were a lion at Astley's circus" and intimated that Miss Derringer might like to join him there, for she had a "soothing manner" and the trick of setting even the hardiest gentleman at ease.

Miss Derringer would like to have retorted that it was unlikely that her appearance would have any bearing on my lord's demeanor. She held her peace, however, and nodded vaguely that she might have a word with the earl if he were not otherwise engaged.

Had she been on true form, she would have chuckled at the double entendre, for it was precisely because he was about to be engaged that he was behaving so abstractedly. Anne, however, was in no mood for chuckling, so the unintended witticism passed unappreciated.

By the time she had escorted her charges to their rooms, handed them over to a waiting dresser and ancient but benign nurse—much to Tom's disgust—it was half past the hour. She then had her own dripping gown to attend to, and recalcitrant locks to set neatly in a topknot. It was the quickest way she knew of dealing with such an abundance of damp strands. Then—and only then—did she allow herself to think of my lord pacing the gallery below stairs. The thought was as unnerving as it was hypnotic.

She thought that this would be the last time in all her life that she would see him as she had learned to love him—single, impossibly debonair and hopelessly, *hopelessly* eligible.

She slipped into the only gown in her ensemble worthy of its elevated name. It was a morning gown of burnished gold, laced impossibly tight and fastened fashionably high. Its understated spencer of emerald velvet was modest, yet nevertheless skillfully revealed the contours of her creamy bosom. The shade exactly matched her remarkable tourmaline eyes, just as the black lacing mirrored the long, sultry lashes that forever framed them.

Anne caught her reflection in the mirror and startled. My lord may think lady Caroline charming. He would have difficulty, however, in regarding her as an antidote. For the first time in her life, Miss Anne Derringer realized she was something rather more than pretty. She was beautiful. She took a deep breath, pondered a while on her motives, then prepared for battle.

Eighteen

"Mrs. Tibbet bade me ask whether your preference is for iced orange or for chocolate."

The earl swung round. Though Anne had been in his thoughts constantly, he had not expected to see her again, in the flesh. Yet here she was, more wild, more wanton and more temptingly beautiful than ever in an organdie creation that left little to the imagination despite its high neck and stiff lacing.

He took a moment before replying, for he was mesmerized by her loveliness and by the dazzling smile she bestowed upon him. He thought he knew her, his gentle, honest, forthright and impudent Anne. He had long since recognized the wit and intelligence that lay buried behind the fear of being labeled a bluestocking. Her humour was an exact complement to his own—acerbic, understated and quite definitely funny.

But this! This was a siren, a wild, desirable dream that smiled upon him with knowing eyes and promised of delights beyond bearing . . . yet she was talking of truffles and tea and commenting on the livery of his butler. . . .

"Augustus?"

"Yes, my lord. It appears it is a six month since he has been supplied with a dress uniform. He would not have mentioned it, you understand, but for the ball that was thrust upon him with such—I hesitate to quote him—'unseemly haste.' "

In spite of himself, Lord Edgemere's lips twitched.

"Baggage! I know you well enough, Miss Derringer, to know that you will not cut up my peace with such nonsensical trifles. I wonder, then, why you tempt me now, in my own gallery, with those beguiling looks and those transparent excuses—diverting, I might add—to hold me in close discussion. If you were Kitty, I would be very much alarmed."

"Well I am *not* Kitty, Lord Edgemere!" Anne resisted the temptation of warning him that this was no reprieve. She was, after all, in battle mode. If Lord Edgemere was about to throw his life away on a common strumpet like Lady Dashford, she would jolly well enter the fray. If required, she would bat her lashes and brazen it out with calm defiance. In the meanwhile, she would offer him a strawberry from the basket on the table. Mrs. Tibbet had thought of every particular.

Lord Edgemere declined, though he regarded her with puzzled amusement. Anne stared at him a full moment before placing a ripe fruit between her rosy lips and slowly nibbling as though nothing in the world mattered except the sensuous enjoyment to be elicited from such a pastime.

Lord Robert, immune to most feminine wiles, watched fascinated as a delectable tongue slowly engulfed the strawberry until nothing was left but the healthy green leaf from which it had been plucked. This Miss Derringer disposed of in a silver salver set aside for just such a purpose.

"Vixen! You seek to disarm me!"

"Disarm you? My lord, whatever can you be talking about?" Anne feigned innocence, though her eyes twinkled brightly, partly from humour, partly from the strange excitement she felt at this particular game. Only, it was not a game. In four hours or less, the Earl of Edgemere would announce his countess. If he made a mistake, he would be forced to live with his decision forever. On the other hand . . . Anne hardly dared to think about the other hand.

Her heart was beating wildly again, and Lord Edgemere was two paces closer to her than he had been before. She stepped back a trifle, but he caught her sleeve and somehow—she knew not how—she was in his arms again. This time, the kiss was fierce and questing and as passionate as ever she could require. This time, his roving hands did not stop at the faint crest of cleavage that peeked modestly from her high-cut gown. They moulded to her contours, and though there was velvet and organdie and kidskin gloves between them, she gasped from the pleasure of it and felt burned as though it had been flesh upon flesh.

Her arms tangled up his back, and she could hear his faint sighs as her topknot loosened to allow her sleek black tendrils a life of their own. They twined in his hand and down his shoulders as she shook her head and opened her lips for more of his sweet mouth upon her own.

As he obliged, she could feel his thigh against hers, and she blushed for the joy of it. He laughed a little, cheek to cheek, then carried her over to the rather grand chaise longue at the far corner of the gallery. The long strides were bliss to her senses until, at last, she recalled a modicum of propriety.

"My lord!"

He laughed and snuggled close to her ear. She could feel his breath tickling her as he spoke. His tone, though mellow beyond belief, was also slightly teasing.

"It is usual, under such intimate circumstances, to revert to less formal terms of address. If I were a duke, for example, you might wish to refer to me as 'lord,' rather than 'grace.' As I am a mere earl, however, I believe it permissible to drop the lord entirely and address me simply as Robert or Rob or—"

"Do be serious!" With an effort, Anne rejected his silent offer of another delectable caress. His gaze had dropped to her ankles, and they were tingling quite unaccountably, despite the fact that he had made no move, as yet, to touch them.

"I *am* serious! When offered a vision of such utter perfection, there can be no possible alternative to a severe fit of seriousness. It is positively damaging to the senses. I feel my doctor would not allow it. Or only," he amended, "in very small doses!"

Anne was so bemused by his hypnotic effect upon her person, that she quite forgot her recently assumed role of siren. Instead, she rather crossly remarked that he was talking a good deal of fustian.

At this, he chuckled good-naturedly but denied the accusation. He eyed her thoughtfully, however, and Anne could not help wondering wither his thoughts were turning. To lady Caroline? Surely not, when his hands were playing idly with her laces and. . . .

"You promised!"

"That I would act the gentleman?"

"Yes!"

"I promised that so long as you were in my *employ* I would act the gentleman!"

"Well, then . . ."

"Miss Derringer, for a woman of your intelligence, your memory is remarkably short! I dismissed you yesterday, if you recall!"

"Dismissed? My lord, I take leave to inform you I resigned!"

"I rest my case! Since you are no longer a member of my household staff, I am released from any rash promise I chose to make!" He triumphantly nestled her closer to him, despite a muffled protest and a valiant effort to extricate herself from the deliciously muscular arms that encased her.

Anne relaxed for an instant, savouring the sensation of being held so securely by the man she undoubtedly loved. He had stopped making advances upon her virtue and seemed content, now, to rest his arms about her and place her head upon his shoulder.

"Robert?" The time for pretense between them was gone.

"My love?"

"Are you truly going to announce your betrothal this evening?"

"Did Lady Caroline say I was?"

"Yes."

The earl smiled in grim satisfaction. "Good. Be patient, my little Celeste."

Joy surged in Anne's heart. He would not call her that, surely, if he was promised to another.

"She was very confident about the matter!"

"Just as she was confident that my gift to her was a necklace of diamonds?"

"Yes."

The earl nodded in satisfaction. "Excellent. The plot thickens."

Anne frowned. "Does that mean you are *not* parting with the necklace?"

The earl merely smiled and placed his immaculately gloved finger to his lips.

"You are being wickedly mysterious!"

"*You* are being wickedly tempting! Meet me at midnight on the library terrace."

"If you are betrothed, I cannot!"

"Not even to use, at last, my precious Herschel telescope? It is two inches, you know."

Anne knew. She also knew he had deliberately evaded the implicit question.

"It is pouring with rain, and the clouds are as thick as darkness itself!"

"It will clear." His lips curved upward in amusement. He could see that his beloved little bluestocking would not pass up the chance, on her last night, to at last glimpse the heavens with an instrument that far surpassed the capability of her naked eye. He watched her mull the proposition over thoughtfully.

"Are you omnipotent, my lord, that you can say it will clear?"

Robert sighed. He was "my lord" again. Still, she had not refused him outright.

"No, but I have lived in this region a long time. There will be the devil of a storm, and then it will pass as quickly as it came. I warrant that by the time the first carriages are called out, the sky will be as clear as crystal and only the soaking land will be testament to the elements. That is the way of it in Kingsbury. Has been for generations. Tonight, the shepherds will heave a great sigh, for the dawn will be sparkling and the sun, tomorrow, will dry out the pastures."

As he spoke, he patted her tendrils into some sort of order and replaced the pins that had set her topknot tumbling. The hair was still slightly damp and the colour on Miss Derringer's cheeks was high. For an instant, he feared she had caught a chill and was feverish. Then he gazed directly into the sea of tourmaline and knew that if she was, it was not from the cold.

"Come, my dear. I promised an end to this charade and an end there shall be this very night. Let me help you set yourself to rights. Though you look bewitching, you also look distressingly, improper! Not that I *mind*, mark you, but the gallery is appallingly public. All we need is for Lord Willoughby Rothbart to take it into his head to peruse the portraits of my late predecessors . . ."

"What a horrible thought!"

"Indeed, particularly if he chooses to sport that lavender and puce waistcoat again for luncheon. My eyes are still recovering from the garishness. By the by, what has become of your suitor?"

"I am more concerned with what shall become of Psyche. Can you have her repaired?"

"Bother Psyche! She was put to an excellent, if unorthodox use! I hope, though, that Sir Archibald is a fair way to recovered."

Anne could not help raising her classical dark brows in surprise. "I should not think you would care overmuch, one way or another!"

"Oh, but I *do,* fair Celeste! It would not suit my plans to have Sir Archibald absent from tonight's festivities."

"Plans?"

"I play a deep game, Miss Anne. I suspect you know it."

Anne nodded. "I collect it has more than a little to do with the matter of the diamonds."

"The diamonds? They are a paltry trifle not worthy of my attention. Be patient, little Celeste, and all shall be revealed. Has anyone attended to Sir Archibald this morning?"

Anne grimaced. "Mrs. Tibbet took in a cold collation at around eleven. He looked like death, by all accounts, and appears to be sporting an egg-sized bump upon his head. Mrs. Tibbet says it looks absurd with the moustaches, and by the state of his temper, he appears to know it."

"Grouchy, is he?"

"Oh, very! He is threatening all *sorts* of uncivilised consequences. I suppose it is fortunate that I shall not be here, past tomorrow, to see the outcome of these."

The earl looked at her hard. "I hope that is not true. I also hope you know me enough to trust me."

"Then, you shall *not* get yourself engaged this night?"

"In all truth, it is my fervent hope that I do." He placed his hands upon her shoulders but was interrupted by the near door of the gallery opening and old Lord Carnaby—the most ageing of the house guests—stepping inside.

It was fortunate that this venerable gentleman was partially blind, for he did not seem to see anything amiss with Miss Derringer's makeshift coiffure, or the fact that she was standing unpardonably close to the gentleman of the household.

He muttered good day, amiably deplored the downpour, poked his stick at several of the portraits in a hazy but agreeable fashion, doffed his ancient beaver skin hat and ambled slowly past. It appeared, for all the world, as though he was promenading in Hyde Park or Covent Street Gardens. Perhaps, thought Anne, he believed he was.

The pair exchanged amused glances. Anne felt a familiar pain, for they thought so alike, shared such a sense of the ridiculous, that the sheer notion of Lady Caroline coming between them was like gall. And yet . . . yet he had not denied his plans to become betrothed. She had asked him as directly as she knew how.

He had said be patient, but what value was patience when the man she loved was throwing himself away on a common slut? And Lady Caroline was that, despite her haughty air and imperious breeding. Was she pressuring him again? Very likely.

Anne took a deep breath. "Lord Edgemere, it is not necessary to sacrifice yourself to that woman! If she is threatening you, call her bluff!"

The worst the world can think of you is that you are a jilt. Not pleasant, perhaps, but believe me, they will get over it. There are much more scandalous on dits to dwell upon. Look at Lord Carnavon . . . the Prince Regent, even, though one grows weary with tales of *his* excesses."

"I find myself singularly disinclined to be placed in that category." The eyes and tone were habitually lazy, but Anne was not deceived. There was a dangerous drawl to his voice, and she could have sworn that the luxurious hazel eyes flashed for an instant.

"Then, she *is* threatening you!"

Robert vouchsafed no reply. Anne closed her dreamy, sultry eyes, took a deep breath, then plunged herself headlong into a world where there was no turning back.

"Your lordship, I beg you to consider! If you *must* marry, marry me instead! I care not the snap of a finger for society! Let them wag their stupid little tongues and call you a cad and a jilt. The worst they can do is give you—and, by extension, myself—the cut direct. Think I care? Not I! Sticks and stones, my lord, break bones. Not whispers and lies."

The earl's eyes darkened with an arrested expression Anne could not quite fathom. He regarded her quietly for a moment or two before allowing his habitual sardonic attitude to return with the slight tightening of his jaw.

"I do believe, my very proper Miss Derringer, that I am receiving my first proposal of marriage! Flattering, albeit highly irregular!" He snapped open a gold embossed snuff box and inhaled deeply.

"A pox on flattery! And as for irregular . . . I had not previously thought you too mindful of proprieties, my lord!"

The earl's eyes gleamed at this palpable hit. "Forgive me, my little Celeste. I am a creature of surprises. When it comes to proposals of marriage, I find that I am singularly inclined to propriety!"

"At the expense of happiness? Don't be such a toplofty gudgeon!" Anne could not believe how bold she had become, throwing caution to the winds like a cast-off mantle. Lord Edgemere loved her. She did not know why, but she was suddenly convinced of that fact. Perhaps it was the stubborn set of his chin, so uncannily like that of Kitty's.

She pressed her advantage home in the moment of

slight hesitation. Amused eyes raked her up and down in the type of scorching manner that caused her words to tumble out in a rush of confusion rather than in the orderly manner in which they had been intended.

"I believe the connection is not entirely ineligible. I have good bloodlines, I am a lady born and bred, I believe I am healthy enough to . . . to . . ."

"Bear my children?" There was now more than a little laughter creeping into the earl's honeyed accents.

"Precisely!" She dropped her gaze, but carried on hurriedly, before she lost the courage. "I would never dream of suggesting this course but for the fact of my newly acquired fortune. You, my lord, shall not doubt my motives."

"Oh, but I do!"

"Beg pardon?"

"I doubt your motives entirely! You speak of breeding and bloodlines. You disappoint me vastly, for I had hoped you'd mention my compelling attraction, my irresistible nature, my—"

"You see fit to tease, my lord!" Anne's tone was reproachful.

"I am in deadly earnest! I do not regard marriage in the same manner that I regard the qualities of my brood mares. Perhaps that is remiss of me, but there, you may set it down to my recalcitrant nature and to the fact that I have always preferred Socrates to Debrett's when it comes to matters of import."

And that, precisely, is why I love you. The words sprang unbidden to Anne's thoughts, but she was not yet so brazen as to voice them. Instead, she assumed her severest tones and scolded him for taking the matter of his lineage so lightly. She deftly skirted the question of his masculine magnetism. She was not so far beyond the pale that she would admit to the undercurrents that threatened to engulf her. If she did, they were both sadly in danger of steering off the point.

Still, Lady Caroline would have him locked in her clutches forever if a willing damsel did not rescue him from her coils smartly. She pressed her case home.

"I assure you I would not take so improper a course if I did not think it appallingly essential!"

The earl responded to her earnestness. He dropped his bored, slightly amused pose and drew her to him. The charade would have to play itself out, but by God, he wanted a conclusion by evening!

"Anne. My beautiful Anne. I thank you from the bottom of my heart."

"Then, you will listen to reason? Lady Dashford—"

He held up his hand. "Hush. I am devastated to have to inform you that I decline your most generous offer."

"Decline?" Anne's heart faltered, and she dropped the hand that had reached out to gently stroke his clean-shaven chin.

"Decline." His voice was firm and his eyes unwavering upon her. "Do not appear so downhearted. I have feelings of the deepest and tenderest . . . no, I shall hold my peace. Tonight, if all the pieces of my well-laid plans fall satisfactorily into place, the boot shall be on the other foot. It is *I* who shall be—damnation!"

"What is it?"

"That is Dartford! I would know the sound of his hooves anywhere!"

"But who could be riding him? The weather . . ."

"Anne, where is Tom?"

"Oh my God! Surely he wouldn't . . ." Even as she said it, Anne knew it was a forlorn hope. Tom had been peculiarly out of spirits that morning. Lady Caroline had been so definite about the betrothal . . . perhaps he had taken it into his head to challenge her. Perhaps he was just in a wild, stormy, defiant mood. He *knew* Dartford was forbidden to him.

"I shall check the nursery wing."

"There is no time. I shall go after the horse. It might just be some high-spirited groom, but I cannot take the chance."

"No!"

My lord did not wait for a reply. He swung out of the gallery and down the front steps with the swiftness of Hercules.

It was left to Miss Derringer to help Lord Carnaby make his second circuit of the room. It was the mark of her breeding that she was able to maintain a civil tongue as she helped him with his cane and rang for a footman.

When the excellent gentleman arrived, she smiled politely and fled.

Nineteen

Lady Caroline purred with pleasure. She had barely greeted Lady Anchorford, her hostess, as she had passed her on the stairs. Miss Wratcham, however, had received a courteous nod of the head. Lady Caroline had not survived the rigours of the season with her reputation intact without knowing who to kowtow to when required.

Once within the portals of her chamber, she had dropped her gracious society pose and rushed feverishly to the dressing table, where she hoped she might find the gift. She was disappointed to find, instead, a posy of flowers. They were perfect blooms—red and scarlet scattered with dewdrops—but sadly, they went unappreciated for all their lovely scent. She noted the luxurious scrawl across the card: Edgemere.

Lady Caroline knew a moment of panic. Had he been teasing her or leading her on? Had he *really* retrieved the diamonds from Sir Archibald Dalrymple, or was she simply dreaming? Come to think of it, all that morning the talk had been about nothing but Sir Archibald's "dashed good luck." What if the necklace was back in his possession? Fury blinded her, so she did not see the small package tucked neatly by her pillow. Hastings had gone to a lot of trouble to get it there.

"Jane!"

"Your ladyship?" Jane entered from the dressing room.

"Was a package left for me?"

"Package? Oh, the flowers you mean! Jeeves—we are walking out together, you know—asked me to set them upon your table. They are charming, I'm sure."

"Don't be foolish, woman! I said *package* . . ." Caroline's voice trailed as she caught sight of the item on her bed. Her relief was profound, though she noted it had been discreetly covered in brown paper. Not the best presentation, perhaps, but so long as it was the genuine article, she cared not a fig for such trifles.

"Thank you, Jane. You are dismissed."

Jane's eyes wandered lingeringly to the bed in synchrony with her mistress's gaze. She was curious about the parcel, but knew it was more than her job was worth to question her mistress in such a mood. No doubt, if she was wily—and she was—she would be able to weasel it out of her at some later stage. She bobbed a curtsy and returned to her work.

There were still several buttons to stitch before the night's flowing creation was ready.

Lady Caroline was heedless of her riding habit as she dived on the bed. She ripped open the parcel, and seconds—a few glorious seconds—later, she was holding her prize. The necklace sat heavy in her hand and sparkled up at her invitingly.

"Yes!" She threaded it through her fingers and lay back upon the high, well-aired bed. Lord Edgemere would be trapped that very night. *He* might regard the gift as an expensive parting present, but he would never be able to extricate himself from the interpretation *she* would publicly place on it.

She shook out the parcel for a note, but found nothing but a blurry half memo "ad. . . ." Admirer! So he was not so indifferent, then, Lord Robert! He must have just stopped himself penning the rest of the missive. Caroline smiled. They would not, after all, deal too badly together.

* * *

The rain was pouring down in torrents as Dartford thundered down the meadows. Tom was by now too frightened to press on to the Anchorford estate, where he had had every boyish intention of confronting Lady Caroline. Up behind him was Edgemere, terrified of calling, lest he startle the boy and cause him to lose his grip upon the saddle. Dartford was the most flighty of his beasts, though undoubtedly the swiftest. The little Viscount Tukebury was a skilled rider and contrived not to tumble as he pulled in the reins and caused the animal to turn. He was flat upon the saddle, drenched to the skin, but he hardly noticed this circumstance, for his eyes were wet with unshed tears. His heart was hammering painfully in his chest, for Dartford was much, much higher than he had seemed in the comfort of the stables. If he fell . . . he shuddered and tightened his grip on the reins. He would *not* fall! That beastly Lady Caroline would not win so easily. She wanted to be rid of him, he knew it. . . .

"Tom!" The earl's words were soft and gentle, but Tom did not hear them. Instead, he clung on for dear life as the horse lost patience and took off into the gloom. Edgemere thought he could detect a wail of fright as the hooves settled into a canter. Restlessly, the earl kicked his own heels in and set off after. If he had had time to brood, he would have been filled with the deepest dread. As it was, he concentrated only on the sound of the hooves galloping in the shadows. If he was to be of any assistance at all, he must keep up. The sounds of running water entered into his consciousness. They were heading for Tom's stream. If Dartford took fright, he might make a bolt for it across the track where Edgemere had first come upon Miss Derringer. Any number of carriages were due to head out in that direction, many to avoid the pike, but most, he was horrifyingly aware, to attend his ball. A collision with one of these would be fatal. The hooves were becoming fainter.

Edgemere increased his pace until Dartford once again came into view. Tom seemed to be hanging dangerously to the left, almost as though he had been unseated but had refused, stubbornly, to release his grip of the saddle. Even now, he seemed to be struggling to regain his seat, slowing the horse down in his efforts. Edgemere seized his opportunity and caught up.

Tom shuddered as he heard Robert's calm, authoritative voice behind him. "Easy does it, Dartford. Steady on, steady there, Tom."

Tom gulped. He knew he was in a great deal of trouble, but he didn't care. Robert was a comfort, even if he *was* a gudgeon for choosing Lady Caroline over their dear, adorable Miss Derringer.

"Can you dismount?"

"I don't think so. He still feels restive."

Edgemere nodded. "I shall lead you back. Can you pass me the reins?"

"I can try."

It took so long for the horses to be positioned side by side that Anne had time, in the interim, to saddle one of the mares and fly—*fly* across the heather to the stream. Somehow, she suspected Tom might head for this haven. When he was not there, she deliberated whether to head on home or push onward toward the Anchorford estate. The child might, after all, simply be reading in the schoolroom. She should have checked! Out of the corner of her eye, she could dimly see carriage wheels—early guests. If they did not see Tom in the mists . . . if he had been thrown, perhaps. . . . She urged her horse forward, taking care that Tom was nowhere underfoot.

"Tom! Tom!" She called out wildly, but her words were lost on the wind. At last, she thought she heard hooves upon the small track in the clearing. The rain had stopped, but her sheer gown was now nothing but a tangle of gold organdie and lace. She squinted into the fog and caught her breath.

A tall, burly man was seated on horseback just a few yards from the fir trees. Anne did not take note of his torn breeches or his grubby stocks. She was more interested in the blunderbuss that was directed squarely at her chest. The rains were ceasing almost as quickly as they had started, but this fact was little comfort as the dripping weapon was cocked and primed.

"Got yer now, me beauty!"

Anne's heart sank. She would know that snigger anywhere. It was the same throaty, heartless noise she had heard when she had been abandoned quite three miles from her agreed upon destination of Kingsbury. She straightened her back, her eyes kindling with anger and an unknown mix of fear and determination.

"Samson! What on earth are you doing here? And put down that weapon at once! It could misfire and cause grievous harm."

"That it could, missy, so climb down from that prime piece of livestock there before I 'ave a mind to try it."

"Dismount? Whatever for?" Anne played for time, her eyes cannily fixed on the ancient blunderbuss. The coachman was so remiss in his duties, the weapon was probably not well enough oiled. Should she risk making a bolt for it? Calling out? The earl was probably in the vicinity, for he was searching for Tom. Tom! Gracious, Samson could not be so iniquitous as to have captured the boy for ransom? A cold chill swept over her.

"Do you have Tom?"

"Tom? What git is 'e?" Samson leered, and, the clinging gown offered little consolation to his victim. "I 'opes 'e aint no gentleman toff what's given yer no slip o' the shoulder!"

Anne shuddered at his vulgarity but offered up silent

thanks. If he thought Tom a lover, he obviously had no notion of the whereabouts of the young Viscount Tukebury.

"It is none of your business, Samson! Now put that gun away. This is the eighth Earl of Edgemere's property, and consequently you run a great risk. If he does not find you, his gamekeeper will. Either man will not hesitate to put a bullet through your head."

"Then, they 'ad better not find me 'ere, 'ad they? Now climb down, Miss *Derringer,* before I lose wot little patience I 'ave. Yer and I got business to attend to."

"Business?" Anne strained her ears to listen for Edgemere. If she could call out, then leap from her mare, the earl might create enough diversion for her to run—or roll, as the case may be—into the thicket. She did not think much of this plan, but it was better than no plan at all. She held her voice steady as she listened for hooves upon the footpath.

Samson looked smug as he edged Lady Somerford's prize bay a little closer. "It be yer lucky day, Miss Anne! I am not going to ravish yer without making sure yer first 'ave yer marriage lines nice and snug in yer pocket. Yer can say *that* fer Samson Weatherby! Right refined I am and that's a fact."

"Marriage lines?" Anne felt her stomach churn. There was more to this incident than mere bad feeling; she could sense it in her gut.

"Aye, yer 'eard me right. Now 'urry up and slide down from yer 'orse before I change me mind and 'ave me way wiv yer before we find the parson."

"You mean to marry me?" Miss Derringer could think of nothing but the blunderbuss that was now pointing rather unsteadily at her stomach. If he had some outlandish notion to wed her, she had less to fear than she had thought. He would not dare to fire for fear of killing her.

"That's wot I said, ain't it? Now that yer as rich as a

nob, I'd be dicked in the 'ead not to leg shackle yer all right and tight."

So! Samson had pieced together news of her good fortune and was bent on turning it to his advantage. She felt sick, for a man with a motive as strong as his would stop at nothing. It was useless to point out that no parson would marry her until banns had been posted. He would merely ravish her and sit out the necessary time before a license could be procured. Anne knew his type. Ruthless and stupid. It was a terrible combination and one that she did not underestimate, for all Samson's clodpole manners.

How could Mr. Clark have betrayed her trust in this manner? Only he, Mrs. Tibbet and Lord Edgemere himself knew of her windfall. She noted the self-satisfied smirk on her captor's face and trembled slightly, though she still made no move to slide off the mare.

"Who told you I had come into a fortune? I am sure *I* have not heard of such a marvel! If I had, I assure you I would not still be hiring myself out as a governess."

Samson's eyes narrowed suspiciously. For the first time, he had doubts. It was true what the wench said. If she was as rich as was whispered, she would be queening it in London rather than acting the servant. He released his breath as rosy visions of the future receded before his very eyes. There would be nary a guinea for his trouble if the rumour had all been a sorry hum. His ruddy face reddened in frustration.

It did not help that Miss Derringer was not so much as whimpering. Cool as a cucumber she was. Not for the first time, he wondered what it would be like to make her lose her studied poise. He would enjoy it, he would, and he needed *something* for his trouble. He licked his lips. Somehow, he must find out the truth. There was no sense in shackling himself to the ice maiden if there was no fortune to be bought for the cost of a ring. Bedding alone would be much more to his tastes. Despite the tension of the moment, he did not miss the intriguing outline of her slender form. It was excessively palatable against the revealing, wet and devastatingly flimsy organdie.

"Not well 'eeled? But I 'ad it off Lord Featherstone's undermaid—a cosy little piece if I say so meself—that yer ship 'ad come in in more ways than one."

Anne heard the slow trot of hooves behind her. Just a little nearer and she would seize her chance and scream.

"Lord Featherstone? What has *he* to do with anything?"

"Toffee-nosed chap. 'as windmills in is 'ead 'e does. Gambles on practically everything that moves. 'as a losin' streak as long as me arm. Mind yer, won by a long shot on that there *Polaris* or whatever. No but thought 'e'd 'ad it in 'im."

Anne nodded. Then, Ethan Clark had not revealed her secret. No doubt his partner, Mr. Wiley, had had a loose tongue when revealing Lord Featherstone's share of the investment. Despite her dire situation, she felt a weight removed from her chest. Betrayal pained her more than greed and vengeance. The hooves—did she hear four pair?—were now close enough to chance her luck. Anything would be better than allowing Samson to carry her off unchallenged into the mists.

"Ere!" Samson saw her move and leveled the weapon just inches from her head."

"Take it easy, Samson! You asked me to dismount, and I am doing just that. I would hardly be any use to you dead or even injured, so I suggest you put away the infernal gun."

Samson wavered for a moment. Anne seized her chance and screamed as she jumped from the side of the horse farthest from the gun. She fell to the ground and gasped as the air was pushed from her lungs from the landing. Almost reflexively, Samson's gun fired. Then she could remember no more but an answering shout and the thundering of hooves.

When Anne opened her eyes, Mrs. Tibbet's was the first face she saw. After that, it was a confusing medley of bobbing copper curls and an overpoweringly exuberant Lord Tukebury, who looked alternately like the cat who had got the cream and a strutting cockerel.

"What happened?"

"Oh Miss Derringer! You missed the most famous fun!"

In spite of her aching ribs, Anne's lips twitched, though her voice was dry as she commented, "Evidently."

"Robert was leading me back—on Dartford, you know—"

"Yes, I know, and I advise it is best not to remind me!"

"Yes, well, anyway! We heard the gun and your scream, and Robert dropped my reins and thundered forward like—like—"

"Like lightning!" Kitty interpolated with relish.

"How do *you* know? You weren't even there!"

Kitty obliged her brother with the most disgusting of faces, causing her beloved governess to lie back against the cushions in despair. Had she taught the little vixen nothing?

"Sorry, Miss Derringer, but sometimes Tom can be the most provoking, pig-headed—"

"Enough of that, children! If you do not stop your quarreling, I shall forbid you Miss Derringer's chamber!"

Mrs. Tibbet was surprisingly fierce. She had just returned with a cup of chocolate and several slices of mouth-watering Madeira cake, and her threat was met with squeals of protest. Nevertheless, it had the desired effect. Tom was allowed to continue with his story uninterrupted, despite several rather baleful glares from his sister.

"The man—heaven knows who he was—reloaded and took a shot at Robert—"

"What?" Anne sat up with a shock.

"It was nothing—winged him, merely . . ."

Mrs. Tibbet nodded to confirm, so Anne unclenched her fist and allowed her arrested breathing to resume a little more normally.

"Then—*then* comes the best bit!" Tom bounced on one foot and hopped up to Anne.

"He came up to Robert—who was cast from his horse—and tried to . . ."

"There, there, Tom! Come to the point! Miss Derringer is looking faint!"

"Well, he came up to Robert and was about to kick him in the ribs when he stumbled and his gun fired again. Dartford took fright—he is a very frisky animal, you know . . ." Anne suppressed a smile at his superior attitude.

". . . and plunged into the fray. I was nearly unseated, but I clung on fast—as tight as I could—and we charged. Goodness! The man gulped with fright and dropped his weapon. He was nearly crushed, but I pulled the reins as hard as I could and missed him by a hairsbreadth!"

The recitation ended with such an excited flourish that Anne laughed out loud.

"Stuff and nonsense, Tom! *Then* came the best bit!" Miss copper curls could not help this outburst despite a warning frown from the housekeeper.

"Robert grabbed the varmint by the scruff of his neck and landed him such a facer I warrant he shall not think straight for weeks!"

Tom was scornful. "How do *you* know?"

"I was standing looking down from the gazebo. I'd come out to look for you."

"You couldn't have seen anything! The place was covered in mist!"

"It had just cleared. See." Kitty pointed outside. "It is all gone, and the air smells heavenly."

Anne could not contain her curiosity. "What happened then?"

"Then?"

"Yes, after his lordship gave him his comeuppance?"

"Oh, then! Then he clear fainted."

"Who? Samson?"

"No, silly! Robert."

Anne spilt her chocolate over the crisp counterpane.

Mrs. Tibbet tut-tutted furiously and sent the little varmints from the room. They took one look at her and scarpered.

Twenty

"He is fine, Miss Derringer. He simply lost a small amount of blood from the wound and the exertion of planting the man a facer . . ."

"He is all right, now?"

"As right as a trivet. He begged me pay you his compliments and inform you that Samson Weatherby shall bother you no more. As we speak, he is bound in custody. It is fortunate that the magistrate is a passing acquaintance of the earl's, for he attended to the matter at once. He was so diligent in his duties that I reckon Samson will not be driving anywhere for a while."

Anne nodded absently, for in truth her concern was less with the scandalous behaviour of the coachman than with the condition of Lord Edgemere.

"You are certain his lordship is not ill? Should a doctor not be called for?"

Mrs. Tibbet smiled. "Call a doctor for such a paltry wound? Certainly not! My lord would not *countenance* such a thing! His man bound up the wound tightly, and the last I saw of him, he was greeting some of the early arrivals."

"Has Lady Caroline arrived?"

"Not yet, and I expect we won't see her till quite late."

"Why ever not?"

"Lady Caroline, I am afraid, always makes a grand entrance. She will arrive when all heads can turn to see her. That, Miss Derringer, was ever her way." Mrs. Tibbet pursed her lips and said no more. By the time she had seen to the tea things, Anne's mood had darkened considerably.

If Lord Edgemere was well enough to welcome guests, he was well enough, surely, to check on her. In her slightly dazed state, Anne neglected to consider the propriety of such an action. It would be unseemly, indeed, for his lordship to make such a gesture when she was confined to her chamber. Mrs. Tibbet glanced at her anxiously.

"Are you certain you have taken no harm, Miss Anne? I mislike those circles under your eyes, and your cheeks seem so pale . . ."

"I am perfectly fine, thank you!" The cheval glass reflecting her image did not seem to think so, but Anne had no patience with such trifles.

"Go, Mrs. Tibbet! I am sure you have a thousand and one things to do what with housing the orchestra, overseeing the food . . ."

"Gracious! The orchestra! I hope I have allowed enough space for the instruments. I settled for the far corner by the potted palms, but I am afraid it is going to be a tight squeeze."

"It shall all be perfectly delightful, I am sure." Anne was not sure, for her heart was breaking. The earl had refused her rash offer—she felt foolish enough about that—and was now going to plunge himself into a betrothal with a woman who was quite contemptible. At best, she was unworthy of the earl's inestimable merits. And for what? For the simple sake of masculine honour. The earl would not stand to be sued for breach. The scandal to his noble name would, incomprehensibly to Anne, be impossible to bear.

Anne hoped she could trust her instincts enough to believe the earl had never been trifling with her regard. He loved her, she could feel it. The undercurrents between them were too strong to dismiss out of hand. So then? So it seemed he was now reduced to having his hand forced by a woman brazen enough to be a doxy. It was a shame, a crying shame. True, he had told her to be patient. But he had also told her he meant to become betrothed that night. And since he had refused *her* humble offer, it could only mean that the detestable Miss Dashford had won.

Anne's indignation was hard to bear. Mrs. Tibbet was looking at her queerly, so she forced a smile to her lips.

"I am much better now, I assure you! Off you go, for the success of the ball depends upon it, I am certain! If I need anything, I have only to ring."

Agatha Tibbet relented. "There is a pitcher of iced lemonade on the dresser. I shall mend your gown, but in the meanwhile, I have put out a rose satin that belonged to Lady Lucinda, the previous Countess Edgemere. She would have liked you."

The words were softly spoken, but Anne divined a hidden quality to them that she could not quite define. It was almost as though Mrs. Tibbet was conferring a blessing upon her. But there! The fall must have shaken her senses, for she was being woefully fanciful for such a prosaic young lady.

"Thank you, but I shall not be attending the ball, you know."

"I know, but it would be a shame to waste such a pretty gown. You are exactly the right size for it, and I cannot think of a better person to wear it." The housekeeper said no more. She couldn't, for she was inexplicably overcome. She squeezed Anne's listless hand once, then shut the door quietly behind her.

"Ah, Sir Archibald! A word with you, please!"

Lord Edgemere looked dapper in a Weston creation of

deep emerald green, nipped tightly at the waist and sporting a diamond pin that sparkled from his eminently fashionable waterfall cascade.

Sir Archibald eyed the cravat with distaste. His valet had spent the better part of an afternoon trying to achieve just such an effect but to no avail. Several discarded neckerchiefs lay upon the bed to tell their sorry story. And as for that pin . . . it must be worth a small fortune at the very least. The best he could manage was a meagre gold clasp encrusted with a rather poor paste ruby. Life, at times, was singularly unfair.

"What is it, Edgemere? Come to gloat, have you?"

"Good Lord, no, Sir Archibald! What *can* have made you imagine such a thing? Allow me."

With a deft twist of his hand he removed his guest's final attempt at the waterfall and snapped his fingers at the watchful valet who hovered anxiously behind him. "Fetch me another cloth, my good man, then be off with you."

"What?" expostulated Sir Archibald.

Lord Edgemere said nothing until he had a crisp neckerchief in his hands. He nodded curtly to the servant, who stammered a bow and looked uncertainly at his master.

"Oh, *go,* Sebastian! Heaven knows, you have already made a dismal mull of things. And shut the door behind you, will you? This house has ears." Sir Archibald glared defiantly at the earl as the handle finally clicked.

"Well?"

"In a minute, Sir Archibald! First things first." The earl stepped forward and placed the cravat smartly about Dalrymple's neck. For an instant, he had the unnerving impulse to choke the life out of the man. Then his smooth civility returned, and he deftly created a complicated series of knots called, in the highest circles, "the lotus." Sir Archibald caught sight of himself in the glass and grunted.

"How the devil did you . . . ?"

"Practice, sir Archibald. Practice and a little flair. There! You look much more presentable, do you not?"

Dalrymple could not help preening a little, though his head still ached and he regarded Lord Edgemere's attentions with the deepest of suspicion. He fingered the neckcloth nervously but allowed his lordship to help him into his well-padded coat. He hoped that the lambs wool would hide his minor imperfections of form, but next to Lord Edgemere's lithe and impossibly muscular physique, he despaired.

"Damn your eyes, Edgemere! What in tarnation do you want with me?"

"I believe the reverse is more to the point, Sir Archibald."

The baronet raised his speckled brows inquiringly. "By which you mean . . . ?"

"By which I mean that if you wish to continue to gain credit through your possession of the diamonds, you will listen most carefully."

Lord Edgemere had struck the right cord. He had Dalrymple's full attention at last.

The ballroom, as Mrs. Tibbet had predicted, was full to the brim. Lord Anchorford's guests had arrived in two carriages, though Lady Caroline had declined the offer of the second barouche, preferring, she said, to arrive "a little later." Lady Anchorford had kindly accepted her claim of fatigue, though she acidly remarked to her husband that Lady Dashford could be relied upon to upset her household by calling up a coachman later in the evening.

Apart from this minor entourage, there were all the country gentry who had been invited from Hampton and Staines to the other side of Kingsbury. Anne would have smiled to note the imposing presence of the Countess of Eversleigh, who glittered with a thousand jewels and an overheavy tiara upon her bluish grey head. Alongside her was Miss Danvers, primly dressed in a brown gown of dull merino. She clutched at her reticule with pursed looks and generally took in the festivities with a jaundiced air.

Festivities they were, for the combined ballrooms were bedecked with flowers, the walls hung with shimmering satins of canary, lavenders and greens. Mrs. Tibbet had outdone herself with the lighting, for she had achieved a radiant effect with hundreds of gleaming candelabras. Chandeliers from the ceiling glittered a breathtaking mix of crystal and white wax. Flickering flames were reflected everywhere in mirrors strategically placed to the greatest advantage. Members of the orchestra were, contrary to all expectation, seated with the greatest of comfort. The discerning guest could just make them out, seated in buttoned leather chairs next to a plethora of potted palms, ferns and cycads.

The dance floors gleamed with beeswax, but already there was very little space left to note the clever parquet work, for it seemed that the whole of England had arrived for the occasion.

Lord Edgemere bowed regally as guest after guest arrived and made their curtsies and legs. No one—not even Mrs. Tibbet, who eyed him anxiously from the gallery—could detect any sign of perturbation. If his arm ached beneath his perfectly fitted sleeve, he certainly showed no outward sign.

"Lady Grafton and Princess Esterhazy! How very kind of you to make the journey!"

"Wouldn't miss it for the world, Edgemere! Society has waited long enough for you to do the right thing by it. No good one of the most eligible bachelors of the decade closeting himself up with a pair of whippersnapper siblings and the old family retainers! I remember the days of your dear mama . . . oh, it was a merry place then!" She looked about her with an interested air. "I see you have purchased a few marbles. Taking up Lord Elgin's interest?"

"I wouldn't be so presumptuous! I do, however, have strong classical interests, and if you care to, I could show you the long gallery where I house much of my collection."

"Hmm . . . tempting, but I wouldn't be so callous as to monopolize so much of your time, Edgemere! The ballroom abounds with young ladies with more pressing claims, I imagine." With a teasing glance she rapped him over the knuckles with her fan and moved on. The queue appeared endless, but Edgemere stood his ground, determined to greet every last one of his guests, many of whom had travelled from as far afield as London and even Bath to grace his home. Considering the ridiculously short notice and the inclement weather, it was a testament both to his quiet popularity and to the novelty of his providing such an entertainment that so few people had declined.

He nodded to one of the upper house staff, and the orchestra struck up soon after. A glance at the hall clock indicated that Lady Caroline, of course, was late. He sighed impatiently. Out of the corner of his eye, he could see Sir Archibald leering at one of the debutantes. He was playing with the folds of his cravat, which irritated Edgemere slightly, for he noted that his excellent handiwork was coming loose. Lord Willoughby Rothbart, true to form, was monopolizing the attentions of Lily Farrington, society's latest heiress. She seemed to be enjoying his company, for she was even now extending her dance card, despite several disapproving looks from her chaperone.

Edgemere resisted the temptation to tap his foot. Where

was she, the vixen? All his plans depended upon her arrival. Ah! He believed he heard the announcement now. "Mr. Arthur Mortimer, Miss Serena Mortimer, Lady Caroline Dashford . . ."

He took a pinch of snuff before bowing pleasantly over Miss Serena's hand and nodding to her father. Then—only then—did he acknowledge Lady Caroline's arrival.

She was magnificent, as he fully expected. She was wearing a satin gown with a band of blond silk crisscrossing her well-endowed bosom. Her draped tunic was a vivid gold, complemented by an open tunic of shimmering silver that was drawn closed at the hipline by a jeweled brooch. Both the longer hem of the gown and the shorter hem of the tunic were edged with wide, embroidered bands of the identical style to the short, puffed sleeves. Her fan was carried shut to reveal the stem, studded in diamonds. Her hair was shining guinea gold, piled up high in an elaborate coiffure and fastened with roses. None of this mattered. The only thing that mattered was that she was wearing the necklace. It glittered and danced upon her neck as though it were a thousand stars, set down from the firmament and emblazoning her person in a manner that overshadowed all her other artifices. Had she been wearing nothing but rags, she would still have looked splendid.

"Lady Caroline. I am honoured." Lord Edgemere took her hand and pressed a kiss upon her palm. From the top gallery, Miss Derringer, arrayed in soft rose, took a step backward into the shadows. She would not, after all, be attending.

Lady Caroline nodded regally, flirted at Lord Robert outrageously with her eyes, tapped him on the shoulder with her fan—to his credit, he did not wince, though she had just nicked his wound—and moved on. Lord Robert was playing most satisfactorily into her hands. Now she had only to spread a few rumours, let slip a few confidences . . . she touched the necklace delightedly. To be sure, it was a talisman. She would have been surprised to see the brooding look upon Sir Archibald's face as he watched her entrance from the wings.

The hour was now quite well advanced. She had missed several quadrilles and the first two country reels. The waltz was about to strike up and she would dearly have loved to corner Edgemere for it. It would have fitted her stratagems perfectly, but the annoying man seemed permanently stationed at the entrance, though no one had arrived for a half hour at least.

"Lady Caroline, may I have the pleasure of the first waltz?" Sir Archibald Dalrymple blinked from the glare of the diamonds. She imagined, however, that the charms of her cleavage were oversetting his nerves, causing him to tug reprehensibly at his neckerchief. She suppressed a slight scowl. If Lord Robert was so disobliging as to be unavailable, she supposed it could do no harm to take a turn with Dalrymple. In truth, after the earl, he was the handsomest man in the room, even if he was a complete gudgeon.

"Very well, Sir Archibald! You shall have that honour, though I swear you had better do something about your neckerchief or I shall seek out Lord Willoughby instead!" She loved setting her rivals at loggerheads. She stared archly at Dalrymple as he muttered an apology and stuffed the whole starched creation into the top of his expensive, if garish, waistcoat. She raised her eyes but made no further comment as she gave him her hand. The orchestra was striking up, and there was no time to seek out another partner. It would do her reputation no good to sit out a dance like a veritable wallflower, so she graciously smiled upon Sir Archibald and took a step onto the floor. Eyes followed the duo, then polite applause.

Lady Caroline preened, for she was in high good looks and the diamonds, she was pleased to reflect, enhanced her creamy bosom and lent her an air of queenly elegance. There was no way out for Edgemere now, for every eye in the hall was upon her. Her possession of such an expensive gift spoke volumes. Edgemere was doomed, for no one would believe he would give a respectable woman such a gift without first asking for her hand.

The waltz ended at last, and she was thankful, for Dalrymple had missed his steps several times. The last had been the most severe, nearly causing a rip in her embroidered blond satin hem. She suppressed a glare but refused the mumbled offer of orgeat. Miss Wratcham was approaching, and she was just the person to sow a few seeds. . . .

"Miss Wratcham! How delightful you look in that gown!"

"Thank you, Lady Caroline. I daresay it is not as *flamboyant* as yours, but it does have a certain flair. May I compliment you on your necklace? A recent gift, if I collect?" She looked slyly at Lady Caroline, agog to hear if the rumours swiftly circulating the ballroom were true.

Lady Dashford smiled. Miss Wratcham could be relied upon to play exactly into her hands. She opened the clasp of her fan and dropped her wrist, so that the silver lace opened to its fullest extent.

"I fear you have divined my secret! How terribly naughty of you, Miss Wratcham!"

Miss Wratcham bent her head closer as Lady Caroline fingered the necklace. "I do declare I am betrothed! Now don't say a word . . ."

"How deliciously marvellous. Did he give you the necklace as a betrothal gift?"

Lady Caroline nodded. "But hush! I know I can rely on your discretion absolutely."

"Oh, absolutely."

Lady Dashford nodded. She clicked her fan shut and smiled as Lord Willoughby begged to sign his name to her card. Miss Wratcham excused herself, for she had something "very particular" to say to her dear friend Lady Dorothea Pilkington.

She was gone before she could notice the faint smirk behind Lady Caroline's best society smile. The deed was done; she had seen to it.

Twenty-one

Miss Anne Derringer dried her eyes and scolded herself for being such a ninnyhammered fool. Lord Edgemere had made his intentions as plain as a pikestaff to her, and she had been too addlewitted to pay any attention to them. She had allowed her sensibilities to overcome her common sense, and that was sadly—sadly—out of character. She could not blame Lord Robert for kissing Lady Caroline's hand. She *did* look like a fairy princess in her flowing tunics and glittering gemstones. Perhaps he was simply reconciling himself to his fate, determined to do the right thing by her even if his heart *did* waver.

Anne had no doubt that it wavered, for she had felt the full strength of his love directed at her, and the monumental power of such a force could not simply be ignored or denied. Still, he had chosen duty and honour before matters of the heart, and it was incumbent on her now to abide by that decision. It would not help Lord Robert if he saw how deeply he was cutting up at her heart or how arduous was the burden he had condemned to her shoulders. He would be bearing the selfsame weight; she could not ask him to endure any more.

Anne sat up with decision, oblivious to the soft folds of cherry rose that shimmered in the candlelight of the cosy nursery room. It would be easier if she left, finally, and allowed him to forge the role he had assumed for himself. She knew that if he could never be a loving husband to Caroline, he would at least be a dutiful one.

With a heavy heart, she began the business of writing a letter to the new governess, whoever she might be. She prayed that Lord Robert would not be so foolhardy as to reinstate his original intentions. If for no other reason, she would speak to him before the night was out. The children deserved that consideration at least. She dipped her pen, then softly inscribed the stages Thomas had reached with his Latin, mathematics and French proverbs. So hard to quantify! Her lips quirked as she remembered some of his quainter—but definitely not repeatable—phrases. And Kitty! She must be allowed to continue with her Gothic novels, for only then might she pursue a lasting interest in literature of all genres.

She hoped the new governess would give them a bit of slack, would mingle humour with discipline. . . . She threw down her pen. Gracious heavens, she was writing a dissertation! She tore up the paper, then sighed. It was useless. And the time! It was late; the children would be sleeping if she did not hurry to make her farewells. It would have to be tonight, though it wrenched her heart, for she would leave by the first post in the morning. Anne was human enough not to want to see Lady Caroline's gloating face at the breakfast table, for undoubtedly the countess-to-be would ride over from the Anchorfords' at first light. She blew out the nursery room's taper, took one last look at the room, then walked slowly to the winding stairs on her left.

"You are engaged to be married, Lady Caroline! How very delightful!" The princess Esterhazy extended a leisurely hand. "And the diamonds are charming. Quite charming!"

"Yes, they are, are they not? Worth a quite extortionate

amount I believe, but then, my betrothed has always been rather generous."

"*Has* he?" The princess looked interested, ever eager for a scent of scandal broth. If Lady Caroline had been accepting expensive gifts before she was engaged. . . .

Lady Dashford realized her mistake immediately. "Not that I have ever accepted anything beyond posies, you understand, but his reputation, as I am sure you know, speaks for itself."

Princess Esterhazy raised her brows. Whatever reputation Sir Archibald Dalrymple had acquired, it certainly had little to do with generosity, or even with the happy circumstance of him being in funds. That was why it was so strange that he had decided to place the necklace into Lady Caroline's keeping. Still, she was not so uncivil as to say as much to his future bride. She merely nodded her head regally. "Well, my dear, when you are Lady Archibald Dalrymple, I shall take it upon myself to call upon you in Green Street."

Lady Caroline nearly choked on her stuffed creole. "You are mistaken, Princess! I am *not* betrothed to Sir Archibald. I cannot imagine where you acquired such a notion!"

"Why, from your necklace, of course! You are undoubtedly a lady, my dear Caroline. You would never accept such a gift from anyone other than your affianced, surely?"

"Yes, but . . ."

"Well then, the diamonds belong to Sir Archibald, therefore . . ."

"No!"

"I beg your pardon?"

"No! You are labouring under a misapprehension, Your Highness! Sir Archibald lost them to Lord Robert Carmichael two nights ago."

"Tush and nonsense, my dear. The heat is probably

addling your brains! I *deplore* these squeezes! However cold it is outside, one can be depended upon to positively *fry* indoors. So many people and all the flames . . ."

Lady Caroline's mind was not on the weather. She had a dreadfully sinking feeling at the pit of her stomach and was determined to dispel her sudden fears immediately. Perhaps the princess was suffering from the heat. Certainly, she appeared quite appallingly confused. . . .

"Excuse me, Highness, I have just one or two matters I must attend to . . ."

"Of course, my dear. You run along and enjoy yourself. Sir Archibald is out on the balcony. I know, for he has been staring after you this age at least."

Lady Caroline stalked off. Sir Archibald, indeed! She would find Lord Robert and force him to declare himself at once. Where *was* the man?

"Lady Caroline, I have come to claim my dance." Lord Willoughby extended a jovial, elegantly gloved hand.

"Not now, Lord Willoughby! I am trying to find—"

"Sir Archibald? I saw him on the balcony about two minutes ago. I must say, Lady Caroline, you are a very sly creature! I would never have thought that you and Dalrymple . . ."

"Will you cease talking about Dalrymple? I have had him up to my ears! What *is* it with everybody?"

"But the necklace, Lady Caroline!"

"What *about* the necklace?" Lady Dashford lost some of her charm when she was angry. She didn't care. Lord Willoughby was small fish anyway.

"You accepted his necklace and announced your betrothal. It is a foregone conclusion—"

"To the Earl of *Edgemere,* you idiot! The necklace was regained by him almost immediately!"

"That is not what *I* hear!"

"Nor I." Lord Anchorford calmly apologized for interrupting and accepted a strawberry from a passing footman. Lady Caroline noticed with exasperation that a small crowd was gathering about them and wished she had been calm enough to keep her voice down.

"Well, it is true. He told me so himself."

"Told you what, Lady Dashford?" The earl seemed to appear as if from nowhere.

"You told me you had regained the diamonds."

Lord Edgemere looked remarkably blank. "The diamonds?"

"These!" Caroline pointed to her neck, as if he was not already dazzled by the gems.

"Ah, those. Yes, they were a sad loss to me, I am afraid. In future I shall be more careful about how I gamble away my property. Nice evening, though, Anchorford!"

"Thank you! I fancy my guests were well entertained . . ."

Lady Caroline felt as though she were going mad. "Then, what is *this?*" She pulled the note from her bodice, and the company gasped at the outrageous display. A few, like Lord Willoughby, grabbed at their monocles, but too late. The note was withdrawn all too quickly.

"This?" Lord Anchorford wrenched the note from her hand. "It is something initialled AD . . . now who could that be?"

"I do believe it is I! Archibald Dalrymple, you know." Sir Archibald looked round apologetically. "I fear my handwriting was a little hasty . . ."

Lady Caroline felt the room spinning.

Some of the primmer dowagers looked at each other significantly. Miss Wratcham stepped forward and glanced at the diamonds' clasp with interest. "Undoubtedly it is Sir Archibald's; I remember the design of that clasp distinctly. There can be no mistaking it!"

"Well, of course it is mine! I won it fair and square! You look wonderful in it, my dear. It is the perfect betrothal present, for I trust it shall remain in our family as an heirloom for years."

Sir Archibald smiled fondly at Caroline. Edgemere had been convincing. She *was* a tidy little piece, and he would have the taming of her . . . perhaps it would be all for the best. At least the diamonds would be safely in his possession again, for though he would not be able to sell them outright without a great deal of squawking from his lady wife, he would at least be able to get credit again. His possession of them was paramount.

"But—" Lady Caroline's lips sealed as she regarded some of the ton's highest sticklers. If she wailed that she had thought the gift from Lord Robert, they would be bound to ask her why she surmised that.

She could not tell them without mentioning previous indiscretions and losing what was left of her reputation entirely. No one would believe, by the odious way he was behaving, that Sir Archibald had never formally proposed and been accepted. Likewise, from Lord Robert's polite but distant manner, no one would consider for a moment that . . . that . . . at least she had the grace to blush. If society only knew! Still, she could not cry out over spilt milk.

Sir Archibald was eligible enough if she could not have Edgemere. She was getting on, after all . . . then there were the diamonds . . . if she refused Dalrymple, she would certainly have to return them. . . . She swallowed and took Sir Archibald's hand.

"I am afraid I am feeling a little faint from the crush, Sir Archibald! I fear I had the most *frightful* delusions just a moment ago."

"There, there, dear, so long as you are recovering now. Perhaps I shall take you out onto the balcony for air? Can someone call a footman for some fruit punch? It is delectably refreshing, you know . . ."

The crowd dispersed with the annoying feeling that it

had just missed some quite delicious scandal Out of the corner of her eye, Lady Caroline could see Edgemere. He had his fist clenched across a marble balustrade, but other than that, his features were immobile. For an instant, their eyes met, and he doffed his impeccable tricorne just a little.

Damn his eyes! The man was not such a greenhorn, after all. He had won. Lady Caroline opened her fan and fluttered her lashes at Dalrymple. Edgemere would not have the satisfaction of seeing her rage. Even as he released his grip and made a polite bow to the Duke of Sedgewick, her tinkling laughter could be heard for several moments outside.

"Tom! Kitty!" Anne puzzled, for though they were undoubtedly abed, they seemed to be sleeping far deeper than usual. She crept in, wondering whether a new taper would startle them. Deciding they were made of sterner stuff, she lit one of the grander wax candles and set it by the beds. Still, they did not stir, but the soft glow shed by the light made the lumps in their beds look rather more suspicious than when she had first caught sight of them. Anne laughed, in spite of her woes.

She should have known! It was too much to expect them to go docilely to sleep with all the excitement below stairs. Never mind that Tom had just sustained a near disaster on Dartford, or that Mrs. Tibbet and she had done everything in their power to tire them out for the evening. The temptation would surely have tried the patience of saints, and dearly though she loved them, Anne knew at once that Tom and Kitty did not fall into that category.

She had better look lively, for there were any number of places they could be meddling in—the stables, the kitchens, heaven forbid, the dance areas themselves. . . . Anne blew out the candle and ran down the corridor. At the very least, she must alert the house staff. If she could find them herself, so much the better. At least she could keep them out of the more dire sorts of mischief. There would be no returning them to their rooms, however. *That* would be too cruel!

She stopped a bit before opening the west wing door. It led off to some of the more public areas, and she was mindful of her dress. Just as well she had remained garbed in the satin. She would not look amiss in the hall, for in truth Mrs. Tibbet had chosen well. It fitted her admirably, and though the pretty satin slippers had been too large for her statuesque figure, the matching rose gloves had been perfect, as had the high waistband secured strikingly with ribbons of cherry rose. She had no adornments upon her throat or arms—these she had long since sold—but her hair was fashioned a la Psyche, with a single fern pressed in at the crown. The effect was devastatingly simple and breathtakingly beautiful, for the fern exactly complemented the tourmaline of her eyes and the cherry rose was a perfect foil to the raven-dark hair. She patted down her skirts and whisked a skein of hair from her eyes. She would have to do, she supposed, if someone caught sight of her. Taking a deep breath, she opened the door and began her quest.

Of course, the scamps were nowhere to be found. She edged her way past several of the dowagers and made her way across the cool marble floors toward the kitchens. Mrs. Tibbet could send the grooms down to the stables and keep a watchful eye on some of her jellies. Anne would not put it past the duo to be helping themselves to some of the desserts rather earlier than the guests.

She was startled when a dapper young gentleman in a double-breasted wool frock coat barred her way to the kitchens and demanded she hand him her card. Bewildered, she stammered a rather vague response. The gentleman looked at her closely, then chuckled. "If I knew no better, I would think no one had told you tonight that you are the very belle of the ball."

"Beg pardon?"

"My love, look beyond you to that clever collection of mirrors. Can you not see the truth of what I immediately perceive? I am a veritable connoisseur, you know!"

Anne smiled suddenly, and her face lighted up so dramatically that the gentleman, for all his years of feminine experience, was almost overcome.

"Why, sir, I do believe you are flirting with me!"

"Really? Why, yes, quite possibly I am! But come, my dear, your name. Edgemere cannot be so grim as to withhold that all to himself."

The smile dimmed. "It is of no consequence, sir. Please, I must get past."

"But your card. I insist on signing my name to it."

"I have no card."

"Have none? By the zounds, now I *swear* I have heard everything. Come, we will go at once to the master of ceremonies and procure you one."

In spite of herself, Anne laughed. "You speak as if we are in the pump rooms in Bath, sir! You *must* know there is no such person presiding, unless you call the *earl* some such thing!"

As if on cue, Edgemere interrupted her laughing reply. "Do I hear my name taken in vain? Cedric, you dog, depart from here at once. I have something very particular I have to say to Miss Derringer!"

Anne's heart missed a beat, for the earl was smiling at her so open-heartedly that she could not bring herself to believe he had just willfully thrown his entire life away.

The unknown stranger looked coolly amused. "So that is the way of it, is it? I must say, Edgemere, you play your cards deep. The whole world and his wife thought it was the cunning Caroline—"

"Stow it, Cedric!" Robert looked daggers at his oldest and dearest friend.

"Miss Derringer, the orchestra is striking up for the third waltz of the evening. Are you certain you do not wish to bestow the honour upon me? Robert is all very well, but he does not share our divine colouring. You note that I, too, have exquisite green eyes and hair as pitch as the night?"

"Doing it too rum, Cedric! Your locks are merely a very dark brown, and as for having the effrontery to compare your green to Anne's . . ."

"Anne? Pretty name, that! Did you know Edgemere swears by Weston, but *I*—I use only Soames of Addington Place."

Anne had no time to comment politely on the skill of his tailor, for with a broad smile and a decidedly impudent wink, he was off behind a pillar and out toward the supper room.

Anne's heart started to beat quite wildly, for Robert was regarding her with such a look of ill-suppressed passion that her knees threatened to fail her and she felt quite unwarrantedly faint.

"Not thinking of swooning, are you?"

"Good lord, do you think me so lily-livered as that? Certainly I shall not make such an appalling spectacle of myself in front of your guests!"

"Ah, but then I could quite unashamedly carry you up to your rooms!"

"Your thoughts need a new direction, Lord Robert." In spite of the severity of her words, Anne's delectable lips curved upward in a telltale manner that caused an answering gleam in the hazel eyes that regarded her so closely.

"Shall I dance, do you think?"

"I believe that is customary at a ball, my lord."

"Then, little Celeste, you will do me the honour."

Twenty-two

Anne glided onto the floor as if in a dream. She did not understand a thing. Lady Caroline was nowhere to be seen, and certainly, there was no sign that any announcement had been made with regard to a betrothal.

The hard lines on Lord Edgemere's brow seemed to be lifted, and his manner was as lighthearted as the day she had first set eyes upon him in the meadow. What had caused this transformation?

She had no time to wonder, for he was guiding her skillfully across the floor, his arm securely about her waist and quite reprehensibly close, she was sorry to note. Or was she? She snuggled a little closer, daringly closing the gap to less than an inch, a circumstance that made his noble lordship the eighth Earl Edgemere smile more than a little as she felt an answering pressure about her shoulder.

"How is your wound, my lord?"

She had to look up to formulate the question and realized, a little late, just why the waltz was considered a trifle fast. Her lips were practically upon his as she tilted her head backward to speak. He would have grinned, but for the fact that his expansive chest was suddenly quite constricted and his breathing rather more shallow than normal.

"I believe, as I look down into those fathomless pools of tourmaline, that my wound is quite, quite healed."

"I meant your *flesh* wound, sir."

"Oh! I collect you meant my *heart* wound."

"That, too."

"I do excellently, my dear Miss Derringer, now that Sir Archibald Dalrymple has finally met his match."

"Sir Archibald? I thought he was in bed with a lump the size of an egg."

"You are behind times, Anne! The lump has receded to a mere bump of hardly any consequence. At all events, he is decidedly *out* of his bed, though I warrant that with the filly he has just bagged, that state of affairs will not last long."

"You talk in riddles, Lord Edgemere! Improper ones, too!"

Robert laughed. "Shall I make you puzzle it out? It would serve you right for looking so damnably splendid when I cannot do a thing about it!"

"That has never stopped you before . . ."

She saw his eyes grow dark and knew she had better stop her teasing.

"Good lord!"

"What is lt?" Lord Edgemere had to pull himself up short to avoid stepping on her feet. Anne had stopped dead in her tracks.

"The children!"

"What about them?"

"They've escaped! They could be anywhere! I was just setting off to find them when I came upon the charming gentleman in the silverthreaded frock coat."

"Charming? I shall cut his heart out. That is Lord Cedric Liverpool, by the way. The Marquis of Salisbury."

Anne nodded. "I must fly! Heaven knows what mischief they are concocting."

"Let them concoct! We are having our fun, why shouldn't they?"

"Because, my dear addlewitted sir, they could be in the stables, your cellar . . ."

"My cellar? Call out the guards. Finish the dance, Anne, then kill them for me with my compliments. Tom is already in for a tongue-lashing over his handling of Dartford."

"So long as it is merely a tongue-lashing."

"He deserves a whipping, but I cannot bring myself to the sticking point when he very possibly saved my life!"

"And mine!" Anne could feel the heat pass between them in a delicious, unspoken, but highly intoxicating manner. The earl squeezed her waist in a shockingly rakish manner considering that all eyes were upon them, but Anne cared not a jot. Indeed, she sighed a little when he reluctantly released his grip.

"See, this delightful dance is ending, so I shall bid you farewell. Farewell, but not good night. We have a date, remember?"

"I remember." Anne's smile was sunshine. "Not for the world would I miss using the Herschel two-inch telescope."

"Baggage! I intend to make you forget star gazing."

"Indeed? What a very strange notion, my lord! By the by, I take it you do not intend to become betrothed tonight."

"My girl, you have a very sorry grasp of my intentions. That is *precisely* what I intend."

"But not to Lady Caroline?"

"Not to Lady Caroline. Sadly, she has already been taken."

Anne's eyes snapped open.

"Taken? By whom?"

"La, Miss Derringer! You are behind the times! To Dalrymple, of course!"

His tone was so innocently smug Anne had to put her pink satin fingers right over her mouth to smother a chortle. So! That was the deep game Lord Edgemere had been playing. How remiss she had been to ever doubt him.

"You shall tell me everything or I shall never speak to you again!"

"I am quite humbled by that threat! Very well, Miss Derringer, have it your way. And now, adieu, for I have promised both Ladies Elizabeth and Mary Bellafonte a dance each."

"Then, they are both very fortunate! I have enjoyed myself immeasurably and only hope I am not punished for my indulgence."

"How so?"

"Tom could be unhitching the coaches, Kitty could be harassing the cook, both could be playing havoc with chamber pots . . ."

"Go!"

As it was, Tom and Kitty were being a great deal better behaved than Anne had given them credit for. Both were charmingly attired in ballroom wear from the attic—Tom looked particularly funny in skin-tight breeches that hung upon him several inches too long—and had secured for themselves a private spot away from the madding crowd but with a clear enough view of the proceedings. They had extracted several silver salvers from passing footmen who now scurried around anxious to retrieve them before the kitchen staff did their tallies. Anne eyed several delicious-looking salmon dishes, some sweet pastries delicately oozing fresh cream and cranberries, one or two platters of ham and stuffed quenelles and a small, rather restrained plate of fresh cheeses.

"Can you spare any of that? I am famished."

"Miss Derringer!" The pair looked at each other guiltily. Anne ignored them and helped herself to a wedge of the salmon.

"Any lemon?"

"No, we tried to cadge some off Hastings, but he threatened to dob us in, so we've had to make do without."

"Poor children. I shall inform Hastings that in the future you are to be served an unremitting supply of citrus wedges."

Tom grinned happily as he threw his sister a cranberry. "*Told* you she was a good gun!"

Anne was first to creep into the earl's domain. The revelry was still going on downstairs—she could see faint hooded shapes in the garden—but she had no taste to return. She was content, at last, to sit and wait.

The strains of Purcell and Handel were almost audible as she opened the familiar door to the balcony and looked out. Lord Edgemere had been right. The storm clouds had long since vanished, leaving the sky as crisp and clear as a band of inky velvet set with diamonds.

It was cool, now, after the crush of the ballrooms. Anne shivered a little, for the ball gown was not sewn with star gazing in mind. Still, she could not help herself. The night was so tempting, and her heart had rarely rested this easy in all her four and twenty years. For the first time, as she stepped outside, she felt she had come home.

The earl bowed smoothly to Lady Inglebury and helped her with her shawls and confections of muffs and scarves. Nothing in his demeanor suggested that he was anxious to get rid of his guests or draw a close to his illustrious party. Only the Marquis of Salisbury eyed him with amused sympathy and even went so far as to help Mr. Mortimer and Miss Serena Mortimer call out their carriages. He was rewarded by an ironic twitch of the lips from Robert, who understood exactly what his illustrious friend was thinking.

At last, it was at an end. The earl thanked Mrs. Tibbet gravely and asked that all the staff be suitably thanked and rewarded. Cedric lingered a little, asking, with a faint curve to his lips, why the earl had not invited him upstairs for port.

"Oh, go take a long walk, Cedric!"

The marquis chuckled. "So that is the way of it, is it?"

"Yes. And if you dare say a single word about impropriety . . ."

"Who, I? That would be very much like the pot calling the kettle black. Besides, I never meddle in matters of the heart. Too damn dangerous!"

"Yes, well." Lord Carmichael's sudden outburst abated as swiftly as it had descended upon him. He grinned. "Sorry if my temper is a little threadbare, my man. The evening has held its fair share of suspense. Then this appallingly long schedule of dances . . ."

"No more than usual, my dear Robert . . ."

"Oh, take that silly grin off your face! You are welcome to my port, but you shall have to, I am afraid, drink it alone. I am certain Augustus shall see to your needs handsomely."

"Then, I am well satisfied, for I have quite a fancy for the cherry brandy you laid down."

"Good! I make you a present of it. And now, I am off!" So saying, his lordship drew his gloves from the table, alternately snatched at his hat and his cane, discarded them both and marched from the room.

It was left to the Marquis of Salisbury to regard him thoughtfully, though his eyes were brimful of silent laughter. The great Edgemere, then, had finally fallen.

"Anne. It seems I have waited an age for this."

"I, too."

"I hope you mean *me* and not my telescope!"

"Now, let me see . . . is it a choice or may I have both?"

"Baggage! Come here and let me kiss you senseless."

"Very tempting, my lord, but I am afraid I shall have to decline."

"What?" His lordship's tone was incredulous.

"There is something I wish you to see. The sky is so clear it cannot just be my imagination. I believe, to the north, I can detect a comet. It has not previously been charted."

The earl looked into her dear, shining, green-dark eyes and was defeated. Her excitement was so palpable it was infectious. Besides, they had their whole lives to indulge in the sort of activity he might have preferred at that precise moment.

"Oh, very well, the telescope wins. Have you handled one before?"

"Never, but I know the theory."

"Good! Then, you shall align it, for I have far better things to look at at this moment."

"Better . . . ?" Anne took in the direction of his gaze and blushed.

"Pay attention, sir!"

"I *am,* Miss Derringer! Here is the key."

He watched as she carefully removed the instrument from his cabinet and laboured to set it outside. Then she seemed to do a series of extraordinary things with it—he was too distracted to note precisely what—and she handed him back the key.

The earl pocketed it absently before nonchalantly framing the words that had been on his mind all evening. "By the by, you *will* marry me, I take it?"

"Oh, of course."

"Excellent, I am glad *that* is settled. Tell me when I can take a peek."

"Now, if you like. There seems to be a tail of gas just short of the constellation."

The earl stepped forward and took a long look. When he had finished, he looked at Anne with amused respect that bordered, rather incongruously, on awe. "Set down the coordinates, Anne. I do believe the Royal Astronomical Society might be interested in this. If it is a discovery, it shall be named after you. Comet Derringer. It has an interesting ring to it."

"No! I will be labeled a bluestocking forever more. I've had my fill of that. *You* shall get the credit, for it was your telescope that confirmed it. It shall be called Comet Carmichael."

"Comet Celeste?"

Anne shook her head. She was determined. The earl adored the stubborn tilt of her chin. So very like his own. Then his eyes gleamed. He wanted to finish with the matter of the comet, for morning was approaching and soon he would, for decorum's sake, have to pack Anne off to her chambers.

"You *did* say you would wed me?"

"I did, my lord."

"Then, I shall get a special license tomorrow, for this comet needs a name."

"You have thought of one?"

"Yes, my dear, stubborn, pig-headed Celeste, I have thought of one."

"And it is?"

"It is Comet Carmichael."

She sank back into him with a satisfied smile. "It shall be named for you, then."

"No, my sweet, it shall be named, after all, for you. As I said, Comet Carmichael."

Her eyes widened as she at last understood the import of his words. Then she giggled.

"Satisfied?"

"Satisfied."

"Good. Then come here and let me kiss you senseless."

Miss Derringer, obedient as always, humbly obeyed.